MURDER AT THE WINTER BALL

Rachel and I finally made our way to our shared office.

"Uh-oh." Rachel grabbed the antique door handle and gave it a sharp pull. "This is locked."

"It *should* be locked." I bent down to examine the door. The ancient copper key, brittle and thin, was buried in the keyhole, the stem snapped off. "It's almost as if—"

"Someone wanted to keep someone in," Rachel finished for me. We shared a wordless glance and raced to the heavy mahogany front doors. I grabbed Rachel before we left the front hall and motioned to the big roll top desk that served as a check in kiosk for guests. The lock had been jimmied and broken.

"Someone took the key and broke it in our office door."

The carefully labeled key rack was missing the copper key now jammed in the keyhole.

We were down the porch in a flash in our heels, the shoes sinking into the now muddy and puddled front grounds. Icy sheets of rain coursed down on our heads, obliterating the last bits of snow. We finally made it around to where our office stood and peered into the room, our hands flanking our eyes against the bright office lights.

Ginger sat at my desk, her willowy frame slumped over and face down . . .

Books by Stephanie Blackmoore

ENGAGED IN DEATH

MURDER WEARS WHITE

MURDER BORROWED, MURDER BLUE

Published by Kensington Publishing Corporation

Murder Borrowed, Murder Blue

Stephanie Blackmoore

KENSINGTON PUBLISHING CORP.

http://www.kensingtonbooks.com

KENSINGTON BOOKS are published by

Kensington Publishing Corp.
119 West 40th Street
New York, NY 10018

All Kensington Titles, Imprints, and Distributed Lines are available at special quantity discounts for bulk purchases for sales promotions, premiums, fund-raising, and educational or institutional use. Special book excerpts or customized printings can also be created to fit specific needs. For details, write or phone the office of the Kensington special sales manager: Kensington Publishing Corp., 119 West 40th Street, New York, NY 10018, attn: Special Sales Department, Phone: 1-800-221-2647.

Kensington and the K logo Reg. U.S. Pat & TM Off.

ISBN-13: 978-1-4967-0482-5
ISBN-10: 1-4967-0482-7
First Kensington Mass Market Edition: February 2018

eISBN-13: 978-1-4967-0483-2
eISBN-10: 1-4967-0483-5
First Kensington Electronic Edition: February 2018

10 9 8 7 6 5 4 3 2 1

Printed in the United States of America

Chapter One

"The groundhog didn't see his shadow!" My sister, Rachel, turned from the television with a look of anguish marring her pretty face. I would've expected her to be upset if the furry little guy *had* seen his shadow.

"What's the problem? I could do with an early spring." We were deep into the snowy season, and I was ready to take a break from burrowing under blankets each night and donning winter boots each day. I loved an excuse to curl up next to the fire with a good book and a cup of hot cocoa, but I'd be thrilled when warmer weather arrived.

"Dakota wants a winter-themed wedding. We need the snow to stick around." Rachel pulled back the heavy gray velvet drapes and peered outside, her eyes anxiously sweeping the grounds.

"I don't think we have anything to worry about," I soothed, joining her at the window. "Everyone knows that groundhog stuff isn't reliable."

Outside was a veritable winter wonderland. A lacy lattice of intricate, icy crystals spread across the library window like a delicate doily. Beyond the glass, the evergreen trees seemed to groan with the weight of a thick blanket of snow straining each branch. Tracks from deer and raccoons were the only patterns etched upon the smooth expanse of white ground. The newly risen sun reflected off the snow with slicing, blinding rays. It was a beautiful, cold, clear February day.

"I just want it to be perfect." My sister spun around and aimed the remote at the television. She turned off the footage of Punxsutawney Phil and paced the room. I was as anxious as her, but didn't want to show it. The crew for the celebrity wedding reality show *I Do* was going to arrive in minutes, and I wanted to show off my B and B, Thistle Park, at its very best.

We were hosting the wedding of actress Dakota Craig, recently anointed America's newest sweetheart. Dakota had fallen into obscurity after starring in a teen soap opera, and had risen, phoenix-from-the-ashes style, this past year with a string of acclaimed film roles. Everyone loved a comeback kid, and Dakota was it. She was also a humble, generous woman, if the emails and phone calls we'd been exchanging these last few months to plan her wedding from afar were any indication.

Her fiancé, Beau Wright, was the reigning king of country music. I'd always thought of him as something of a lothario, and there had been a lot of speculation about his hurried engagement to Dakota. But he'd been gracious and polite in the few dealings we'd had planning his nuptials. I couldn't say the same for Dakota's mother, Roxanne, who behaved like a stage mother on steroids.

My cell phone buzzed in my pocket.

"Is it the crew? They're officially late." Rachel crowded next to me to peer at the screen. I stifled a groan.

"It's Helene again." Helene Pierce was once almost my mother-in-law, until I'd called off the wedding to her son. I counted my lucky stars nearly every day for that decision.

"How many times has she texted this morning?" Rachel arched a perfectly plucked brow.

"This is the fifth. Not counting the three phone calls and two emails from her. All before the sun came up. I haven't even had my second cup of coffee." I typed back a hasty but professional reply to her query and hit SEND. I jammed my cell phone back into my dress pocket. I promised myself I'd take a sterner line with my arch nemesis turned client. "She knows the crew of *I Do* is arriving today. She's trying to rattle me."

And it was working.

I wondered for the thousandth time what I'd been thinking when I'd agreed to throw a modern-day debutante ball, free of charge, for the posh Dunlap Women's Academy, at the behest of Hurricane Helene. The Winter Ball was to be held in two days, encroaching on filming for the reality show. It would be a tight turnaround, not one I'd ever agree to in saner moments. But I had needed a mammoth favor, and Helene had granted my wish as the worst incarnation of a fairy godmother a girl could have. And now she'd called in her chips. I was at her constant beck and call. Thank goodness Helene was rattling me from afar. She was ensconced in her second home in Boca Raton.

And although being nearly two thousand miles away kept her from popping in unannounced, she still harangued me each day via Skype, text, and phone to check on my plans for the Winter Ball.

"Did we take on too much?" I turned to Rachel in a moment of panic. The start of a headache began to spread between my eyes. "How will we pull off the Winter Ball, finish planning Dakota's wedding, and film for *I Do*?"

Rachel waved her hand and dismissed my worries, but her keen green eyes told a different story. "You pulled off Whitney and Ian's wedding in a month, all while renovating the house. We've held half a dozen weddings since. You could do this in your sleep."

I took a steadying breath and slowly let it out. "I'd just feel better if everyone were on the same page with the Winter Ball plans. The Winter Ball Committee directed me to ignore Helene's choices, and she's going to go ballistic when she finds out." Not only had I had to listen to every whim, concern, and demand from Helene, I'd also had to keep her in the dark about not honoring those wishes. It turned out I wasn't the only enemy Helene had. Her adversaries at the school had used her absence and snowbird status to undo all her plans for the ball. I checked my watch and let out a gust of air. "And I wish there were more time between the Winter Ball and Dakota's wedding."

Rachel snorted. "You didn't really have a choice. Let's just make lemon slushies out of the crummy lemons we've been given."

My sister was right. Being featured on a popular

reality show was just what we needed to advertise our B and B and wedding-planning business. Rachel and I had spent the last two weeks with a bowl of popcorn between us, watching every previous episode of *I Do*. We were nervous about appearing on television and wanted everything to go off without a hitch. The show was edited to highlight drama between the wedding planners, venue owners, celebrity couples, and the host of the show, Adrienne Larson. But I was determined for the Thistle Park B and B to come across in a good light, with minimal shenanigans.

"Besides," Rachel continued, bringing me back to the present, "we have an unlimited budget for this wedding. It's going to be spectacular." Her eyes gleamed with Gatsby-esque plans for Dakota and Beau's big day.

"We have to take their personal style into account, Rach," I reminded my sister. "Dakota isn't a fan of bling and razzle-dazzle, as far as I can tell." The bride's selections had been tasteful and restrained, and seemed to value sentimentality over opulence. But Dakota's measured choices hadn't stopped Rachel from living vicariously through her, and she'd suggested some over-the-top details that Dakota had politely declined. Roxanne, Dakota's mother, was all too willing to advocate for a flashy wedding. I'd logged some tense time already during conference calls with the bride and her mother. I'd deftly deferred to Dakota, and Roxanne had eventually come around. Still, the wedding plans so far seemed to be a compromise effort between dueling mother and daughter, and I hoped Dakota was genuinely happy.

"Ooh!" Rachel whipped around from the window, her wavy, honey-kissed tresses fanning out behind her. "I see a van coming down the driveway."

The two of us raced from the library to the front hall and stationed ourselves expectantly at the front door. I smoothed down the checked black and plum merino dress I'd donned for the occasion and tucked an errant curl behind my ear. Rachel shimmied the skirt of her spangly navy shift down a few inches and fluffed out her hair.

"This is it," I whispered to my sister.

"Our chance to put the B and B on the map!" We practically wriggled with excitement and barely contained ourselves from flinging open the heavy front door until the cheerful clang of the bell sounded.

"Mallory and Rachel, wonderful to finally meet you." The woman perched before us on the front porch was adorned in icy blue finery. She wore an exquisitely tailored Alexander McQueen coatdress in a vivid periwinkle. It probably cost more than my whole wardrobe. Lozenge-sized aquamarines graced her earlobes. Her tiny feet were ensconced in creamy suede, red-soled, high-heeled boots. I stared at them with incredulous eyes. I couldn't figure out how she'd made it from the production team's van and up the front walk without a single drop of moisture falling on the buttery leather. A jaunty fawn-colored cloche hat protected her shining, perfect cap of flaxen hair. She swept into the hallway and removed white angora gloves. She gave my hand a firm shake, with cold fingers.

"You must be Adrienne. Welcome to Thistle Park." I ushered the host of *I Do* into the front hall, where Rachel stared at her designer outfit with eyes agog. Adrienne Larson had impeccable taste, an artist's eye, and a will of steel. She'd earned the moniker of Ice Queen through subtly vicious yet outwardly polite battles with wedding planners and celebrity brides on *I Do*. I admired her choices and the suggestions she made on the show, and secretly hoped she'd approve of the wedding plans I'd come up with. But I also hoped she wouldn't meddle too much. Adrienne was a formidable figure on screen, and not one I wanted to tangle with anytime soon. I'd vowed to outmaneuver her overbearing suggestions about Dakota's wedding.

The rest of the crew filed in, and introductions were exchanged. The director, Xavier, was deferential and pleasant, his blinding white teeth on full display as he smiled and shook our hands. The light crew and cameramen didn't seem ruffled by Adrienne's presence. After a few minutes, I relaxed. We gathered in the parlor before a roaring fire and chatted with the crew over croissants, fruit, and coffee. We were about to start a tour of the house when a familiar black Accord advanced up the driveway.

"Garrett's here," I mused to Rachel. "I wonder what's up." I eagerly threw open the door before he had a chance to ring the bell.

"What a lovely surprise." I tilted my head back to receive a brief kiss and smiled at my boyfriend.

"I can't stay long. I'm dropping Summer off at school." Garrett's usually warm voice was tense and distant. I took a step back, but held the lapel of his black wool overcoat.

"Is everything all right?" I tried to tamp down the edge in my voice.

"I just realized something. Last night, I watched an episode of *I Do.*" His gorgeous hazel eyes were pained.

I laughed and let go of his coat, the tension broken. "Totally not your style, but I appreciate you checking in to see what I'm up against the next two weeks."

A wave of panic seemed to wash over Garrett. The laughter died in my throat.

"I should have watched it sooner. Mallory—"

"The TV crew is here. I saw their van." Garrett's thirteen-year-old daughter, Summer, peeked her head around the massive front door. Her heart-shaped face was surrounded by a cheery red ski hat. Her eyes were eager and bright.

"Summer, I told you to stay in the car." Garrett's voice was clipped and strange. I stared between him and his daughter, confused. She scooted around the open door and stood in the front hall, seeming to search for someone.

A plate crashed in the parlor.

Summer ran to Adrienne and almost knocked her over with the force of her embrace. Adrienne hugged Summer back with impossible fierceness and slowly raised her tear-stained eyes. They were heavy with a mixture of sadness and elation.

"Mom! You came back!"

* * *

The air in the room was heavy and stifling. All was still as Adrienne wiped her waterproof mascara with a tissue and Summer gazed at her with a look of adoration. My eyes darted back and forth between Summer and Adrienne at one end of the room, and Garrett before me, as if I were taking in an Olympic Ping-Pong match. Summer and Adrienne continued their hug, and Garrett's stunned visage took on an increasingly perturbed cast. He'd initially appeared flummoxed and stricken, but his disbelief was quickly distilling into lightning-hot annoyance.

"Summer." Garrett's voice was a strange, strangled mixture of anger and eerie calm. "You're going to be late for school."

I couldn't believe he was focusing on the mundanities of getting to school on time when Summer was calling Adrienne Larson her mother. I didn't know the specifics, but I knew enough. Thirteen years ago, Summer's mother had run off to Los Angeles a mere two weeks after Summer was born. She'd left Summer with Garrett and only seen her daughter a handful of times since. I had known Summer's mother's name was Adrienne, but I hadn't realized the host of *I Do* and Garrett's one-time love were one in the same. And from the look of shock on Garrett's face, he hadn't realized it either. Garrett rarely spoke of Adrienne, and when he did, it was with much angst, even after all these years.

"But, Dad, Mom just got here. I'd like to stay

and see the show being filmed." Summer's hazel eyes sparkled as she pleaded with her father. Adrienne gazed at her daughter, her mauve lips composed in a straight line. She placed a delicate hand possessively on Summer's shoulder and raised her chin. She shot Garrett a look of defiance, almost daring him to say no.

I took a step closer to Garrett in a silent show of support and struggled to process what was happening. I had a hard time reconciling the Adrienne I'd heard of in the context of abandoning Summer and Adrienne as the host of *I Do*. The way Summer keenly and fiercely clung to the woman she'd called Mom was muddying my views, too. Garrett's perception seemed addled as well. He appeared to be weighing his options.

I could see how Garrett and Adrienne's good looks had both contributed to Summer. She'd gotten her platinum hair, heart-shaped face, and ethereal manner from Adrienne. But their styles were diametrically opposed, with Adrienne clad head-to-toe in her trademark light blue, save for the red soles of her Louboutins. Summer had a casual tomboy affect, and just this past July had consented to chop off the inky black hair she'd dyed.

I studied Garrett. From her father, Summer had inherited her prodigious height, a smile that crooked up on one side, and soft hazel eyes that more often than not held dancing laughter but could also be smoldering and serious. Right now, Garrett's eyes looked anything but amiable. He went with the simplest way of diffusing tension.

"We can discuss spending time with your . . . mother on the way to school. C'mon, Summer, you don't want to be late." Garrett's voice was at once stern and pleading. Summer reluctantly gave up her spot next to Adrienne, but not before she graced her with another fierce hug. She crossed the parlor with a wistful glance for her mother and stood beside Garrett.

"See you later, Mom?" Summer's eyebrows rose in anticipation, and Adrienne let out a merry peal of laughter.

"Yes, sweetheart, we'll be seeing a lot of each other."

Summer lit up at her mother's pronouncement and doled out another electric smile, her magenta braces flashing.

"I'll see you at the car." Garrett offered his daughter a warm smile, and she seemed to relax, the tension of the moment gone. Summer gave me a hug on her way to the front hall. She left her father to face off with Adrienne.

Garrett waited until we could hear the heavy mahogany front door slam shut.

"You have a lot of explaining to do, Adrienne." Garrett's words came out in a strained string of hisses, yet he managed to remain barely civil. "For example, how did it happen that Summer seemed to know you'd be here, but I'm just finding out now?"

Adrienne's pale petal lips lifted up in a lilting smile. Her cool demeanor was back, her nerves unflappable. The only sign of the scene that had just taken place was a little bit of smeared mascara at the edges of each eye. "If I'd told you beforehand, I'm sure you'd have arranged for Summer to be out of town, or otherwise unavailable."

Garrett shook his head, a lock of nearly black

hair gracing his forehead. "That's not true, and you know it. Summer would give anything to see more of you, though I'm not sure why. If you'd contacted me, I would have arranged for you and Summer to have plenty of time during your stay in Port Quincy. I would never do anything to keep you two apart. You've done enough of that yourself over the years for me to have to contribute to your disappearing act." I could practically see the frost in the air.

Adrienne gasped and a delicate hand fluttered to her throat. The director, Xavier, came to her side and placed a fortifying hand on her arm.

"Let's not get testy, folks." He was dressed head-to-toe in black, with a black merino hoody, a black silk T-shirt, black cargo pants, and black Adidas shoes. Thin wire frames rimmed his piercing amber eyes, the bottom of the glasses resting on his sharp, tanned cheekbones. His silver hair provided his only pop of color. He carried a Lucite mug of a malodorous green liquid. He stopped to take a sip of the concoction through a wide straw before advancing toward Garrett, his arm sliding from Adrienne's shoulder. I caught a whiff of patchouli as he crossed the room.

Is he just supporting Adrienne as the director, or is there something more going on between them?

"I don't want Summer to be late." Garrett ignored Xavier's admonition and headed for the door, all but dismissing him. But not before leaning down to grace my lips with a fleeting kiss.

I felt hot eyes boring into the back of my neck and swiveled around to take in Adrienne. A look of clarity and realization seemed to kindle in the splintery cold depths of her icy blue eyes.

Uh-oh.

I had a feeling it wouldn't be so easy to deftly sidestep Adrienne Larson's famously meddlesome ways for the next two weeks.

Adrienne wasted no time in taking over. She instantly forgot her role as estranged mother and shook off her emotionally charged encounter with Summer with swift aplomb, like a snake shedding its skin. She didn't seem embarrassed over her public reunion with her daughter and scoped me out with new vigor. She morphed into hostzilla with startling alacrity. The Ice Queen was in full effect.

"Girls." She folded her hands crisply in front of her and flicked her blue-eyed gaze up and down, taking in my and Rachel's appearance. I raised an eyebrow. I'd just turned thirty this year, and usually a title of ma'am was more affronting. But somehow I could detect a dismissive strain to Adrienne's appellation of "girls."

"You simply must change. These outfits won't work on camera."

I gazed at my checked plum dress and felt a slow heat climb my neck.

"What's wrong with my outfit?" My voice came out in a squeak, and I vowed to calm down. I'd been going for professional and sleek when I'd chosen the dress this morning. It smoothed out my curves and the pretty checkered pattern provided some visual interest.

"The small pattern will show up on film as wavy lines. Do you have something solid you can change into? And it's a smidge frumpy. You'll want something a bit more form-fitting."

I thought I was off the hook, but Adrienne was just starting. Her laser-sharp gaze settled at the crown of my head. "Your hair . . . could you straighten it? It's a little unkempt."

My hands fluttered to the messy bun I'd carefully constructed out of my unruly, sandy curls. I'd been going for a tousled, beachy effect, but I guess that wasn't the end result.

She cocked her head and studied me. I barely refrained from squirming like a bug under a microscope and diving behind my sister for cover. "And that necklace is a bit much—it distracts from your face."

I fingered the statement necklace of violet and silver beads Garrett had gifted me for my birthday and finally found my voice. "Oh no, this one stays."

She turned to Rachel without waiting for my response.

"The glitter on your dress will reflect too much off the lights. It's distracting." Her eyes lingered on my sister's prodigious bustline. "As is the neckline. Do you have something a little more demure?"

It killed me to admit it, but I secretly agreed with Adrienne about my sister's dress. Still, she felt comfortable in it and was rocking her look, so I stood closer to Rachel in a sign of solidarity.

Rachel's mouth was hanging open in apparent shock. It took a lot to render my sister speechless.

Rachel snapped out of her shock and I felt her bristle next to me. To her credit, she didn't blush or flinch. She stood tall, drawing up all five feet and nine inches of her height, aided by her strappy gold sandals. She narrowed her pretty almond-shaped green eyes and leaned over Adrienne.

"This is the dress I'm wearing today. I don't believe the director has a problem with it."

Xavier materialized out of thin air and inserted himself between Adrienne and my sister like an NFL referee about to break up a skirmish.

"Ladies," he soothed, his voice melodic and instantly calming, and his teeth as white and blinding as the pristine snow outside, "we'll have plenty of time to work out wardrobe for the later shoots. Let's just get a few things in the can today." His amber eyes appeared large and calm behind the giant wire frames, and his mouth ticked up in an easy, pressure-diffusing smile. I felt myself calming down by marginal degrees. Xavier's skin was luminous despite his being in what I guessed was his late forties. I wondered just what was in the smoothie concoction he kept sipping—perhaps water from some fountain of youth.

"There is a reason Adrienne always wears pastels," he whispered to my sister and me with a smile. "They're perfect on camera."

I heard the camerawoman behind me muttering, "Just because Adrienne's dating the director, she thinks she *is* the director."

So that answers that question. Adrienne and Xavier are an item.

"This house is quaint, but it'll film well." Adrienne turned around in a slow circle, our offending outfits forgotten. I'd heard Thistle Park described many ways, but never heard it as quaint.

She took in the lofty ceiling of the parlor, complete with a newly restored mural. "Xavier tells me your business is rather new. How many weddings do you two have under your belts?"

"We've hosted weddings nearly every weekend since early November. We've never done a celebrity wedding, but Dakota and Beau will be well taken care of."

Xavier announced we'd begin shooting soon, and the crew got busy setting up a matrix of wires, lights, and mikes.

"Why don't you tell us what you'll be doing over the next twelve days in preparation for the wedding?"

I beamed, eager to show off the plans Rachel and I had worked so hard on since November.

"We'll begin with a run-through when Dakota and Beau arrive tomorrow. I'll set up a representative table to give them an idea of their reception, and we'll do a formal food tasting as well. . . . Wait, are you filming this?" I swallowed and stared into the camera pointed at me. I stopped my patter and self-consciously tucked an errant curl back into my bun. Adrienne rolled her eyes and let out a belabored sigh.

"We'll be shooting nearly everything this week,"

Xavier explained. "You never know what gems we'll find in all the film."

"Ouch!" Rachel had pinched me through the folds of my apparently frumpy dress.

"Pull it together," she hissed. "You're letting Adrienne rankle you."

"Maybe this isn't worth the free publicity after all," I whispered back to my sister as the camerawoman readied herself again.

"Of course it is. And you've handled way worse than the likes of Adrienne Larson." Rachel flicked her magenta-lacquered nails in the host's direction. She paused for a moment. "Although seeing her with Garrett"—she blew a strand of honey-kissed hair from her forehead—"that was intense." Worry gathered in Rachel's eyes like an impending snowstorm.

"Ready?" Xavier offered a kindly smile.

I steeled myself and began again, determined not to get rankled.

You better get used to the cameras—they'll be all up in your business for nearly two weeks.

"Um, as I was saying. We'll do a formal food tasting and meet with our florist, Lucy Sattler. Later, we'll make centerpieces together."

Adrienne smoothly sidled up to me, her face agog. "I don't think *I Do* has ever featured a celebrity bride making centerpieces for her own wedding."

I tried not to look wary, now that I knew I was being filmed. "Dakota wanted to incorporate authentic parts of her hometown, Port Quincy, and try her hand at crafting some of the decorations for her wedding." There. I'd calmly diffused Adrienne's query. "Rachel will show us all how she came up with the idea of Dakota and Beau's wedding cake, and we'll take you on a tour of downtown Port Quincy."

"Cut." Xavier nodded in my direction. "That was just what we needed."

I let out a breath and joined Rachel.

That wasn't so bad.

If I could just forget the cameras were there and act like myself, reality TV would be a snap.

"A tour of Port Quincy? I went to college here, and I must say, there isn't a lot viewers will want to see highlighted. It's a sleepy little town." Adrienne arched a perfect blond brow and waited to see if I'd take the bait.

"But that's what I love about it," I answered slowly, thinking of how I'd ended up in this town. I'd been engaged to be married here, but never imagined I'd jettison my law career, leave Pittsburgh behind, break up with my fiancé, and inherit his grandmother's mansion. But here I was, ensconced in this quirky and gorgeous house I'd turned into a B and B, in business with my sister, and dating a wonderful man. I couldn't have been happier with the way things had turned out. I loved my new hometown and never wanted to leave.

"Port Quincy may be sleepy, but it's also filled with amazing people. It's charming and welcoming, and I'm happy to call it home. I hope you'll get to know it over the next few days and see for yourself how wonderful it is."

"Great job. You're a natural." Xavier offered me a serene smile, and it was only then that I realized I'd been filmed again. I reveled in his even-keeled manner and wondered how he managed to be with a woman riddled with such high-strung perfectionism. I wondered how Garrett had managed as well. I shook off that thought and vowed to give Dakota and Beau a lovely display of Port Quincy hospitality.

Chapter Two

The next day dawned clear and cold and still. I stayed in bed for a few minutes in my aerie perch of a third-floor apartment and gathered my thoughts for the week ahead. I finally arose just before the sun showed its face and puttered into the kitchen to make my guests a meal. I recalled Xavier's green smoothie and fixed a breakfast with his apparent health consciousness in mind: egg white and veggie omelets, whole wheat bagels, fruit, chocolate black bean muffins, and an array of green teas and coffee. The crew appeared to have slept well despite the time difference from California and dug in with appreciative murmurs. Xavier did commandeer my blender to whip up another pungent shake, this one a concoction of berries, tomatoes, and beets. He took an appreciative slug and let out a sigh. Adrienne picked at her omelet and gave him a contented smile.

"Your outfit is perfect, Mallory," she said as she brought her dishes into the kitchen.

"Thank you." I beamed, secretly pleased the Ice Queen had given me her stamp of approval. Maybe she'd just been grumpy and jet-lagged yesterday. It was a new day, and I'd try to start fresh with Adrienne, despite the millions of questions I had for my boyfriend, Garrett.

"*Your* outfit, however—" she began, sliding her baby blue eyes over to Rachel. Today my sister had donned skintight leggings with little purple hearts scattered over the cloth and a voluminous pink sweatshirt that hung off one shoulder. "Perhaps—"

"No way, Jose." Rachel stopped loading the dishwasher and shook her head, the honey-kissed brown waves fanning out. "Xavier hasn't said anything about my clothes, and he's the only one I care about."

I hid my smile and took Adrienne's dishes, pleased that my sister wasn't taking any guff. Adrienne pursed her lips and wheeled around on her heels. She minced out of the kitchen without a backward glance.

Before we could even comment, a black car rolled into the driveway.

"This is it!" Rachel set down a dish and nearly yanked me from the kitchen. "Dakota and Beau are here!"

The crew gave us amused smiles as Rachel pulled me through the dining room and into the front hall. We made it to the door as the celebrities got out of the car and watched them advance up the long herringbone brick path, cleared of ice and snow.

Beau held the car door open for his fiancée,

and Dakota Craig emerged. On the red carpet, she was all glamor and minimalist, chic style, her dark blond tresses gathered in chignons and buns. Her style in everyday life translated to clean-cut lines and simple clothing. Her long hair was gathered in a loose braid, and she wore gray leggings and an oversized navy sweater beneath her camel coat. I thought I caught a glimpse of red hair at the edges of her temples, but it may have been a trick of the light. Only her sunglasses and her boots, which looked like they cost the amount of some of the smaller weddings held here, revealed her status as a movie star. She carried her own luggage and climbed the stairs to the porch quickly. She pushed her sunglasses into her hair and enveloped me in a quick hug.

"Thank you for throwing this together so quickly." Her famously large violet eyes sparkled and I was surprised to see a smattering of freckles beneath them that didn't show up on film.

"It's a pleasure. I hope you enjoy staying here. We're going to throw you an amazing wedding."

Dakota turned around in a circle, taking in the vast front hall. "It's just good to be back in Port Quincy again."

When I had been contacted about hosting Dakota and Beau's wedding, I'd been shocked to learn Dakota had been born and partially raised right here in Port Quincy, Pennsylvania. Her mother, Roxanne, had moved her to L.A. when she was three to star in commercials, but she'd returned each summer and still considered Port Quincy to be home.

"This is my fiancé, Beau Wright."

"Pleased to meet ya." Beau swept down to kiss my hand, sending me into a fit of giggles. He repeated his antics with Rachel, his southern drawl in full effect, and earned another set of nervous laughter. Charm oozed out of Beau's tight, nonexistent pores. He was as old as Dakota, thirty-one, but didn't quite look it. Perhaps this was because he shielded his complexion from the sun with his wide ten-gallon hat. He removed it and promptly set it down on a lamp. I whisked it away and set it on a table where it wouldn't catch fire. Beau's glossy dark curls shone in the indoor light. He removed his coat, revealing a denim shirt and black jeans, completing his look with his trademark cowboy boots. Beau was simply hotness personified, Michelangelo's David come to life in an unpretentious country package. Beau and Dakota were an unlikely match, one the tabloids liked to speculate about. But they seemed genuinely in love in the dealings I'd had with them over the phone and on Skype, and I was eager to give them a perfect day.

Beau offered me a folksy smile and turned to take in Rachel again. This time, his gaze was borderline lecherous. His famous, preternaturally blue eyes, rimmed in impossibly long lashes, settled on my sister's prodigious bust line. Dakota didn't see it, but I did, and I drew in a sharp breath. He quickly looked away. I wondered if I'd imagined it.

My sister had been through a rough series of relationships this year and had sworn off dating completely back in November. That hadn't stopped the men of Port Quincy from following her around like the Pied Piper of Hotness everywhere she went.

Rachel had changed her attitude about men, but not her signature come-hither style of dress and demeanor. She left a passel of smitten and drooling men in her wake whenever she ventured into town, as they trailed after her to no avail.

It was probably best for her to take a break from men, but she'd been tetchy and off her game for months. She embraced her new celibacy like a nun. She was often grouchy, pious and somber.

But she had no problem setting Beau back in his place. She gave him a side eye powerful enough to peel the paint off the front hall walls. He had the impudence to return her look with a lazy wink.

Uh-oh.

Maybe what the tabloids said about Beau's roving eye was true. I wasn't the only one to witness Beau's performance. Dakota's mother, Roxanne, had brought up the rear and seen it all. She set her bags down in the hall with a huff and shook her head at Beau, who was now carefully studying the glass bird chandelier above him.

Roxanne looked much like her daughter Dakota, if Dakota had aged twenty years and spent much time on her self-preservation. She was a sturdy study in silicone, peroxide, and Botox. She had the same wide cheekbones as her daughter and massive violet eyes, but her lips were trending toward serious duck face. Her hair was an ashy blond in contrast to Dakota's rich golden hue. Only her hands gave away her age, as the knuckles were swollen, the skin paper thin and aged. Her nails sported a meticulous French manicure but were careworn.

One of Roxanne's bags began to shimmy and shake.

"We're here, Pixie. You can come out now."

Who's Pixie?

A low, guttural growl emanated from the Louis Vuitton carry-on at Roxanne's feet. She carefully unzipped the bag and parted the top. A tiny Shih Tzu with long, diaphanous black and white hair bounded from the leather satchel and yipped with glee, turning around in a tight circle on the marble floor.

"Is mama's little girl adjusting to the time change?" Roxanne picked up the pup and nuzzled her under her chin. I bit back a smile when I realized Pixie and her owner bore a certain resemblance. Roxanne wore her long, platinum hair over her shoulders, with a small bunch gathered at the top of her head. Pixie sported the same look, her eyes also large like her owner's, but black and lustrous. Both wore leather, Roxanne's in the form of buttery black pants, and Pixie's in the form of a metal-studded collar.

"I didn't know you were bringing a dog, but welcome, Pixie." I knelt to run my fingers over her long, silky black and white coat. She stood on hind legs and executed a neat doggy extension of her paw.

"Oh, she's a ham," Roxanne clucked over her dog. "It appears everyone in the family has the acting gene."

I idly wondered how Pixie would get along with my cats, Whiskey and Soda, but pushed the thought aside.

"Xavier." The color drained from Roxanne's face

as she took in the director, who'd just advanced down the stairs.

"Roxanne, what a pleasant surprise." Xavier leaned in to plant an air kiss on the momager's cheek, leaving her completely nonplussed. Her hand fluttered to her face, and she excused herself to powder her nose.

What's up with that?

After cursory introductions and the checking in of Dakota, Beau, and Roxanne's luggage, we got down to brass tacks in the library. Dakota and Beau nestled together predictably on the gray velvet love seat, while Roxanne sat imperiously on a yellow chintz chair that resembled a flowered throne. She'd seemed to have recovered from her odd reaction to Xavier. Adrienne, Rachel, and I flanked the fireplace. The cameras were soon rolling.

"We'll go over the basic details of your ceremony and reception. Then, later today, you'll visit with your bridesmaids, and we'll pick up their dresses at Silver Bells, the bridal shop." I didn't add that I had a few last-minute details to shore up with the headmistress of Dunlap Academy, for whom I was throwing the Winter Ball. Ginger happened to be Dakota's maid of honor, so I figured I could mix in a little business this afternoon when we went to see the bridesmaids.

The fire crackled and popped merrily, and lazy snowflakes pirouetted down from the sky outside the wide bay window. I felt more comfortable in front of the cameras today and hoped soon I wouldn't even notice they were there. Roxanne was doting on Pixie, Dakota was nodding eagerly, Beau was checking out my sister, and Adrienne's mouth was twisted in a frown. She picked up my idea book for Dakota's wedding and flicked through the binder, her disdain growing with each perusal of the page.

"The color palette is a bit spare, no?" Adrienne blinked innocently enough, but I could spot her tactic a mile away. She often made suggestions to the celebrity brides at the eleventh hour so that the wedding planners on the show would have to scurry and execute new ideas on the eves of weddings.

"It's a black and white theme, and it's just perfect." Roxanne must have watched a few episodes of *I Do* and was ready to head Adrienne off. "I chose the palette myself. Pixie was the inspiration." The Shih Tzu barked upon hearing her name and jumped down from the window seat to return to Roxanne.

They designed the wedding around Pixie? This is news to me.

"Yes, but a few pops of color might be nice." Adrienne turned to Dakota, her face expectant. "Perhaps a nice pink or red accent woven through would tie it into the month a bit better and not appear so stark."

Dakota cocked her head then nodded slowly. "Yes, pink is my favorite color. A bit of pink *would* be better."

"Mallory, how did you not know the bride's favorite color!" Adrienne tsked lightly and settled back into her chair, her work done.

I gritted my teeth and remembered I was on camera.

"We discussed incorporating pops of pink or

red, but ultimately decided not to. We can add them in now. I'm sure it won't be any trouble."

Yeah, right.

Valentine's Day was just around the corner, and my florist would be busy enough serving the denizens of Port Quincy without having to change plans midstream on Dakota's wedding. But I'd have to work something out, since I'd just been challenged on camera.

"I'll talk to the florist." My cheeks burned as I recalled lobbying for some pink accents for Dakota and watching her get outvoted by her mother.

"No, no, no! It's strictly black and white." Roxanne crossed the room and snatched the idea book from Adrienne's arms. Pixie jumped down from the yellow chair and barked while she followed Roxanne. "This is an Ascot-themed wedding, just like the race in *My Fair Lady*."

Dakota sighed and took Beau's hand, resigned to her momager's wishes. Roxanne had proved over the last few months to be the ultimate mother-manager with a vise-like grip on her daughter's career and plans. She made Kris Jenner of the Kardashians look like Little Bo Peep.

"Ladies, all that matters is that I'm marrying the love of my life." Beau's drawl broke the tension and he leaned down for a showy kiss. All the women sighed, except for Rachel, who stared at him warily.

Adrienne and Roxanne squared off for the next hour, agreeing on nothing except the fact it was a travesty the B and B didn't have an on-site gym.

"I'm happy to give you day passes for the two gyms we have here in Port Quincy." I gritted my teeth and procured the passes, wondering what I'd gotten myself into.

The bride, groom, and my sister and I left to meet with Dakota's bridesmaids and finish some last-minute Winter Ball plans.

"I give them a year, tops," Rachel whispered as we headed out the door.

I hated to agree.

We all piled into my roomy and rattly 1976 tan station wagon, a boat of a car I'd christened the Butterscotch Monster. It had begun to snow again, and we headed down the now-slippery Sycamore Street toward the east side of town.

"I haven't been back to Dunlap Academy in ages," Dakota breathed, taking in the undulating hills of Port Quincy. "It was my favorite time, being in school."

"I thought your favorite time was now, being my best girl," Beau drawled, pulling her closer to him despite her seat belt. She giggled like the schoolgirl she'd been and nestled in his arms. I decided to take a chill pill. Sure, it had *seemed* like Beau had been checking out Rachel, but maybe that was just part of his folksy affect. I'd reserve judgment and push the tabloid murmurings from my head.

We pulled up to the gates of the Dunlap Women's Academy, and I marveled for the umpteenth time at the opulence and fake bucolic splendor. The grounds hunkered behind a wrought-iron fence with the school's crest bearing a lily and a rose imprinted on each panel amidst a riot of black metal curlicues. The school and dormitory seemed to rise out of a mist, a fortress of pearly white stones complete with towers, heavy wooden doors, and flags waving from turrets. The colossal, castle-like building, built at the end of the nineteenth century, perched on a snowy crag overlooking the Monongahela River. Young women skated on the pond on the southern end of the campus, their scarves streaming behind them in long ribbons, woven with the school colors of green and blue. Some built snowmen under the leaden and snowy sky, and laughter could be heard everywhere.

I was holding the Winter Ball as a favor for my arch enemy and once almost mother-in-law, Helene Pierce. Helene had helped me renovate Thistle Park in record time last October, and the price she'd exacted had been steep: host and pay for the Winter Ball for the Dunlap Women's Academy, a coming-out party for fifty debutantes and their dates. The ball was usually held in the grand ballroom at the school, but it was under renovation this year. The school had needed to come up with an alternative fast. I'd had no choice but to comply, and now it was time to pay the piper.

But the ball would be tomorrow, and then I'd be free from Helene once and for all. In fact, she wasn't even due to arrive in Port Quincy until just before the ball. She was currently in Boca Raton, a reluctant snowbird, since it required that she give up her spot on the Winter Ball Committee.

That hadn't stopped her from calling, texting, and badgering me every chance she got. She'd even taken to using Skype to grill me about the ball, the camera aimed at her forehead as she yelled into the speakers.

And there was one catch to all of Helene's orders. While the cat is away, the mice will play, and it was no surprise Helene had other enemies besides me. The Winter Ball Committee had decided to ignore Helene's wishes now that she wasn't lording over them in person. They'd directed me to come up with a fresher, more modern take on the staid debutante ball, and I'd been happy to comply. I'd tried to warn Helene that some of her edicts were not going to happen, but she'd just steadfastly insisted I do her bidding. She would be in for a heck of a surprise tomorrow when she saw I hadn't carried out her numerous orders. But it would be a fait accompli, and there would be nothing she could do.

I gulped as I turned my boat of a station wagon into a parking space and hoped Helene wouldn't make a scene tomorrow. Which was why a shiver trickled from the nape of my neck down the length of my spine when I caught a stinging whiff of Calèche as we reached the headmistress's office.

"Oh no—"

"She's here." Rachel grabbed my arm and spun in a slow circle, as if Helene would leap out of the shadows.

Dakota and Beau sent us quizzical but amused looks. "Who's here?"

"You're here!" Ellie Barnes, the drama teacher and one of Dakota's bridesmaids, ricocheted down the hall and embraced the couple. "I'm so excited for your wedding!"

Dakota and Ellie jumped up and down, laughing and chatting, an amused Beau looking on. The women were of similar height, about five foot seven, but Ellie's hair was a rich, dark chestnut. She had an interesting, angular face, and a rollicking laugh that begged you to join in on the fun with her.

"I'll give you a tour of the school. So much has changed." Ellie linked arms with Dakota and the women nearly skipped off, Beau following, not a moment too soon.

"I expect all of my plans for the Winter Ball are in order."

The icy chill returned as I whipped around to face Helene Pierce. She looked the same as ever, suited up in one of her Chanel jackets, this one an electric blue with green and silver threads. Her gumball-sized Mamie Eisenhower pearls, pinched lips, and tan pantyhose completed her look. Boca Raton had added a bit of a tan to her frowning visage, and her pageboy fanned out around her ears, gray and teased to perfection.

I gathered my will and straightened up, reaching out to Rachel for support. "What a pleasant surprise, Helene. You're back a day early." I chickened out and used a tactic from my days as an attorney and provided her with a little white lie of omission. "The ball will be splendid." I gulped and pressed on. "You won't be disappointed."

No, you'll just be enraged beyond belief. Hurricane Helene will morph into Mount Vesuvius.

Helene nodded regally, her large sapphire teardrop earrings swinging like pendulums against her ropy neck. I'd taken my marching orders from the Winter Ball Committee comprised of students, parents, and teachers at Dunlap. If Helene wanted to have it out tomorrow, she'd have to go through them.

"Mallory, Rachel, so glad to see you." The headmistress of Dunlap emerged from her office, willowy and smiling and welcoming. Ginger was the picture of calm and competence in her gray suit, cut elegantly to fit her spare and slim frame. Her ever-present tablet nestled in her arms and against one hip, as one would carry a toddler. Her dark curls were twisted up in a bun atop her head, anchored by purple butterfly clips, her only splash of color. Ginger Crevecoeur was the youngest headmistress in the school's history, and she had plans to revamp the staid boarding school into a more modern experience for the young women attending. It didn't seem like Helene shared her ideas.

"I'd like to have a word with you." Helene turned to face Ginger. My grilling was apparently over.

"While I'd love to have a chat, Helene, I have a meeting with a parent." Ginger sent Helene an amused look and made her way down the hall to her office. But Helene wasn't done with her, and no one put Helene in the corner.

"You will not dismiss me, girl." Helene's talon-like hand reached out to grab Ginger's wrist, keeping her rooted to the spot. Ginger sighed and glanced at her silver wristwatch.

"You have two minutes."

"I've heard from my sources that you have plans to admit men to Dunlap. I'll have you know the school will never be coed. I will not let you besmirch the founders' intentions."

Rachel lost it at that point, giggling at the word "besmirch." I had to agree. It sounded like Helene was invoking constitutional law over an argument about a boarding school.

"I knew you were a student here quite a while ago." Ginger paused. "But I didn't know you were here when the school was founded in 1892." A smirk gathered at the corners of Ginger's lips as she volleyed her quip. Helene gasped, and two spots of color lit up her papery cheeks exactly an inch above the peach rouge she'd applied.

"I shouldn't even deign to discuss these matters with you here," Ginger continued, disgust now marring her delicate features. "But you know as well as I do if something doesn't change, there won't be a Dunlap Academy. Enrollment is down. We face some hard choices. We'll vote next week."

"It's a good thing my sources told me something was afoot." Helene drew herself up in her kitten heels and rolled her shoulders back underneath her shoulder pads. "I will gather my forces and we will defeat you."

Ginger smiled, unflappable as I'd always known her to be, and started down the hall, dismissing Helene.

"And the Belle of the Ball tomorrow will wear the Winter Ball tiara." Helene crossed her arms and actually stomped her foot like a petulant two-year-old.

Ginger turned around and shook her head. "It's too valuable, Helene. It'll reside in the school's safe until we decide by committee what to do with it."

"That's why I've convened an emergency vote to take place this evening over Skype with the board members about what to do with the tiara."

Helene smiled, her bicuspids showing, lupine and triumphant.

She'd finally succeeded in rattling Ginger. "You wouldn't dare. Only I can convene an emergency meeting. Consider it cancelled. Now, if you'll excuse me, I have real work to do. I'm modernizing this school and making it better, not a place mired in anachronisms and petty feuds as you'd like it to be."

Ginger finally left Helene in the hall and advanced toward her office, her long legs churning to make her meeting on time. I got some satisfaction taking in Helene's face as Ginger left her in the dust. It wasn't often that someone got the last word with my once almost mother-in-law. Rachel and I followed Ginger to wait our turn outside her office to go over some last-minute Winter Ball plans.

"You're late." A tall man dressed in an exquisite pinstripe suit paced in front of Ginger's door like a caged tiger, his lined face drawn into a sneer. A few drops of sweat fell onto his collar.

"Yes, Sterling, I do apologize. Why don't we head into my office—"

"Do you know how precious my time is?" The man stopped pacing and executed a hairpin stop in front of Ginger, rendering them almost nose-to-nose. The lights gleamed off his slicked-back hair, and he showily checked his Rolex. "I wait for no one. This meeting is over."

Sterling Jennings.

I recognized the man as the premier heart surgeon at the McGavitt-Pierce Hospital here in town. His face was plastered on several billboards proclaiming his services.

"But, Dad, what about the lacrosse team?" A young woman cowered in the corner, seemingly embarrassed by her father's performance. She was Nora Jennings, a student member of the Winter Ball Committee, and I sent her a little wave. She returned it, her cheeks turning pink, before she stood and followed her father as he stalked out of the room.

"That was intense." I sucked in a deep breath of air and decided being a headmistress was as stressful, or perhaps more so, than dealing with bridezillas and meddling mothers of the bride.

"I'm used to working with parents who have an inflated sense of importance." Ginger chuckled and ushered us into her office. The room was a soothing study in several shades of purple with a butterfly motif and pleasantly soft lights. "Not to mention board members like Helene who think they run the school and can't wrap their heads around the idea that there's a new sheriff in town." Ginger shook her head and gave an increasingly bitter laugh. "Helene is head of the old guard around here, but the school needs an injection of new ideas." She paused dolefully. "Or there won't be a school anymore."

"You never told me Dunlap was having problems." Dakota peeked her head around the corner, and Ginger rose and crossed the room to give her a hug.

"Don't worry about it." Ginger batted away her concerns with a flick of her hand and sent Beau a shy, inclusive smile. "We've faced closure before and have always been able to head it off."

"I was so happy here," Dakota mused. She crossed the wide office to peer out the window at the girls playing in the snow. "I'd hate to see it close. Do you need money for the school?"

I admired Dakota's straightforward offer, but Ginger shook her head. "It's time you stopped bailing me out." She smiled and turned to me. "Dakota footed the bill for me and for Ellie when we were in high school. She used her earnings from *Silverlake High* to pay our tuition, and I've always meant to pay her back."

Dakota had made her fame in the early 2000s on a teen soap opera, *Silverlake High*. Rachel and I had eagerly watched the show each day after school, and I still had a hard time separating Dakota from her character on the show. It had gone off the air after her costar died on set in a horrible accident, but I couldn't quite remember the details.

"You still have it!" Dakota squealed and picked up a silver picture frame from Ginger's desk and turned to show us the picture. A teenage Dakota stood flanked by Ellie and Ginger, all dressed in the Dunlap uniform. A young man stood behind them, and the four teens laughed with apparent joy.

"What is *that*?" Rachel had stopped looking at the picture and stared in shock at a gorgeous tiara laid out on an impossibly faded bed of red velvet.

"This is the famed Winter Ball tiara." Ginger set the picture of her teenaged self on her desk with a fond pat and picked up the gleaming crown with precise movements. "The workers renovating the ballroom found a time capsule in the cornerstone.

There was a rumor about a tiara, but everyone thought it was rhinestone. It turns out it belonged to a robber baron's daughter who attended a hundred years ago. She was crowned the first Belle of the Winter Ball and donated her tiara to be used for each subsequent Belle."

Rachel licked her lips, itching to don the diadem. It sparkled in the low light, a lattice of hundreds of tiny stones throwing off mini prisms across Ginger's desk.

"They're mine-cut diamonds," Ginger explained, reverently placing the crown back on its velvet perch. "There's no way we're putting this puppy back into service. There's a reason it was whisked away and secretly placed in the time capsule almost a hundred years ago. You can't have something like this lying around all year. Helene will just have to use the cut-glass crown we've been using for the Belle of the Ball." And with that, Ginger entombed the crown in a safe behind her desk.

Rachel and I smoothed out some last-minute details regarding the Winter Ball. Soon my sister and I left with Dakota, Beau, and Ellie, as we made our way downtown to pick up bridesmaids dresses.

Sterling Jennings climbed into an Alfa Romeo with his daughter in tow and gave us a dark look as he pulled out in front of us, cutting us off.

Ginger is a lovely person, but she sure has a lot of enemies.

The tension rolled off my shoulders as the gates to Dunlap Academy closed behind me.

"Tomorrow is the ball," Rachel reminded me, taking in my furrowed brows, "and then this mess will be over and we can focus on Dakota's wedding."

We were thankfully alone, since Ellie was driving the engaged couple.

"There's no way I'll ever agree to host two events so close together again."

Not like I have a choice.

Dakota had insisted on a Valentine's Day wedding, and Helene wouldn't budge on the Winter Ball date either, so we would make the most of the two events and just deal. The amount of money Dakota and Beau were paying me for their wedding made my head spin, and easily covered the cost of the Winter Ball I'd been tricked into hosting.

"We just need to get through the next day, and then we can breathe a sigh of relief."

Rachel and I parked and made our way on the slippery sidewalk to Silver Bells, the bridal store owned by my dear friend Bev Mitchell. It was decked to the nines in February splendor, a canvas of pink, red, and silver. A dress form clad in a voluminous cream tulle gown took up most of the front window. A frilly red parasol hovered overhead, protecting the dress from the rain of red and silver hearts suspended from the ceiling. A male mannequin hovered nearby, down on one knee, a sparkling ring at the ready in his hand for a proposal.

We pushed open the door to the store, the eponymous bells chiming pleasantly to announce our arrival. The store was overrun with girls from

Dunlap Academy getting their final fittings in before tomorrow's ball. It smelled like teen spirit, the air redolent with sweet adolescent perfume and fruity bubble gum. The melee of girls nearly filled the space with their poufy gowns. The store was alive with high-pitched chatter, and the students' energy was infectious.

"This is a lot fancier than our prom." Rachel took in the young women in their pale gowns, and I had to agree. The Winter Ball's dress code demanded white dresses, and most of the debutantes had purchased wedding gowns to fulfill that edict. The twenty girls laughed and gamboled around the store, which was decimated as if a horde of locusts had torn through a wheat field. Scraps of cream and ivory ribbon littered the floor like the aftermath of a battle waged in silk and taffeta.

I spotted Nora Jennings in the back of the store, glancing around rather furtively. A slight young woman with platinum waves grabbed Nora's hand and slipped something inside. Nora quickly traded her a small parcel and disappeared into her dressing room. I blinked, not sure what I'd just witnessed.

"Girls, girls, settle down now. Let's get this wrapped up." Bev, the store purveyor, bustled about, rolling up tape measures and putting pins back into cushions. She'd swathed her apple-shaped frame in a poppy blossom tunic, black pedal pushers, and cherry red flats. She nestled her rhinestone cat's-eye glasses in her tall blond beehive and gave Rachel and me fleeting air kisses as she rushed by.

Dakota had beaten us to the store and was trying on one of her wedding dresses, which she'd brought from Los Angeles, for a final fitting. She stepped from the dressing room and the store went silent.

"Oh, honey, you're perfect." Roxanne gazed in rapture at her daughter as Dakota turned a slow circle in front of the mirror.

"Arf!" Pixie gave an appreciative bark and sniffed Dakota's hem, her curly little tail motoring in a helicopter blade-like frenzy.

Dakota's gown was for the reception, a daring stark white sheath slit up to the thigh, covered in tiny silver beads. The teens oohed and ahhed, and began taking pictures. Some furtively snapped Dakota with their phones, while others were not so clandestine. Dakota didn't seem to mind, and she paused for a few selfies with the students from her alma mater.

"Leah!" Dakota turned from the mirror and rushed forward to embrace one of the teens, a tall girl wearing tortoiseshell glasses and a simple cream satin gown. The girl's most arresting feature was a near yard of vivid purple hair streaming over her shoulders and down her back.

"Mallory, this is Ellie's little sister, Leah, my final bridesmaid." Dakota introduced me to the girl, who bore a strong resemblance to Ellie with her angular face and deep-set, near-black eyes. But it was hard to focus on the similarities between the sisters without getting caught up in Leah's orchid-colored tresses. I could now take in the left side of her head, which was shaved, the better to expose a large gauged earring and a tiny flower tattoo on her neck.

"I can't wait for your wedding! Welcome back." Leah's voice was surprisingly girlish and high despite her punky looks.

Bev bustled over with the bridesmaids' dresses as the girls from Dunlap slowly changed and headed out the door, most of them dawdling to get a closer look at Dakota.

Ellie and Leah emerged from their dressing rooms and executed careful shimmies, as the mermaid-style dresses didn't afford them room to take full strides.

"They're fantastic." Roxanne sipped from the flute of champagne Bev had given her and beamed at the women as she stroked Pixie's long coat. "Chic and stark and bold."

Dakota nodded, impassively taking in the off-the-shoulder black silk mermaid gowns. "It'll be so elegant." Her words were the right thing to say, but there was no heart behind them.

"She hates it," Rachel hissed into my ear, thankfully barely audible.

I nodded, agreeing with my sister. Dakota wasn't happy, and it was becoming apparent that not all of the choices she'd agreed to, as her mother ran roughshod over her wishes, were sitting well with her. I wanted Dakota to be happy, and began scheming for a way to incorporate some of her real wishes for her wedding.

Whatever those are.

In our phone conferences over the last few months, Dakota had acquiesced to Roxanne's suggestions, and now she was stuck with a wedding not entirely of her choice.

But I had a ball to throw in the next twenty-four hours. I vowed to make Dakota's day right. Just as soon as I put the Winter Ball in the rearview mirror.

Chapter Three

It was the day of the Winter Ball. A warm front was due to move through, threatening to turn the dazzling snowy display outside into a soupy mess of rain and mud. But inside my B and B it would be winter splendor, and I hoped the students and the Winter Ball Committee would love it.

"I can't believe we're doing all this work for a glorified prom," Rachel grumbled as she put the finishing touches on the hundreds of petit fours she'd whipped up. "These girls better appreciate it!"

"Tell me why again you consented to handle this event the same fortnight as Dakota and Beau's wedding?" Adrienne appeared at my shoulder, already dressed in eveningwear for the festivities that would begin within the hour. Xavier thought it would be fun to feature the Winter Ball as a small segment of Dakota's wedding episode, since Dakota once attended Dunlap Academy. Adrienne had been happy to comply.

I plastered a serene smile on my face and answered Adrienne as calmly as possible. I'd since talked to my boyfriend Garrett about Adrienne, and as his initial shock in seeing her had worn off, he'd given me some pointers in dealing with her.

"Don't let her know she's getting under your skin," he'd admonished last night over the phone.

"Who said she's getting under my skin?" I'd replied, a little hurt.

"Oh, I know Adrienne, and she definitely will," he'd warned before we'd hung up.

I blinked back at Adrienne. "I owed a favor to someone at the school. It couldn't be helped."

Adrienne raised her eyebrows, waiting for me to go on.

"Don't you worry—this event will go off without a hitch. Then Rachel and I can turn to Dakota and Beau's wedding full throttle."

I wheeled around and left Adrienne before she could offer me another piece of dubiously well-meaning advice. I surveyed with satisfaction the front and back halls, where the bulk of the ball would take place.

The front hall held twenty tables, the discreet place cards glittering on each setting of china. I'd enacted the Winter Ball Committee's seating chart to a T, and while most of the debutantes were from out of town, I did recognize some of the names of families that passed for high society here in Port Quincy. They were the names of people who had once been invited to my wedding to Keith Pierce, Helene's son, that thankfully had not gone off.

The color palette for the Winter Ball was right up Adrienne's alley. It was a wash of pale blue, frosty gray, and vivid periwinkle. Fish lines ran across the high ceilings and suspended hundreds of shimmery silver snowflakes. Pale blue linens dressed the tables, and antique snow globes depicting miniature scenes from Port Quincy graced each table. The globes were fashioned from Mc-Gavitt Glass, the company once headed by the former owner of this house, a captain of industry. Cream and silver candles marched down each table, and waiters lit them carefully in preparation for the beginning of the ball. Hundreds of blue flowers spilled from vases all around the cavernous room. There were snowball-like clusters of periwinkle hydrangea and stately irises quivering in tall gray vases. Deep lupine stalks rose out of bases of dusty miller, and a sea of phlox covered the side tables. All of the flowers had been flown in from South America by way of our florist, Lucy, at the Bloomery, and I turned in a slow circle to admire the Winter Ball Committee's plans come to life, executed by yours truly.

I'd ignored every whim decreed by Helene from her stay in Boca Raton. She'd wanted a coral canvas with gold accents to play up the one hundred and twenty-fifth anniversary of the school. She'd intoned that the girls would dine on watercress sandwiches and beef Wellington. We'd be having spicy tapas and sushi instead, as well as a DJ rather than a swing band.

"I hate blue flowers." Dakota appeared at my side, shuddering, her thin arms wrapped around her stomach. She wore a simple dark green velvet cocktail dress for the event, which she'd agreed to emcee as the school's most famous alumna.

"I'm sorry," I sputtered, caught off guard by the

vehemence of her pronouncement. "We'll be sure not to have any blue for your wedding."

Dakota shook her head in apology. "It's okay. I just didn't know this event would have a blue theme."

Why does she hate blue flowers?

I pushed the thought out of my head as Helene waltzed in the front door. She soon shucked her mink coat and tossed it with a flick of her wrist at the coat check. The heavy jacket landed on the poor attendant, who yelped and hurried to hang it up.

Helene was in rare form. She wore a silky floor-length salmon dress, which I recognized as her Bill Blass. Sequins and seed pearls liberally encrusted the matching brocade jacket. Helene would be right at home on an episode of *Dallas,* circa 1985. She was outfitted in prodigious shoulder pads befitting a Pittsburgh Steeler.

Rachel leaned down in my ear. "Nancy Reagan called. She'd like her wardrobe back." My sister was wearing a daring fire-engine-red halter dress for the event, with a smattering of glitter fashioned as starbursts. I was in a simple black sheath, so I could buzz around all evening and unobtrusively make sure things were running smoothly.

I stifled a smile at my sister's comment. But it was soon wiped off my face as Helene spun in a slow circle, taking in the blue splendor. Her face contorted into a mask of rage, her coral lips pursing and unpursing as she sputtered and quaked.

"What have you done!" She minced over with surprising speed, her kitten heels striking the marble floor so hard I feared they'd spark. "I gave you very specific instructions on how to execute this ball, and instead, you created this abomination!"

A waiter cringed as he passed, readying a large tray of tapas and sushi for the debutantes who would be arriving at any moment. Helene plucked a piece of spider roll from the platter and dropped it back in disgust.

"Raw *fish*? Have you lost your mind?"

I feared she'd have an aneurysm, but stood my ground.

"You weren't on the Winter Ball Committee, Helene. I had to follow their decrees, not yours."

Helene stood still for a moment. The room went eerily still as the waitstaff paused to see what she'd do.

"You're *fired*!" She pointed at me with a knobby finger, dripping in carnelians, her hand quivering with anger.

"You can't fire her," a calm voice sighed from across the room. Ginger, clad in a gorgeous black velvet suit, materialized at my side. She put a steadying and protective arm around my shoulders. "Mallory, you've done a magnificent job. The Winter Ball Committee will be so pleased."

Helene's mouth hung agape, at a loss for words for once in her life. But I knew it wouldn't last.

"It appears it's too late to reverse this travesty of a ball," Helene breathed, a gleam glittering in her eyes. "But at least some traditions will be resurrected as they were meant to be." She reached into her rather large beaded evening bag and pulled out the Winter Ball tiara. The hundreds of tiny old mine-cut diamonds winked and blinked in the light of the chandelier.

"You didn't dare." Ginger's voice was low and murderous as she lunged for the crown. "How did you get it?" She stopped herself from wrestling the delicate snowflake headpiece from Helene's hands and buried her fists in her suit pockets.

"I had your secretary open the safe." Helene's smile was wide, wolfish, and triumphant. "It appears you don't run everything at Dunlap Academy."

Ginger finally seemed rattled by Helene. She was a vision of restrained anger. She opened her palm.

"Give. Me. That. Crown."

Helene shrugged and deposited the crown in Ginger's outstretched hand. "Provided the Belle of the Ball gets to wear it tonight. Then we can add it to the vote next week in front of the board whether the tiara is worn each year. And don't think I don't have the votes to make it happen."

"Are you threatening me?" Ginger took a step toward Helene, towering a foot over her, her willowy frame like a twanging live wire.

"I'm just stating the facts. I will do everything going forward to depose you as headmistress. Your ideas for my alma mater are downright dangerous." Helene drew herself up to full height and took a single step closer. "If you attempt to make the school coed, it will be over your dead body."

She swished away, the sharp fizz of Calèche stinging my nose, leaving Ginger holding the tiara. We both deflated.

"She shouldn't make threats like that." My voice was small.

"Believe it or not, I'm used to it." Ginger regarded the tiara as if it were a live snake. "Do you have somewhere safe to put this for the duration of the ball?"

We retired to my office and locked the tiara in the small room. The headpiece reposed in the middle of my desk, the delicate snowflake lace lattice of platinum and diamonds twinkling in the low light.

"It must be worth a small fortune." I'd once found some very coveted paintings in this house and almost paid for them with my life. I wasn't keen on having something so expensive lingering in my office.

"I had it appraised this week. It's worth fifty thousand dollars."

Rachel let out a low whistle and walked into the room, reaching out a hand to touch the spray of diamonds. "Not chump change."

Ginger ruefully shook her head. "If it were up to me, this tiara would be transported to Christie's auction house posthaste. The school could use the money. But," she sighed, the stress of her altercation finally catching up to her, "Helene is actually right about this. The board will vote next week about whether we keep the tiara and use it as part of the Winter Ball tradition each year, or if we sell it or donate it to a museum. I'm surprised no one dug it out of the cornerstone years ago and raided the time capsule like King Tut's tomb."

A growing sound of chatter spilled into my office from the hall. The ball was beginning, and the students and their dates had arrived. Ginger hurried out of the room with her tablet firmly ensconced in her arms, the electronic device swathed in a case of rhinestones, almost transforming it into a fancy clutch.

I locked the door firmly behind me and didn't give the tiara another thought.

The Winter Ball was in full swing. It was a blinged-out pageant, more in keeping with the razzle-dazzle Rachel craved for Dakota's wedding. Adrienne, wearing a sleek gown in periwinkle silk, flitted around the ball interviewing girls for clips for *I Do*, and the camerawoman shot Dakota welcoming the girls to the ball as the alumna emcee. To my consternation, I saw Helene giving a lengthy speech on camera, and chatting up an amused Xavier.

The debutantes and their dates from the nearby boys' private school spun and danced beneath a behemoth disco ball in the back hall, the spinning decoration reflecting the blue gel lights.

Ginger walked around and talked to her students, who appeared to adore her. She attempted to talk to Sterling Jennings, who seemed to be chaperoning the event, but he wouldn't give her the time of day and sidestepped her every approach.

The evening culminated with the announcement of Belle of the Ball. Ellie clapped and whistled as her little sister, Leah, was announced the winner, and Dakota turned expectantly to receive the gorgeous snowflake tiara to place upon Leah's glossy purple chignon. Leah's angular and punky looks had been transformed, and she made a perfect Cinderella. Her tortoiseshell glasses were gone, and she'd perfectly dressed up her understated cream satin gown with a large rhinestone snowflake pin. I realized her orchid hair perfectly complemented her angular face. The crowd of young women and their dates began to buzz with anticipation when the crown didn't materialize and the minutes stretched by.

Help me, Dakota mouthed from the stage, awaiting the appearance of the tiara.

"Where's Ginger?" I searched the crowded back hall over my sister's shoulder.

"I haven't seen her in a while." My sister scanned the room for the headmistress to no avail.

"It appears the headmistress has disappeared with the tiara." Helene's voice rang out through the back hall as a stunned Dakota stared at the microphone Helene had just ripped from her hands. Helene stood triumphant, her coral lipstick bleeding into the lines around her mouth, her eyes flashing.

"That's not true!" a young woman called out uncertainly as the buzzing in the hall increased.

"This is getting out of control. We've got to find Ginger."

Leah stood stunned in front of her classmates, a crownless Belle of the Ball. She eventually left the front of the room as her classmates made their way to the coat check.

The large man-in-the-moon clock had struck midnight, and it was time for the girls' carriages, or limousines, to turn back into pumpkins. The long, sleek cars lined up in the front drive, their tailpipes giving off plumes of white smoke as the hot exhaust collided with the frigid, rainy night air. The debutantes were antsy to attend the usual post-ball breakfast at a local diner, then head back to their castle boarding school. As we called out for Ginger, the girls limped around, dangling high heels from their fingers, rubbing their throbbing feet, swollen from dancing. Their dates stifled cheek-splitting yawns and dug their hands in their pockets, taking them out again to check the time on their fancy watches.

Rachel and I finally made our way to our shared office.

"Uh-oh." Rachel grabbed the antique door handle and gave it a sharp pull. "This is locked."

"It *should* be locked." I bent down to examine the door.

Crap.

The ancient copper key, brittle and thin, was buried in the keyhole, the stem snapped off.

"It's almost as if—"

"Someone wanted to keep someone in," Rachel finished for me. We shared a wordless glance and raced to the heavy mahogany front doors. I grabbed Rachel before we left the front hall and motioned to the big roll-top desk that served as a check-in kiosk for guests. The lock had been jimmied and broken.

"Someone took the key and broke it in our office door."

The carefully labeled key rack was missing the copper key now jammed in the keyhole.

We were down the porch in a flash in our heels, the shoes sinking into the now muddy and puddled front grounds. Icy sheets of rain coursed down on our heads, obliterating the last bits of snow. We finally made it around to where our office stood and peered into the room, our hands flanking our eyes against the bright office lights.

Ginger sat at my desk, her willowy frame slumped over and face down. A massive arrangement of blue hydrangeas, lupines, lady slippers, and irises stood at attention next to her.

"Get a rock, something, anything!" My shrill voice cut into the night air as we rushed to get to Ginger.

Rachel handed me a copper frog decoration nestled at the foot of the bushes. I broke the window, gasping as the glass cut into my flesh. I unlocked the sash and Rachel boosted me into the room.

"I can't breathe. . . ."

A heavy chemical smell, bleach and something else, eddied in my nostrils, searing the delicate skin. I gasped and made my way to Ginger. I flipped up her palm, feeling for a pulse. I felt my vision flicker, my lungs screaming for air. Tears streaked down my face, and I gagged over and over again.

My last thought before everything went black was about the woman whose hand I held.

She was gone.

Chapter Four

I awoke to pandemonium, a sea of raccoon-streaked teenage faces peering down at me.

"All right everyone, give her some air."

Truman.

I closed my eyes again, thankful the chief of police and my boyfriend's father, Truman Davies, was here. To handle whatever the hell had just happened.

"Thank God." Rachel leaned close to my face, her green eyes misty and bright. "Don't ever scare me like that again!"

"Ginger—"

I sat up and was gently pushed down by Rachel, who tucked a velvet pillow under my head.

"Don't worry about her," she said hastily. Her eyes strayed to the right, where I could see my office. A white cloth draped over a still form.

"She's dead, isn't she?" My voice was at once hoarse and flat. I closed my eyes and welcomed the hot tears, which soothed the searing pain making my eyeballs itch and burn.

Rachel nodded, not meeting my gaze. I sat up, and this time she didn't force me down, but helped me to my feet. Girls gathered around the doorway to the office, still clad in their Winter Ball gowns. Other students stood in the rain, waiting for their limousines like bell-skirted apparitions rising out of the mist. They wept, holding each other up, and their dates from the neighboring boys' school stood stunned and subdued. The attendees had gone from young men and women at a coming-out party to celebrate their youth to veritable adults forced to contemplate death in a single tragic night. They were stony faced and shocked, bleary-eyed and infinitely tired.

And above the wail of the ambulance and the muffled sniffles of the students was a more disturbing caterwaul.

"Where is my tiara?" Helene screeched, frantically pulling at the sleeves of Truman's partner, policewoman Faith Hendricks.

"Mrs. Pierce, we'll get to the bottom of this, but not with you hanging on me." Faith crisply removed Helene's talons from her uniformed arm and deftly sidestepped her, her blond ponytail swishing in apparent annoyance.

"I can't believe you're worried about that stupid tiara at a time like this!" Ellie shot Helene a murderous glance with her near-black eyes as she supported a sobbing Dakota.

"Isn't it obvious?" Helene's voice rose an octave higher than usual. "Someone killed the headmistress to get the tiara. And while you all stand around here, they're getting away!" Her eyes darted toward the open front door, where flashlights could be seen through the raindrops, men and women combing the soupy lawn for evidence.

"We've called in reinforcements from neighboring towns, and they're searching the grounds," Faith announced. "Just calm down, Mrs. Pierce, and let us do our job."

Dakota bawled, hysterical in Ellie's arms. Her fiancé seemed too subdued to tend to her. Beau was nearly catatonic, stone faced and pale, all the folksy mirth drained from his countenance. He ineffectually patted Dakota's back and she wailed, her breath coming in wracking jags.

All the gaiety from a successful Winter Ball was gone. The jaunty party atmosphere was gone in a cloud of noxious gas.

"Chloramine vapor, to be exact."

"Excuse me?" I sat weakly in a chair in the parlor and Truman stood before me, eagle-eyed and attentive even at this late hour. His presence soothed me, but not as much as Garrett's. My boyfriend rushed into the room and gathered me in his arms, murmuring into my hair.

"I came as soon as I could. Dad called and let me know what happened." He drew back and scanned my face. His gaze caught on my eyes, which, I could see in the gilt mirror above the sideboard, were a brilliant, unsettling red. I nestled into him, breathing in his familiar scent of spearmint and oranges. He wore his black wool coat over a pajama top, half tucked into jeans. I steadied my cheek against his chest and felt my tears dampen his coat.

"That vase was filled with what I'm betting is a mixture of bleach and ammonia," Truman explained as Garrett settled me onto the appropriately named fainting couch. "Which produces chloramine vapor."

"That's why you're told never to mix cleaning products." I shook my head as if trying to clear a fog. "But who would have done this to Ginger? Why now, and why here?"

Truman let out a gust of air and began pacing the parlor. He'd hastily donned his official uniform, and his black shoes squeaked on the hardwood floor.

"Ginger called me this afternoon," he admitted in a low voice. "She wanted to keep me apprised about a situation with a student."

We were all silent for a moment, the buzz of the young women growing louder and louder.

"So she knew of a crime committed by a Dunlap student?" I pinched the bridge of my nose, a massive headache coming on.

"Or she knew of someone doing something to a student," Truman mused, shaking his head. "I was testifying in court this afternoon and didn't get her message until late. If only I'd called her back earlier."

We all turned to see the paramedics leading Ginger's body out the front door, her form shrouded in white.

"I have to do something." I stood, a wave of dizziness overtaking me.

"Just rest," Garrett soothed, handing me a cup of tea Rachel proffered.

"But the girls, we've got to get them home." The

debutantes milled about the first floor in a daze, exhausted and spent. Their white gowns, crisp and festive hours ago, seemed wilted and mussed.

"No one's going anywhere," Truman growled. "Not until I've questioned everyone." He turned to leave the room when the odious man who'd refused to meet with Ginger yesterday appeared in the doorway.

"You can't be serious." Sterling Jennings stood with his daughter, a quivering Nora, and donned his coat. "We're leaving at once." His words were filled with bluster, but he ran a hand over his slick hair with a nervous, trembling movement.

"Sir, this is a crime scene investigation. These girls may have seen something of interest. A detail that appears insignificant to them, but may have bearing on the murder of Ginger Crevecoeur. No one leaves until I say so."

Truman placed his hands on his hips, his hazel eyes dark and stony.

"Do you know who I am?" Sterling advanced into the room, his voice dangerously quiet. He was willing to throw his weight around as a premier heart surgeon, but I doubted Truman would care.

"Mr. Jennings, I'm not requesting that you stay. It's an order." Truman stepped closer to Sterling's face, the moisture beads from the rain in his salt-and-pepper hair quivering. "Now get out of my way."

Truman brushed past Sterling and Nora and began issuing directions for the limousines to depart, since the girls would be spending more time than they'd bargained for at Thistle Park. The young women anxiously called their parents on their cell phones. I had no doubt a small army of attorneys would descend upon my B and B come sun up.

But the most strident objector to being held at my mansion was Helene. "The perpetrator absconded with the tiara. You should be out looking for it!" She jabbed her bony finger in Truman's face.

He snarled with barely controlled ire, "Don't tell me how to do my job, Mrs. Pierce." Helene harrumphed down the hall, muttering about how the Winter Ball fiasco was entirely my fault.

The sun eventually rose, turning the black sky to murky gray as the rain continued to pelt down.

Garrett helped me and Rachel cobble together a breakfast for the hundred guests who were trapped at the B and B for questioning. We dug into the deep freezers in the basement and made a banquet of sausage, bacon, pancakes, and scrambled eggs. It was in direct contrast to the delicate and varied menu I'd put together for the Winter Ball, but I figured the girls would need something fortifying, plus it was all we had. I put in a call to the Greasy Spoon Diner to bring some extra meals to round out our provisions. The diner usually hosted the debutantes after the Winter Ball and would be wondering why none of the teens and their dates had showed up.

The Winter Ball attendees reluctantly picked at their food, some too upset to eat. Others dug in as if starved, thankful for the meal we'd made to feed an army of confused, sad, and gossiping girls. Gallons of tea and coffee were consumed, as the students and chaperones struggled to stay awake.

"I've got to go," Garrett apologized, dropping a

kiss atop my head. My fancy bun had long unraveled, and my heels had been left in the muddy ground beneath my office window. "Be careful." He pressed two more kisses into my now-bandaged hands and left me in Rachel's care to see Summer off to school and get to work. I felt eyes boring into the back of my head and turned, startled, to see Adrienne watching me through narrowed eyes.

The day dragged on, and Rachel gleaned snippets of updates from Truman and Faith. Ginger's ever-present tablet was missing, in addition to the diamond tiara. The pouring rain had erased any footprints from the grounds. And the fine dusting of black fingerprint powder had yielded nothing so far, as most of the attendees had worn elbow-length gloves.

The girls' tears had given way to jagged bouts of sleep and naps snatched on the many chaises and couches scattered around Thistle Park. It was 4 PM before the last of the girls, chaperones, and their lawyers drove away, and I felt like I'd spent the longest night of my life coming to grips with the Winter Ball Disaster, as Rachel and I had started calling it.

"Well, this is a colossal nightmare." Truman sat on the couch next to me with an unsuppressed *oof*. Faith sat down too, a study in contrasts. Truman was in his fifties, a vision of what Garrett would look like in twenty years. His six-foot-four frame sagged into the cushions, and his ample belly strained the buttons of his police uniform. Faith was in her mid-twenties, her face fresh and dewy, her ponytail ever perky. They made a great team, and if anyone could get to the bottom of what had happened to Ginger, it would be them.

"Who are your suspects?"

Truman usually didn't like to share details of his investigation with civilians, but seeing as my B and B was the scene of the crime, I hoped he'd relent this time.

He dragged a heavy hand across his brow and sighed. "Who isn't?"

"Oh, c'mon, we all know who did it." Rachel took a swig of coffee and made a face, her pretty green eyes baggy and puffy from lack of sleep.

"You know something I don't?" Truman leaned forward with interest.

"She means Helene. Isn't it obvious?" I put my feet up on an ottoman, willing myself to stay awake. I carefully unwrapped the bandages on my hands and examined the cuts from breaking the glass to get to Ginger. Thankfully, they were pretty superficial. "Helene has it out for Ginger. Yesterday afternoon, before the ball began, she threatened to kill her."

That got Truman and Faith's attention. Rachel and I detailed Helene's threat to Ginger regarding Dunlap turning coed.

"There's a big vote next week," Ellie said as she came up behind us and sat down.

Truman opened his mouth, perhaps to tell her to scram, then thought better of it. "Go on," he implored.

"I'm Ginger's best friend, and I teach at Dunlap too. Attendance is way down. The economy is hurting everyone, even the types of people who can afford to send their daughters to boarding school. Ginger said if we don't consider a merger with the boys' private school down the road, there may not be a Dunlap Academy in a few years."

Ellie caught a glimpse of herself in the gilt mirror and gasped, grabbing at a passel of tissues to wipe at her mascara trails.

"She also wanted that tiara," Rachel added.

"She got Ginger's secretary to get it out of the safe at school and brought it to the ball, even though Ginger had forbidden it." I leaned back in the deep cushions of the couch, warming to the idea of Helene behind bars. "She had it out for Ginger—you have to see that."

"Be that as it may, I got nothing out of her. She lawyered up faster than you can say 'no comment.'"

"She despised Ginger," Ellie muttered, tears streaming down her face anew. "Every new idea Ginger had to make Dunlap a better place, that witch opposed it. I think Helene just got tired of Ginger and took her out."

We fell silent for a moment, until Faith piped up. "And what about Sterling Jennings?"

"It was Helene," I reiterated, latching desperately onto the idea of my arch nemesis finally getting her due.

"He *was* awfully upset today at the school," Rachel admitted, sending me a silently mouthed, *I'm sorry.*

We told Truman and Faith about Ginger's missed meeting with the heart surgeon and his storming off.

"He's the worst," Ellie chimed in. "His daughter, Nora, didn't make the lacrosse team, and Sterling thought he could bribe his way into getting her on the team."

Truman questioned Ellie about disgruntled students, but Ellie insisted Ginger was a well-loved headmistress.

A young cadet entered the room and asked to speak to Truman. To my surprise, he allowed her to speak in front of all of us.

"I secured Ms. Crevecoeur's apartment," the young woman officiously began. "There were two wineglasses there, one with lipstick marks, one without."

Truman sat up sharply. "Was Ginger seeing someone?"

"Yes," Ellie began.

"No," Dakota finished. "She was my best friend too, and she never mentioned anything."

Ellie took her friend's hand and motioned for her to sit down. "Ginger *was* seeing someone—it was just very hush-hush. She said she wasn't ready to disclose who it was."

Dakota looked as if she'd been slapped. "I never knew. Why wouldn't she have told me?" Beau joined her, caressing her hand. "Don't worry, Dakota. She's still your best friend. Was." My head snapped up as I took in Beau's voice. His folksy twang was gone, replaced with straight-up, thick tones more at home in New Jersey.

Is his southern accent fake?

Beau cradled his fiancée in his arms as she bawled once more.

The camerawoman discreetly panned out, taking steps away from us.

"What are you doing?" Truman was up like a shot,

advancing toward the crewmember. "No filming my crime scene!"

"But I've been filming all night," she began, a flash of fear skittering across her face.

"What?"

I'd never seen Truman so angry.

"I want every bit of film from this evening's event. Now."

"Whoa, whoa, whoa." A whiff of patchouli permeated the air, and Xavier materialized at the camerawoman's arm.

"I'm the director, Xavier Morris." He held his hand out to Truman, who didn't take it. "Let's just discuss this like adults, shall we? I can't hand over the footage yet. It's all in the contract."

"I don't give a damn about your contract," Truman nearly roared, somehow keeping his voice low, which only served to make it more menacing. "I want that film, now."

The two men retired to the back of the house to hash out an arrangement, and I finally turned to a weepy Dakota.

I suspected the wedding was off, and she did nothing to make me think otherwise.

"I can't get married with my maid of honor murdered." She shook, oblivious to Beau's arm wrapped around her shoulders.

"I don't blame you, sweetie." I was willing to scrap the whole damn thing. "Why don't you try to get some sleep? I can make you some chamomile tea." I placed a hand on her knee, eager to get up and do something, anything to help her.

"I don't think I'll ever be able to sleep again."

"Would you consider sleeping pills? I think getting a few hours of rest would really help."

Dakota shuddered as if I'd suggested she ingest poison.

"I can't take sleeping pills. My mother used to slip them into my dinner when I wasn't sleeping enough on the set of *Silverlake High.* I'd get really stressed, and it led to insomnia."

"Your mother *drugged* you without your consent?! That's illegal!"

I must have sported a supreme look of horror at the idea of Roxanne drugging her teenage daughter to make her sleep, because Dakota switched modes and tried to put my mind at ease.

She shook her head. "She didn't mean any harm. My mother always wants the best for me."

"The wedding will go on." Roxanne stirred a healthy helping of Splenda in her coffee mug and placed her hand on her daughter's shoulder. She was dressed more like a teenybopper than a middle-aged woman, in a minuscule leather miniskirt, combat boots, and a tiny sweater. She cradled Pixie in one arm, the pup wearing a matching leather bow atop her head.

It was the next day, and Rachel and I had finally cleaned up every offending scrap of evidence of the Winter Ball. Although the cuts weren't deep, my hands were screaming with pain, and I'd changed my bandages several times. But I was bound and determined to scrub all vestiges of what had initially been a successful event from the B and B. Truman had grudgingly given me the go-ahead to clean the mansion, every room save for my office. I'd happily obliged. I didn't ever want to step into the once-cheery room for as long as I lived.

I'd convened a meeting with Beau and Dakota around the octagonal breakfast room table to discuss the formal dissolution of their wedding plans, but Roxanne had caught wind and inserted herself into the situation.

"But is that what *you* want?" I turned to Dakota, concerned that the woman who had drugged her daughter still had the power to steamroll her.

"I'm not sure what I want," Dakota whispered, looking to Beau for help.

"You have to keep your brand in mind," Roxanne said in a soothing, singsong voice. I was officially creeped out. Even Pixie the pup seemed to give her a dubious look, her blackberry eyes wide and incredulous, her doggie tongue hanging out.

I left the breakfast room to retreat to the kitchen and busied myself with the teapot. I placed a plate of blueberry scones and apple cinnamon biscotti on the table with jittery hands. A woman who felt nothing for the death of her daughter's maid of honor was just the kind of woman who could have perpetrated the crime.

"Mallory."

I jumped about a foot in the air and whirled around to face Adrienne. She'd stayed up through the Winter Ball aftermath with all of us, yet she'd recovered well, her face smooth and impassive. I wondered if the show hostess took sips of Xavier's fountain-of-youth smoothies to stay looking so perfect.

"I took the liberty of typing you up a script." She thrust several pages into my hands, and I stared at them in confusion.

"A script? But isn't this supposed to be reality TV?"

Adrienne sighed as if I were an especially dim student and shook her head, her shining platinum hair falling back into place when she stopped. "I can tell this is going to be an especially boring episode of *I Do,* and I thought I'd help you out."

"*Boring?*" I was incredulous as I readied the tea on a tray. "Are you freaking kidding me?!"

"Truman"—her mouth twisted in a frown as she mentioned her daughter's grandfather's name—"succeeded in convincing Xavier to release most of the film up to this time. So we're starting from scratch. It's like the Winter Ball never happened." She waved her hand in the air, as if to make all the bad events of yesterday evaporate with a flick of her fingers.

I felt like picking my jaw up from the floor.

"It may not make it to TV, but the reality of Ginger's murder was as real as it gets, Adrienne."

"Which is what Xavier is trying to argue. But Truman wouldn't hear of it." She sighed. "He always was hardheaded. Not much has changed there." I knew how Truman felt about Adrienne leaving his granddaughter Summer when she was only two weeks old. Hardheaded wasn't even the half of it.

"Death is not a spectacle for reality TV." I heard my voice getting shrill. I picked up the elaborate tea set and scones and headed to the breakfast room, utterly disgusted.

"We're all set." Roxanne beamed at me, her hand gripping the shoulder of a miserable Dakota.

Pixie now sat in Dakota's lap, attempting to lick her face to make her feel better. "The wedding will go on."

"Is this what you want?" I sat at the table and leaned toward Dakota.

"It is." Her eyes were laden with infinite sadness, but she seemed to have had a genuine change of heart. No doubt helped along by her pushy mother. "Ginger would have wanted me to get married. Right, Beau?"

Her fiancé nodded, placing his hand over the large diamond sparkling on her left hand. "Ginger couldn't wait for us to get married, and we're going to follow through." His countrified accent was back, but now that I suspected it wasn't real, I could pick it apart at the edges. The vowels were a little too long, the twang a bit too studied.

I sighed and went over the wedding plans with them as the ever-present cameras rolled.

We had no time to waste with all of the prior footage confiscated, and made our way through the sodden muddy grounds to the carriage house to film Dakota crafting her centerpieces. Rachel and I had set up a representative table a few days ago, and the mock-up was waiting for us, gleaming and festive as if nothing horrible had happened.

Dakota and Beau's wedding was to be a study in black and white, an Ascot *My Fair Lady* theme. Our sample reception table featured long silver branches woven together with fresh pine boughs. The evergreens were befitting of a winter wedding, but more in line with the outdoors than like a Christmas holdover. Through the foliage, I'd threaded shiny black metallic beads, which would reflect the light of the chandeliers in the front hall. Fist-sized clear and black crystals nestled among the pine boughs and branches. Our florist had dropped off the sample table flowers with the Winter Ball arrangements, and fragrant lily of the valley and big, stately calla lilies shared tall and stout silver vases. Stark white china, trimmed in silver, held smaller pewter plates. It was a bold and sophisticated theme, and if I could admit it, a little cold and clinical. If Pixie had truly inspired Roxanne to push for these plans, none of the pup's warmth was present. But I'd whipped up the setting according to Roxanne's whims, with some small suggestions allowed by Dakota.

Rachel came out with a sample menu of escarole salad, lemongrass soup, ceviche, salmon with capers and endive, spicy basil short ribs, and a black and white checkerboard cake. She explained to the cameras how we'd taken Dakota and Beau's palates into consideration while choosing and tweaking the menu.

"Well done," Adrienne murmured. She looked pained to admit the tasting was a rousing success, under the sad and crazy circumstances. "It will be a sophisticated Valentine's Day wedding, not something cheesy as I was expecting."

"Um, thanks, I guess." I wasn't sure if she'd given me a compliment or an insult.

"Mom!" Summer bolted into the carriage house and enveloped Adrienne in a bone-crushing hug.

"Oh, sweetie." Adrienne buried her head in Summer's short blond hair, and I felt a rush of pathos for the woman who barely got to see her daughter.

But that was her choice, a voice in my head reminded me.

"You've executed my mother's plans very well," Dakota said in a low voice as she sidled up to me, tearing me from thoughts of Summer and Adrienne.

"That's what I was afraid of. Dakota, it's not too late to make some changes to bring this wedding more in line with what you *really* want."

"Are you sure?" Dakota's violet eyes sparkled, and we made tentative plans to meet sometime tomorrow when the cameras weren't rolling.

The cameras filmed as Dakota, Rachel, Summer, and I spray-painted dried branches from the grounds a brushed silver. Things were going as well as could be expected, until Adrienne inserted herself into the shot. She was doing her usual host narration, setting up the scene for the eventual viewers and asking us mundane questions about the wedding craft.

"And here we have my daughter," she said, with obvious fondness.

"Cut." Garrett stood in the doorway to the carriage house, his gorgeous hazel eyes blazing.

"Who said that?" Xavier swiveled around to take in Garrett.

"Who gave you permission to film Summer?" Garrett motioned for Adrienne to join him outside.

"But, Dad—" Summer started to join her father and mother, but Garrett held up his hand.

"Not now, Summer. I need to have a word with your mother."

We could hear their argument from outside, in smatters and bits, though I could tell they were both trying to keep their voices low. I heard the words *custodial, guardian,* and *permission* flying about and gathered that Summer wouldn't be appearing on *I Do* anymore.

"I wish they'd stop fighting."

Summer stood with tears streaking down her elfin face. I slung my arm around her shoulders and we exited the carriage house.

Chapter Five

I couldn't get Summer's stricken face out of my head. I tossed and turned all night, my head hot on the flannel pillowcase. My mind replayed Adrienne and Garrett's fight. I'd been in Summer's shoes once, decades ago, when my own parents' marriage had imploded. It hadn't been pretty, and my heart ached watching the tears gather in Summer's huge hazel eyes.

Garrett and Adrienne had stopped their argument as soon as Summer and I had emerged from the carriage house and they'd taken in how upset their daughter was. They'd both gathered her up in their arms, murmuring apologies. Summer had left with Garrett, and Adrienne had spent the rest of the afternoon silently observing the crafting process, for once at a loss for words.

The sun hadn't yet peeked its face over the horizon, and rain thrummed in a staccato rhythm on the rooftop of my third-floor attic apartment. I idly wondered how Dakota's black and white winter-wonderland-themed wedding would play out now that the snow had been washed away. We could no longer have a planned sleigh ride, and the ice crystal motif might look a bit silly. I recalled Dakota's impassive face as I'd presented the wedding ideas and a headache of doubt crept across my brow.

The cast and crew of *I Do* slept below. At 5 AM, I gave up my fruitless quest for sleep and padded down the back stairs as quietly as the creaky wood would allow. My calico cat, Whiskey, followed behind me, and Soda, the orange kitten, raced after her. They'd been wary of traveling downstairs after catching a whiff of Pixie the Shih Tzu, and stayed close behind.

I planned on whipping up a scrumptious breakfast for my guests. I smelled the aroma of coffee as my foot connected with the final step, and my pulse accelerated. I flicked on the lights in the cleverly disguised industrial kitchen and screamed.

"You scared the living daylights out of me!"

"Sorry." Dakota offered me a wan smile and held up a small French press. "I couldn't sleep, so I helped myself to some coffee."

I sighed and sank into a chair across from the bride. "Make that two of us."

Dakota rubbed her eyes with the cuff of her green silk bathrobe. "I can't believe I let my mother convince me to go on with the wedding." She cast a glance in the direction of the front hall and my crime-taped office and shuddered. "All I can think of is Ginger at your desk. This isn't a time for a wedding celebration."

I couldn't agree more.

I let her go on, to see if she could talk herself out of her wedding.

"But I do want to marry Beau. And I think Ginger would want me to go through with the wedding. I just wish it weren't so soon."

I emptied the remaining contents of the French press into a large yellow polka dot mug and clasped one of Dakota's hands in mine.

"What do you *really* want?" I reminded her of my promise yesterday to rework her wedding, as much as time would allow.

She gave a weak laugh. "To go back in time and save Ginger. To never have agreed to be on this silly reality show. To stand up to my mother and get the wedding I really want. To honor Ginger's memory in some way." A small smile broke through the heavy sadness. "And to marry Beau."

"Why are you doing the show anyway?" I blurted out, emboldened by the deep, rich coffee and the edge from lack of sleep. "No offense, the show usually features D-listers." I clapped a hand over my mouth as the last part slipped out.

Dakota leaned back in her chair and laughed, her chuckles clear and bell-like. The sound was a welcome change from the tears of yesterday. "After *Silverlake High* went off the air and my roles dried up, I was considered a D-lister. Until the last three indie films I landed. I promised Xavier I'd do *I Do*. He was the director on *Silverlake High,* and he launched my career. I feel like I owe him." She stopped, suddenly pensive. "Our careers both took a nosedive after *Silverlake High* was cancelled. I feel like working with him again on this pet project of his is coming full circle." She leaned back in her chair and closed her eyes. "I just wish there were a way to still get married, but honor Ginger as well. It won't be the same without her here."

"You could honor her somehow." The wheels began turning in my head.

"You don't think it would be too macabre, incorporating Ginger into the wedding?" Dakota leaned forward, cupping her mug of coffee.

"Not if you're celebrating Ginger's life. It would be untraditional, but the circumstances are a little crazy right now. You could overhaul everything and do what you really want, and honor your maid of honor, too."

Dakota nodded slowly, warming to the idea. I grabbed a legal pad and pen from a drawer and we got to brainstorming.

"What about Ginger?" I gently prodded.

"I want to honor her the day of my wedding. I wanted her to stand next to me, to be by my side on one of the biggest days of my life." She stared dolefully into her coffee cup, her wide violet eyes overcome with a sudden wave of sadness.

"We could have a memorial for her in the morning," I said slowly, trying to picture how the day would work. "I could talk to Ellie and the other teachers at Dunlap. They must want to plan something too."

Dakota slowly nodded. "I think Ginger would appreciate that."

"If Roxanne wasn't in the picture, what would you have chosen?" I sat expectantly, pen poised in hand.

Dakota placed her hand under her chin, her large Asscher diamond flickering in the kitchen's lights. "For the ceremony, I'd want to be outdoors.

I don't even care what the weather's like. I want to see the stars. Maybe we could have a short ceremony in the gazebo." A small smile tilted up the corners of her lips. It was the first genuine display of excitement, however muted, I'd seen her have for her wedding plans.

"And the reception?" I scribbled down ideas for an outside ceremony and urged Dakota to go on.

"It's cheesy as hell, but I picked Valentine's Day for our wedding for a reason. I'm in love with the holiday, and I'd have a red and pink and white explosion." This pronouncement brought out a genuine grin, and I vowed then and there to create Dakota's vision, despite the fact that her nuptials were a mere nine days away.

"It'll be tight with florists already inundated with regular Valentine's Day orders," I cautioned. "But let's see what we can do." I flicked through a mental Rolodex of the three flower shops in Port Quincy and couldn't wait for the business day to begin so I could start placing pleading calls.

"Just one thing." Dakota clasped my hands in hers. "We have to keep these new plans a secret from my mother."

I retracted my hands and gulped. Roxanne would freak out the day of the wedding when she saw the red and pink and white palette. I replayed the scene of Helene's displeasure and meltdown at the secret Winter Ball reveal in my head and swallowed hard. A surprise wedding would be fun, but I was admittedly squeamish.

"Are you sure? Wouldn't it just be better to tell her you've had a change of heart?"

Is Dakota really that scared of standing up to her mother?

I thought of Dakota's revelation that her mother used to drug her and shivered. My own mother, Carole, was a formidable force, but even she wouldn't stoop to that. Maybe I'd do things on the sly too if Roxanne were my mother.

Dakota sighed. "You have no idea what she'd do if she found out we're jettisoning her carefully laid plans. This has to be a secret, Mallory, or it won't happen. Besides," she laughed, "planning a secret wedding and the final reveal will make for great TV."

"Will Beau be on board?" I'd planned many a wedding with the bride or her family in charge, the groom a silent afterthought. I wanted to make sure he was on board too before we dug into the new plans.

"Oh, he'll love it. He likes surprises, and he'll really dig getting one over on my mother."

"If you don't mind me asking, why did you let her make all of the choices in the first place?"

Dakota sighed and ran a hand through her golden hair. She revealed the slightest touch of red roots. I hadn't been imagining them earlier.

"My mother has worked tirelessly to build my career. She pushed me, hard, even when I wasn't sure I wanted to stick with acting." Dakota sounded grateful, but I wasn't so sure I would have been in her position. "We were *poor* poor for so long, I'm talking no food in the fridge and the electricity turned off. Roxanne sacrificed a lot to make my career happen. And as a result, it's never enough for her." She sighed and looked down at her massive ring. "Roxanne wants me to do every commercial, sponsorship, and role that comes my way. She's always thinking of my brand. I appreciate she wants to take care of me, in a way. It just gets a little stifling." She paused and her eyes strayed to the carriage house out back. "And it's a shame that the wedding my mom planned won't get used."

I cringed at the thought of the waste of decorations and food. An idea percolated and eddied in my tired brain.

"I gave away my wedding once," I began slowly.

"You were engaged?" Dakota sat up straighter.

"To Helene's son," I ruefully admitted. Dakota burst out laughing.

"You sure dodged a bullet there."

I grinned, not insulted by her statement. "I thank my lucky stars every day that I didn't go through with it. I ended up giving my reception to a bride in need of a wedding. We could do the same for the black and white design."

Dakota's violet eyes sparkled. "But who would want to take on the wedding exactly as Roxanne planned it?"

I grinned. "I know just the guy."

"*Guy?*"

"Owen Holloway. He runs the Helping Hands Foundation." Owen wanted to throw a black-tie auction and event to raise funds for his foundation, but he didn't quite have the money to pull it off. He'd also been maddeningly unspecific when I'd told him what I could do with his minimal budget. I'd put Owen's gala on the back burner, but now I could seamlessly transition Roxanne's choices into a black-tie auction. A fully formed event falling right into his lap would be just the thing Owen's foundation needed.

The glimmer in Dakota's eyes grew, and she nodded. "Perfect."

I glanced at the big red cuckoo clock over the stove. "We only have about half an hour before I really need to start breakfast. Let's sketch out the new wedding plans and I'll make calls this morning."

We put our heads together and hunched over the legal pad, my fingers flying to record every idea. We'd welcome the cheesiness factor, and go for a hopelessly romantic Valentine's Day theme. If we could get them, Dakota would have peonies and ranunculus in luscious bunches of petal pink, magenta, and blood red. I could order tablecloths in pink and berry, and fill bowls with pink marbles and floating red candles. We'd have pale princess pink and rose snowflakes in metallic paper strung above the guests. The ceremony would be outside, and the small reception would be held in the Thistle Park greenhouse, which we'd transform with red, white, and pink flowers. I grew more and more nervous as our ideas grew, and batted away the doubt that hunkered on my shoulders. Would we be able to pull it off? I'd have my answer in a few hours.

"And now the menu."

"I want rich comfort food," Dakota declared, looking longingly at the bell jar of doughnuts I kept in the kitchen for my guests. "I've been dieting since I was ten, and on this one day I'd like to eat to my heart's content." A far-away look registered in her violet eyes. "What I *really* want is a peanut butter cake. With chocolate and bananas."

I tried and failed to suppress a surprised grin. "You mean like an Elvis sandwich wedding cake?"

Dakota laughed in assent and we put our heads together to come up with the rest of the menu. We scrapped the chic, health-conscious foods from the black-and-white wedding and planned on a menu of gourmet comfort food. There would be basil tomato soup, smoked salmon macaroni and cheese, lamb meatloaf, seven-cheese loaded potatoes, and bacon and scallion green beans. I'd ask Rachel if she could create a banana and peanut butter cake with chocolate icing, and we'd have an assortment of stouts, red wine, and cherry chocolate martinis.

"My dress will be bursting at the seams!" Dakota crowed.

"What's going on here?" Roxanne's slippered foot alighted on the last step of the back stair. She set Pixie on the floor and the tiny Shih Tzu trotted over to Dakota for pets and kisses. Roxanne's violet eyes took in our sheaf of notes. I crossed my hands over the yellow paper and beamed.

"We're just going over some details for your daughter's big day."

"You made the right decision, Dakota. Ginger would have wanted this." Roxanne smiled, but it didn't reach her eyes.

Two hours later, I'd made breakfast and fed the cast and crew, placed some calls to Port Quincy's florists, and set up a meeting with Owen Holloway to gift him Dakota's reception. Dakota had a fun morning fluttering about, whispering news of her secret wedding plans to Beau, Rachel, Xavier, and the crew. But then she'd seemed to realize Ginger wouldn't be there, and excused herself to wipe her eyes in the corner, a box of tissues at the ready. Dakota appeared exhausted from cycling through the emotions of mourning Ginger and trying to get excited for her new wedding plans.

The only people who didn't know about the secret wedding were Roxanne and Adrienne. The two people who would undoubtedly flip out the most when they found out. I tamped down the feeling of dread that bubbled up whenever I thought of how the Winter Ball surprise had gone with Helene. Especially if defying her had led Helene to murder Ginger.

At 10 AM, my sister and I piled into the Butterscotch Monster with Dakota and Beau. We headed downtown to meet with Owen Holloway. The fickle February weather continued to confuse and delight, as spring had arrived early. I rolled down my window, breathing in the fresh air the rain had brought and delighting in the sun on my arm. The temperature was in the mid-sixties, and I was glad we'd changed Dakota's wedding from a winter theme to something more traditionally Valentine's Day.

Beau gallantly opened the back door for Dakota and linked arms with his fiancée as we entered Owen's foundation building, an aging yet charming, skinny art deco suite of offices in the heart of downtown Port Quincy. HELPING HANDS was emblazoned above the scrolled copper patina doorway. The large front room buzzed with people sitting at card tables, calculators and computers in front of them.

"It's tax season, and Helping Hands is doing taxes for free," I explained to Dakota and Beau as a volunteer ushered us inside. I saw Ellie's little sister, Leah, volunteering, bustling around the room with a clipboard, handing out pens and cups of coffee, her purple hair swinging behind her. Her punky looks garnered a few sidelong glances, but she offered a smile to each person she saw. She gave us a friendly wave.

"And this is—"

"—Dakota. It's been too long."

"Owen Holloway," I ended lamely, not realizing Dakota and Owen obviously knew each other.

Owen stood before Dakota, taking her in, a guarded yet eager look stealing across his pleasant features. His auburn hair waved back from his forehead, matched and balanced by his thick beard. His chunky black glasses framed his warm, whiskey-colored eyes. He was dressed in his usual garb, a plaid shirt—today's was black watch in shades of blue and green—and his ever-present dark washed skinny jeans, cuffed at the bottom, and brown boots. An infectious smile stole over his face, but he held back from embracing Dakota.

Dakota blinked, flustered, and her arm fell from Beau's. She nervously raked her hand through her hair, the diamond winking under the fluorescents. A slow flush climbed up her throat and obliterated her freckles. Beau took in her reaction and cleared his throat. His eyes were narrow and missed nothing under his ten-gallon hat.

I could understand her reaction even if she didn't seem to have some history with Owen. Owen Holloway was the quintessential boy next door all grown up, a blend of dark Clark Kent good looks mixed with a dash of hipster. The philanthropist ran the foundation his parents had started, and he was a quiet and steadfast member of the Port Quincy community, offering his foundation's solutions to those who needed them the most. And did I mention he was gorgeous?

Rachel had been at Pilates or jiujitsu, or getting a manicure each time I'd met with Owen, and had never experienced his quiet and steady charm. But today she didn't overlook Owen, nor the moony-eyed glances Dakota was sending his way.

"I'm Rachel," she purred, licking her lips. Her celibacy pledge was seemingly forgotten.

"Mallory's sister." Owen tore his eyes from Dakota and shook hands with Rachel, including her in his warm smile.

"And I'm Beau Wright." Dakota's fiancé shook Owen's hand with unnecessary force, making the foundation owner wince. His New Jersey accent was back in full effect, the twang evaporated in a puff of anger.

"Oh my gosh! I can't believe I didn't introduce you," Dakota tittered, remembering Beau at last. She linked arms once again with her fiancé, and he visibly relaxed.

I stood back and observed the meet-and-greet like an armchair anthropologist. Beau was vastly annoyed, still sizing up Owen. Dakota seemed to have more natural chemistry with Owen than with her actual fiancé. I wondered if Dakota and Owen had ever been an item.

"Well, I'll leave you ladies, and gentleman, to your plans." Beau tipped his hat in Rachel and Owen's direction and gallantly swept Dakota up in a dramatic dip kiss. His country, folksy accent was back, now that his temper was in check. The whole time we'd been standing around in the front room, people had been snapping pictures of Beau and Dakota on their cell phones, and now the audience cheered and whistled.

Okay, so maybe you're wrong about them.

Beau and Dakota seemed to have real affection for each other. I chastised myself for playing closet marriage counselor instead of wedding planner, although I sometimes did think my couples should be seeing a counselor before they plunged on with their weddings.

Rachel and I followed Dakota and Owen as we made our way to the second floor of the building.

"Tell me what you have in mind," Owen invited, when Rachel, Dakota, and I were arrayed before him in his office, settled in comfortable chairs. Dakota filled him in on gifting her original black and white reception to stand in for the Helping Hands fundraiser, her face animated and convincing.

Owen laughed, taken with the idea. "This is perfect. And the best part is that I don't have to figure out the details of throwing a big, fancy party. You're the best, Dakota." His whiskey eyes turned soft as he stared at her a bit too long. Dakota swallowed and looked down at her lap, but when she lifted her face, her eyes were shining.

If these two were never together, they should have been, I thought to myself. Rachel was narrowing her eyes at Dakota, and I could practically read the thought bubble above her head. I willed her to calm down. Something may have been going on between Dakota and Owen in the past, but she was an engaged woman now.

I looked away to avoid the tension building in the room and my eyes alighted on a picture on Owen's desk. It was the same one that sat in repose on Ginger's desk, in a butterfly frame, featuring a young Dakota with vivid red hair, as well as Ginger and Ellie. I gasped when I realized the young man in the picture had been Owen.

Owen saw me looking at the picture and took in my startled look. "The three musketeers, and me." A gentle smile graced his handsome face, creating a dimple in his left cheek. "I met Dakota and Ginger and Ellie when they started volunteering at my parents' foundation while they attended Dunlap Academy." His smile slowly dissipated. "I can't believe Ginger is gone."

A soft knock at the door startled us all. Leah poked her head in, clipboard in hand. "Hi, Dakota."

"Leah's going to be a bridesmaid in my wedding," Dakota said carefully, almost seeming to rue any mention of her nuptials to Owen.

He nodded impassively and turned to the young woman. "What do you have for me?"

"The stats on this morning's tax open house." She passed along the clipboard and blew her heavy purple bangs off her forehead. "I need to go back to school—"

"—to study and write another paper," Owen finished for her with a grin. His smile faltered. "Ginger was worried about you, Leah. She said you were working around the clock to make sure you get into Harvard. She thought you needed to take it easier."

Leah grew somber at the mention of Ginger. "I can't believe my mentor's gone." She brushed off his concern at her working too hard and bid us all farewell, sweeping from the office, her long preternaturally purple hair swinging behind her.

Owen sighed and tented his hands in front of him. "To tell you the truth," he admitted, "Leah's work is slipping. I think she's spread herself too thin, and doesn't have time to do volunteer work."

"She's just trying to please Iris," Dakota explained, a worried expression clouding her pretty violet eyes. "If there's one mother who drives a harder bargain than mine, it's Ellie and Leah's mother, Iris. Nothing pleases her. She'll stop at nothing until Leah wins a full scholarship to some Ivy League school and Ellie makes something of herself."

I sat up sharply. "Isn't being a drama teacher at an exclusive girls' school enough?"

Dakota shook her head sadly. "Not for Iris. She wanted Ellie to be headmistress at Dunlap, not Ginger."

"And look where that got her," Owen added, a streak of vehemence tingeing his words. "Who in the hell would want to hurt Ginger?" He leaned back in his whining leather chair and stroked his beard.

"Um, Helene? Duh," Rachel piped up, an exasperated look on her face. "She's going down once and for all."

Owen nodded, a lock of dark glossy auburn hair falling onto his forehead. "I know Ginger was gearing up for a fight with a faction of the board of trustees for the school, led by Helene. Ginger wanted to make the school coed in a last-ditch effort to save it, and Helene opposed her. Helene controlled the old-guard members, while most of the younger teachers and some parents were on Ginger's side."

"You sure know a lot about what's going on at Dunlap," Dakota said carefully.

"Ginger and I had dinner often," Owen admitted, shyly studying the stats Leah had dropped off.

"Oh?" Dakota asked, her voice high and tight. She looked at Owen sharply, waiting for a reply, and received none.

"But there's one thing bothering me," I filled the tension-filled space. "Helene doesn't do her own dirty work. I couldn't picture her in her evening gown mixing up bleach and ammonia in a vase."

"It could have been thieves after the tiara," Rachel mused, checking out her chipping manicure. "The *Eagle Herald* paper ran a big feature story last Sunday about finding the diamonds in the time capsule. Helene was even quoted in the story saying how happy she was that the tiara would crown the Belle of the Winter Ball. It was like an open invitation to come steal it."

"Whatever happened, now one of the three musketeers is gone." Owen picked up the picture from his desk and lovingly traced Ginger's face, letting out a sigh.

"We'd better go," Dakota offered, standing and cutting the meeting short. She plucked the picture from Owen's hands and stared at it fondly. "We were so happy then." The smiling group of teens gazed back at her, frozen in time.

Owen and Dakota shared one more miserable look as we filed out of the office. All save for Rachel, who hung back, her vivid pink nails standing out against the arm of Owen's plaid shirt. "I'd love to have dinner with you sometime." She blinked her almond eyes up at Owen, the lashes full and fluttering. I had to hand it to her, my sister knew how to go after what she wanted in life. She had none of Dakota's hesitancy, and it usually served her well.

Owen seemed startled, a deer caught in the high beams of Rachel's intense gaze.

Watch out, boy, she'll chew you up.

"I, um . . ."

"Say yes." Rachel parted her lips, an expectant smile quivering on her cupid's-bow mouth.

"I—yes." He smiled with relief. "Sure. How about tomorrow night?"

"Pick me up at seven?"

I left my sister to hash out the details of her date and ran smack into Dakota, who was leaning furtively in the doorway. She sent a hurt, hot glance at my sister, then settled her spine ramrod straight as we left the Helping Hands Foundation.

"Is there a salon nearby?" Dakota asked, her face set and determined.

"Yup," Rachel answered, a triumphant grin on her face. "I need to get my nails done for my date with Owen tomorrow. Let's go." She linked arms with a stunned Dakota and pulled her along down Main Street.

We left the salon an hour later, a sparkly silver acrylic set of nails for Rachel, a blowout for me, and a vivid, shining wave of red locks for Dakota. I'd grudgingly taken Adrienne's advice to heart and straightened my curls, wondering if the smooth and temporary overhaul of my frizzy, sandy hair would play well on camera.

Dakota looked more like the teenage picture of herself with her hair dyed a bright carrot red.

"This is my real color," she explained, holding a tress up in front of her eyes. "My mother had me dye it a golden blond to downplay the red."

"That's nuts!" Rachel shook her head. "You look great as a redhead."

"Thanks," Dakota breathed, her annoyance at Rachel's date with Owen temporarily forgotten. "Roxanne always claimed I looked too *Anne of Green Gables* with my real hair and freckles."

"More like Julianne Moore," I piped up. We'd pulled back into the drive of Thistle Park and advanced up the walk to the front porch. The sun warmed our faces and fluffy white clouds littered the sky. If the trees weren't so barren, it would seem like late spring.

"What have you done? Your *hair!*"

Ruh-roh.

Roxanne met us in the front hall, her face a mask of anguish and despair.

"Arf!" Pixie got into the mix and churned in circles around Dakota, the Shih Tzu's barks high-pitched and accusatory.

Roxanne seemed more in dire straits over the color of her daughter's hair than she had upon learning about Ginger's demise.

"I thought I'd go back to red. My *real* hair color." Dakota fluffed a few strands, daring her mother to object and flaunting her new do. Dakota had finally grown a spine, as if her fiery hair had infused her with a jolt of much-needed confidence.

"I just don't know if that's going to work with casting," Roxanne muttered, following her daughter down the hall.

"Well, I can always dye it again," Dakota snapped, brooking no more discussion on the matter.

"Your ceremony dress arrived," Roxanne seethed, pointing to the corner of the parlor where a gigantic trunk stood. The back corner of the room had been overtaken by a Hooverville of boxes and packages from adoring fans who had found out somehow that Dakota and Beau were getting married at Thistle Park. Whiskey and Soda tore into the room, prancing up the pyramid of boxes and settling at the top to observe us, sphinx like, statue-still, their ochre eyes blinking.

"Well, aren't you going to try it on?" Roxanne rubbed her hands together in anticipation.

I handed Dakota a pair of scissors from a drawer in a letter desk, and she cut the string and tape from the packaging. We oohed and ahhed appropriately as she revealed a heavy vanilla cream satin ball gown, complete with fur trim at the hem. It was quite different from the reception gown she'd tried on in the Silver Bells bridal store.

"Fake fur, of course," Dakota assured us, twirling with the dress held in front of her. "I didn't do a PETA ad to wear real fur on my wedding day."

Adrienne poked her head around the corner, the camera crew drawing up the rear.

"That dress would have been perfect a few days ago with all of the snow," she mused, a mischievous look dancing in her blue eyes. "But I'm not sure if it's quite right for the weather now."

Oh no. I can see where you're going with this.

I already had a secret wedding to plan, and Adrienne was up to the usual shenanigans she'd pulled on other episodes of *I Do,* where she tried to get planners to change their ideas in the eleventh hour to foment some drama for the camera. I was going to put into action the riotous display of red and pink while keeping up the ruse of the black and white wedding, and I'd be wheedled into doing nothing more.

But Roxanne was nodding, warming to Adrienne's critique. "I'm afraid she's right, Dakota," Roxanne sighed, for once agreeing with Adrienne. "Your old winter wedding plans will never do."

"They're going to have to," I said firmly. Adrienne and Roxanne left the room, buzzing about new wedding plans, my admonition not taken seriously.

"Something smells divine," Dakota breathed, changing back into her leggings and cardigan behind an antique cherry blossom screen.

"It's the peanut butter cake." I dropped my voice. "For your secret wedding."

"Let's go try some!"

"I'll be right back with a slice."

I left Dakota to finish changing and headed for the kitchen. I pushed open the door to the butler's pantry on the way to the breakfast room and kitchen.

"Allow me—"

There stood Beau and Rachel, caught in what looked like a compromising clinch. Beau appeared to be reaching for a cup, but stopped at the last second to press my sister against rows of china and silverware. He leaned in for a kiss.

Chapter Six

"Get off of me!" Rachel grabbed Beau's arm and pinned it around his back. He screamed in pain, but Rachel wasn't done. She'd attended jiu-jitsu lessons for the past three months to blow off steam, and now she showed off the fruits of her labor. She bent over and flipped Beau onto his back in a neat roll, where he landed in a huff and stayed there. He weakly waved his arms and legs like an overturned cockroach, a moan escaping his chiseled lips.

"I think she broke my freaking back." His voice was definitely all Jersey now.

An antique platter with orange peonies painted around the edges rolled, toppled, and crashed to the floor, splintering pieces of china every which way in a clattering cacophony.

"You—you hussy!" Roxanne caromed around the corner, her hands on her hips. The crushed platter crunched beneath her feet and Beau finally realized he had an audience. Roxanne swept a barking Pixie from the floor before she could pad over the broken china, and the little doggie gave several short, accusatory barks.

"I am *not* a hussy. He assaulted me!" Rachel pointed a sparkly silver nail in Beau's direction. A moment's worth of chagrin alighted on his impossibly smooth face, but flitted away a second later, replaced with something more calculated.

"That's not how I see it, miss. I was just reaching for that cup that was too high up for you to grasp." He shook his head sadly, casting a sympathetic glance at Rachel.

"If my sister says you came on to her against her wishes, then that's what happened." My eyes narrowed to slits, and I had to still my hands at my side.

"What's going on here?" Dakota leaned against the doorframe, her eyes wide.

"I was helping Rachel get a cup," Beau explained, his voice half-twangy, half not. "She misinterpreted it and laid me flat on my back!"

Dakota tsked softly, holding out her hand for Beau to grasp.

She believes him?

Dakota helped Beau up to his feet and turned expectantly to me. "Do you have a broom? I'll help clean up this platter."

I pointed her in the direction of the kitchen, stunned by her easy acceptance.

My sister stood, still breathing hard on the side of the butler's pantry.

"He tried to kiss me," she said in a clear, low voice.

"I know what I saw, too," I replied.

"And . . . cut!" Xavier nodded to the camera-woman and took a step back.

"You *filmed* this?" I stood incredulous and disgusted as I realized the whole fiasco with octopus-armed Beau had just been memorialized forever for *I Do* viewers.

"This will be our highest-rated episode—I can feel it." Xavier practically rubbed his hands together with glee.

A waft of smoke overtook the decadent peanut-butter-cake aroma and curled around the corner of the butler's pantry.

"Oh no, my cake!" Rachel zoomed around the corner to rescue her confection, knocking into the camerawoman, I observed with some satisfaction. It was too late. The smoke detectors all around the first floor started blaring out a clarion warning.

That cake isn't the only thing going up in flames.

An hour later, things were under control, but I felt like I resided in the Twilight Zone. Dakota believed Beau hook, line, and sinker. He'd concocted some silly story about Rachel asking him to help her reach some china, and how she'd slipped in her heels, falling against him. But I know what I saw, and I'd bet Dakota knew too. I think Roxanne reminding her of her contract to finish this episode of *I Do* and the brand-enhancing qualities of a marriage to one of country music's biggest, if not waning, stars might bring had something to do with Dakota's change of heart as well.

"I believe my fiancé." Dakota's words were impassioned. I think she did believe him. We were sitting in her room, the lovely purple honeymoon suite outfitted with pansies and violets and lots of French cream accents.

My nerves were frayed and I couldn't help delivering a jab in solidarity with my sister. "You believe your fiancé, or you believe what you want to believe?"

Dakota winced at my bull's-eye zinger and stared at her diamond. "I know what people say about Beau. But I love him. And he would never cheat on me," she announced firmly.

"I'd like to save you a lot of trouble." I took a deep breath and waded in. "I know what I saw. And I believe my sister."

Blood was thicker than water, and I didn't need this fizzy celebrity Perrier version of water anyway. If I could convince Dakota that her fiancé was a no-good, down-and-out lothario, she'd thank me later.

"I believe my fiancé, Mallory. Rachel didn't do anything, but neither did Beau. It was an honest mistake. He's about six inches taller than her, and she was reaching for that cup." It was all true, up to a point. But then he'd leaned down in an unmistakable stance, about to deliver a kiss that just barely hadn't happened.

I'd seen Dakota beamed in on my television nearly each day after school. She was an exemplarily gifted actress. And she was playing her finest role right now.

Why does she want to marry Beau so badly?

I shook my head, the silky straight hair treatment

I'd received at the salon feeling strange and adding to my feelings of being out of sorts.

Dakota sighed and stood. "The show must go on."

I reported back to Rachel and the two of us held a conference.

"I want to cancel this whole thing." I paced around our third-floor apartment, still mad at the gall and lies spewing from Beau. "It'll be tight with the bills coming through for the Winter Ball, but we don't need Beau's business. I'm not sure if I can cancel some of the things we ordered for Dakota's wedding, but we can try—"

"Stop." Rachel held up her hand. "I want to follow through with this abomination of a wedding. If Dakota wants that slug, she can have him. I still think the business we'll get from being on *I Do* is worth it."

"But—"

"No buts. I can handle myself just fine." Rachel raised her chin with infinite dignity and extracted a small vial from her pocket. "And the next time that rat bastard takes a step toward me, he'll get an eyeful of this."

It was the little spray bottle of mace our mother had gifted us at Christmas.

"Now that's something I'd like to see."

Rachel and I headed down the stairs to the kitchen, a united force. Beau and Dakota had retired to their room, and I helped Rachel by making the chocolate frosting for the peanut butter wedding cake that she'd started to bake anew. My heart was no longer in the process, but I would fulfill my contract to Dakota with aplomb.

Adrienne dug around the crisper in the refrigerator, amassing ingredients for another smoothie for Xavier. She closed the door with a snap and leaned in to stare at a photograph of Garrett, Summer, and me at a pumpkin patch. She stood stock-still for a moment, and then began to chop veggies and fruits furiously, reducing the mountain of roughage to a tidy pile ready for the blender.

"You must be very close to my daughter." She tilted her head toward the picture and pressed the button on the small appliance. The machine whirred and ground the veggies and fruits to bits.

She didn't wait for my reply and silenced the machine.

"I have a proposition for you."

I braced myself for whatever was coming.

"I don't mean to create more work for you, but—"

Yeah, right.

"The winter theme simply won't do for this wedding. I was thinking of a new, early springtime palette."

"It's too late," I said flatly, crossing my arms. "It's impossible to change the plans at this date."

Okay, not technically impossible, since I was still going to go through with the new plans for Dakota's secret pink-and-red-themed Valentine's Day wedding. But one wedding change was enough.

"But you have a nearly unlimited budget." Adrienne blinked innocently, then turned to the concoction in the blender. She poured it into a tall, clear glass, the smoothie a deep aubergine color, much like amethyst-tinted sludge. I caught a whiff of blueberries and fish oil.

Xavier breezed into the room and deposited a

kiss on Adrienne's cheek. He took a delighted sip of his smoothie. He confirmed my suspicions. "Antioxidants from berries and beets and a whole host of omega threes. It can't be beat. Care for a sip?"

"Um, no thank you."

Blech.

"Have you seen the footage from this afternoon? This will be the most watched *I Do* ever."

I couldn't tell what disgusted me more, Xavier's glee at future ratings at the expense of Dakota and Rachel's dignity, or his odoriferous drink. Scratch that. His naked hunger for better ratings and the patently dramatic definitely bothered me more.

A single thought skittered through my brain.

What if Xavier arranged for Ginger's death to drive up ratings? A murdered maid of honor for a celebrity wedding would sadly be a draw.

I batted the thought away like a pesky mosquito.

Don't be preposterous.

"Adrienne is right, you know," Xavier continued, wiping away a streak of purple from his upper lip. "You really ought to change the wedding to accommodate the early spring. It'll showcase your talents as a wedding planner."

I closed my eyes and took a nice, deep, fortifying breath. I exhaled and offered what I hoped was a beatific smile.

I will be a calm sea of equanimity, I chanted to myself.

"Of course."

Adrienne's smile faltered. She'd obviously wanted a blow-up over the last-minute demand to change plans.

* * *

Rachel and I worked all afternoon to come up with a warmer-weather-themed plan. We were filmed as we worked, and I'd finally gotten used to the ever-present cameras. Rachel had stopped acting in the presence of the crew, and she settled into a comfortable rhythm, tweaking recipes and humming to herself.

I explained the new yellow sunshine theme I'd come up with for the warm-weather, early spring nuptials. It turned out the little furry groundhog had been right. I'd met briefly with Dakota and we'd agreed to keep up the ruse. I could showcase my planning skills for the camera, and I'd turn this wedding plan into a theme for Owen's foundation's event.

"The color palette will be lemon and cream, with navy and sage accents," I explained to the camera. "We'll use some of the silver accents from Dakota's original wedding, like the vases and plates. But we've completely overhauled the wedding. We'll have new paper lanterns in cream and yellow starbursts, and pale butter runners. Guests will now dine on citrus salad, lemon sole, and tangerine chiffon cake."

The camera panned to Rachel, and she explained how she'd decided on that particular cake flavor.

"We'll also serve Arnold Palmers, shandies, and lemon drop cocktails," my sister explained, gesturing to a beautiful display of the drinks.

Xavier smiled as he said cut.

"You ladies are naturals." He beamed. "And for what it's worth, Rachel," he whispered, "about Beau? I believe you."

"Thank you," she whispered.

Xavier sighed. "Everyone seems to know about Beau's apparent inability to keep his hands to himself." He made a face. "A lot of women go along with it because he's a star. I'm glad you set him in his place."

Rachel sampled her cake, jabbing her fork into the slice with a bitter stab. It jounced against the plate and made a high-pitched squeak.

"Who just goes around kissing whomever he wants?" Her face was incredulous as she took a bite of delicious tangerine chiffon cake.

"Listen, ladies, I have a proposition for you. I have a new show idea, and the producer is struggling to find the right talent. I think you two would be perfect, and I'd like to recommend you. Let's go somewhere for dinner tonight and discuss."

He graced us with a dazzling smile that didn't create any lines in his face and swept from the kitchen, leaving me and my sister stunned.

"What do you think he has in mind? Are we getting our own show?"

"Let's hope not," I blurted out, bursting Rachel's bubble.

"Give it a shot! I have to change."

And with that, Rachel raced up the back stairs to our apartment.

Chapter Seven

Xavier's elusive pitch dangled and buzzed in my brain for the rest of the afternoon. I had one more task to complete before dinner. I headed over to Ellie Barnes and her mother's nursery to discuss the secret wedding plans and to set up a game plan for overhauling the Thistle Park greenhouse for Dakota's reception. I'd completely renovated the mansion and the grounds this past fall, including the greenhouse. But the glittering glass space stood quiet and still, awaiting my not-yet-finished ideas to fill the space with flowers and plants.

I pulled the Butterscotch Monster into the Barnes's Nursery grounds, bypassing the pretty, low-slung yellow farmhouse with green trim where Ellie resided with her mother. Her younger sister, Leah, lived at Dunlap with the other boarding school attendees. I idly wondered what it would be like to live under the same roof as a mother so intent on pushing her daughters to greatness as Iris Barnes was. It couldn't have been easy for

Ellie. I thought Leah currently had the better deal, living at Dunlap Academy.

The Barnes's Nursery was made up of several interconnected greenhouses, a collection of pleasing clear domes joined together with long glass hallways. The effect was that of a sparkling group of beehives and igloos, the plants inside different shades of viridian, yellow, and red. The lush, impossibly warm air from the greenhouse hit my face and surprised me as it always did. It was warm for February, but the greenhouse was downright tropical.

"Yoo-hoo, Mallory." Iris Barnes came clucking over, her face set in a welcoming grin. She pulled me in for a hug, and I acquiesced, thinking what a warm, motherly woman she was. A tiger mama, that was. Iris Barnes at first glance came across as yielding and pliant, her demeanor that of some kind of muted earth goddess, with a soft corona of fuzzy brown hair, and none of the angularity of her daughters' faces. She was short and stout, almost as wide as she was tall, and she wore orange gardening clogs with wool socks and faded jeans. She spent her days presiding over her beloved nursery business. When she wasn't fomenting her daughters' takeover of the world. Iris's favorite topic of conversation was the brass rings her Ellie and Leah were grabbing and reaching for. If there was one woman who was a pushier mother than Roxanne, Iris was it.

"Have you heard the news?" She practically bounced on her foam gardening clogs, her hands clasped together within her rough cloth gloves. "Ellie's been made headmistress!" She waved around a sharp pair of shears, and I took an involuntary step back.

"That's fantastic." I offered Iris a steady smile and congratulated her on behalf of her daughter.

But Ginger had to die for that to happen.

"I always wanted Ellie to do something with her life, and now she's followed through." Iris took in my shocked expression and tut-tutted. "Now, I know she is a wonderful drama teacher, but I always thought she could do more. Ellie is always the bridesmaid, never the bride." A dark cloud seemed to pass over her round face. "I never worry about Leah—she has ambition. She'll get into Harvard, you know. Now, paying for tuition, that's another matter."

A tiny trickle of awareness danced across my shoulder blades. What if Iris had been involved with Ginger's death so Ellie could become headmistress?

Before I could plunge further into that line of thought, Ellie herself ducked into the greenhouse.

"There's the newest headmistress!" Iris clapped her hands together again and Ellie blushed.

"Oh stop, Mom." She was wearing an official-looking suit, and her angular face was alive and exhilarated.

"But what Ellie really should be doing is acting, not just teaching drama and serving as headmistress. Ellie is a wonderful actress, did you know? Much better than Dakota." Iris sniffed with disdain and removed her gardening gloves to prepare for our meeting.

"Mom! Don't be ridiculous." Ellie seemed to

want to quiet her mother and motioned us back to the office part of the nursery.

But Iris persisted. "Ellie deserved to be on that show. That silly little man with his health shakes got it all wrong."

Is she talking about Xavier?

Ellie rolled her eyes and readied a pot of coffee. "Back when we were eighteen, Dakota arranged an audition for me. This was when Caitlin Quinn was on strike from *Silverlake High*."

I wracked my brain. Caitlin Quinn was the actress who had died from some horrible accident on the set, something having to do with a gas leak, if I could remember right.

"Caitlin had been holding out for more money, and she was the star of the show," Ellie reminded me. "Xavier was the director, and he had a lot of input on who was to replace Caitlin. He was considering me after Dakota arranged the audition." Ellie seemed equally wistful and relieved.

"And he should have cast you." Iris pouted, pouring a cup of fragrant steaming vanilla coffee into a green mug embossed with the Barnes's Nursery leaf motif and name.

"We were all visiting the set when Caitlin died." Ellie grew serious. "Dakota, Ginger—"

"Ginger was there?" I broke in.

Ellie nodded. "Me, my mom, my sister, Leah, and Ginger thought it would be fun to be on set, and Dakota arranged it. No one was working because of Caitlin's strike, and we had the sound stage to ourselves."

"And you were there when Caitlin had her accident?"

So this isn't the first death Dakota's been involved with.

Ellie looked pained. "Unfortunately, yes."

But not as pained as Dakota, who had finally joined our meeting. The actress strode down a row of red-leaved plants with a frown marring her face. I wished I'd heard her come into the greenhouse.

"Are you talking about Caitlin?" Dakota had turned white, her freckles vividly standing out from her pale skin. I did a double take. I was still getting used to her newly dyed red hair.

"Have a seat, dear," Iris tried to smooth things over to no avail. I wondered how much Dakota had heard, and if it had included Iris stating that Ellie was a better actress than Dakota.

"Please don't bring it up. I have guilt every day over what happened." Dakota's hand fluttered uncertainly up to her mouth.

Why would she have guilt about what happened to Caitlin if it was an accident?

Ellie nervously switched subjects and we turned to the business of making Dakota's secret wedding a reality. I put thoughts of Caitlin Quinn and accidents in Los Angeles in the back of my brain and turned to the pressing tasks at hand. We were running out of time to plan Dakota's wedding and soon might have to fall back on the black-and-white wedding plans.

"We need to transform the greenhouse," I announced. "Right now, it's just soil. We have a blank canvas, which is good, but it won't do on its own."

I'd planned on filling the large space, which

could accommodate dinner for fifty, with a mixture of perennials and vegetables. But I didn't have the greenest thumb, and so far the greenhouse had remained fallow since its renovation in the fall.

"What about bleeding hearts?" Ellie paused and cocked her head. "We have a bumper crop of them ready each Valentine's Day, and not all of them are spoken for."

We followed Ellie deep into the greenhouse to a section overtaken by a sea of bleeding hearts, the blooms dramatic with white heart-shaped buds atop quivering red teardrops.

Dakota reached out to finger a plant. "Oh, these are just perfect."

I nodded and pictured how the bleeding hearts would look. "I talked to a florist I don't usually work with, who will try to get in the red, pink and white blooms in time for us to make arrangements in vases, too. We can set the vases on each table so the bleeding hearts don't have to carry the whole theme."

My usual florist couldn't tackle Dakota's changed plans. I'd had to beg the other two florists in Port Quincy. The owner of the Petal Shop had balked at my request at first, since Valentine's Day was the busiest day of the year, until I named a dizzying sum authorized by Dakota and Beau to make it happen. I hated to throw money around to get the job done, but I guess that was part and parcel of being part of this celebrity wedding.

"And I was thinking we could release some butterflies in honor of Ginger," Ellie tentatively offered. "Since they were her favorite."

Dakota enveloped her friend with a crushing hug. "That's perfect." Her eyes grew wistful. "I can't believe she told you she was seeing someone but didn't tell me." Hurt pooled in the violet depths.

Ellie sighed and dug her hands into her pockets. "She wouldn't tell me who she was dating, but she must have had her reasons."

"But we were the three musketeers," Dakota persisted. "If she couldn't tell us, who could she tell?"

Owen seems to know a lot about Ginger's life, especially if they dined together once a week. Maybe he knows.

Iris brought me back to the task at hand and explained how many bleeding hearts she estimated it would take to fill the empty beds in Thistle Park's greenhouse. We walked around the nursery to broker the purchase of some other white and pink flowers to round out the display.

"We'll need to plant the flowers ourselves," Iris warned, "and it won't be easy work. You'll have to wear gloves, too. Bleeding hearts give some people a slight rash. They're mildly poisonous if ingested in high quantities."

"Well, no one's eating them, so I think we're okay." I reached out to touch a delicate bell-shaped bloom of a diminutive mauve flowering plant with lustrous, dark purplish black berries.

"Don't touch that!"

I pulled my hand back as if I'd singed myself and jumped.

"S-sorry." I moved from the plant and turned with what must have been a quizzical look for Iris.

"That's belladonna," she said with utmost seriousness. "Also known as deadly nightshade. It's highly poisonous, and unlike bleeding hearts, you don't need much."

I shivered and retracted my hand, still scratched and bleeding from breaking the glass in my office to try to save Ginger.

I headed home to shower and get ready for dinner with Rachel and Xavier. I wondered again if we were to be offered our own show. My sister and I showed up at Pellegrino's restaurant at seven, eagerly looking for the director. We settled into a discreet, deep wooden booth in the corner, Rachel straining her neck to catch a glimpse of Xavier. Tiny blush candles in miniature heart candelabras graced each table, and little magenta gerbera daisies winked from small silver vases in an understated nod to the Valentine's month.

A whiff of Calèche wafted over and I froze.

Helene, I mouthed to my sister. I needn't have warned her, as my arch nemesis's voice soon followed.

"She simply ruined the Winter Ball—she was aiding and abetting with Ginger Crevecoeur. If she thinks she can get away with that, she's got another think coming."

My heart sped up as I wondered if Helene was talking about me. I craned my head out of the booth at an unladylike angle and caught a glimpse of my old fiancé, Keith, and his new fiancée, Becca Cunningham. Keith nodded and encouraged his mother to go on, taking in every word. But Becca slunk lower in her seat, the black stripe of her part highlighted against her blond hair. She stared into her lap and seemed to wish to disappear.

A strange rush of pathos crested and crashed over my shoulders. Keith had cheated on me with Becca, and his own grandmother had let me in on the trespass. I was wary of Becca, but I had to remind myself that it was Keith who'd decided to step out on our engagement. Becca had made no such pledge.

I'd spent many an evening right here in Pellegrino's with what I'm sure was a similarly miserable look on my face, listening to Helene hold court as the reigning queen bee of Port Quincy. Most of that time had been planning my wedding, or Helene's second wedding, as I liked to think of it. I'd ended up crafting a ceremony and reception to please Helene's every whim. It was my first gig as wedding planner, however inadvertent.

"I'm off to powder my nose," Helene announced to Keith and Becca. "When I get back, we'll continue planning your wedding."

I shivered at her pronouncement. I wouldn't wish wedding planning with Helene on anyone, even the woman who had sort of stolen my once fiancé. Becca sagged in her chair and watched Helene's retreating back with a look of utter relief. Keith continued digging into his dinner.

Oblivious as usual.

"I just know she murdered Ginger, and she's going to get away with it," Rachel seethed, watching Helene mince off to the restroom on her kitten heels.

"I'd agree, but she wouldn't use a mixture of

bleach and ammonia to do it." I was pretty certain Helene had never met a cleaning product in her life, and she wouldn't be aware of the dangers of mixing the two chemicals.

"Ladies."

Xavier had arrived in all his Zen glory, and I put the thought of Helene out of my head. I basked in the positive energy of his megawatt smile and glanced around to see if he'd brought one of his ubiquitous smoothies. His hands were empty, and he apologized for being late.

He chatted shop for a while, beating around the bush until our orders were taken. Rachel and Xavier got salads, and I ordered capellini pomodoro.

"I had a string of bad luck after *Silverlake High* went off the air," Xavier mused. "Caitlin Quinn was our star, although Dakota would have eventually eclipsed her. When Caitlin passed away, the show was cancelled, and I had to remake my career."

He took a sip of green tea and winced. "Reality TV transformed my career. It's what I'm meant to do. I'm always looking for a new idea, and I have a great one."

Rachel eagerly leaned in, her salad forgotten.

"The network wants to do a show focused on regular, everyday couples. Interest in celebrity weddings is waning. There's one on every weekend, some special or other."

He pushed his wire frames down his nose and looked at us each in turn.

"I've been keeping my eye out for a certain talent for the show. And you two are just what I'm looking for."

Rachel couldn't suppress a squeal, and I had to admit I was excited too.

"You two will be great. You have just the right mix of girl-next-door appeal with a little extra zing. I appreciate how the two of you work well together as sisters, but you have your differences too."

"I think viewers will really connect with the small-town aspect," I gushed, thinking a show held at the B and B with normal weddings would be fun. Maybe we'd even get some creative input, and the show wouldn't need to focus on the divisiveness that can sometimes go along with wedding planning. "People will fall in love with Port Quincy."

Xavier's face fell. "There's one thing. This is a destination wedding show, not one based in Port Quincy." He raised his brows over his glasses expectantly, his silvery spiky hair catching the light.

I felt the air whoosh out of my lungs. "Destination weddings?" I felt like Charlie Brown with the football yanked away at the last second.

But Rachel was glowing. "I adore traveling. Oh, Mallory, this is so exciting!"

"We'll film four months of the year. Do you have someone else to run the B and B?" Xavier winced again as he took a sip of wine, and I wondered if there was something wrong with it.

A frisson of annoyance replaced my concern. Xavier was acting as if Rachel and I would immediately be on board.

"This is the opportunity of a lifetime," Xavier continued, seeming to sense my hesitance. "You'll get free publicity, your star will rise, and so will business back home at your B and B."

I wasn't so sure I could leave Port Quincy. Things were getting more serious with Garrett, and the B and B was already doing well, thank you very much.

Rachel looked worried. I could see a campaign stirring in her pretty green eyes. My sister was indomitable when she wanted something, and she wanted this show.

Dessert arrived, black coffee and fruit compote for Rachel, more green tea for Xavier, and tiramisu for me. I took a delectable bite of the creamy dessert, and then began to choke.

There, before me, Garrett led Adrienne into the dining room, his hand on the small of her back. He steadied her as she tripped on her towering red-soled Louboutins. I knew it was a fake falter, because no one could walk on those stilts better than Adrienne. When I made a rare attempt to walk in heels that high, I had the ungainly gait of a flamingo. But the shoes seemed like a seamless extension of Adrienne's appendages, rendering her a graceful gazelle.

Xavier excused himself to use the restroom, the pained look returning to his face.

"Why aren't you paying attention?" Rachel practically hissed. She took in my stricken face and wheeled around, taking in my beau with his former flame. "Oh. I get it now."

Xavier returned, clutching his stomach, his face a mask of pain.

"I'll get the check, ladies. Think about my offer."

He settled up, and a light bulb seemed to go off in his head. "You two handle so many weddings.

Do you have any tips on proposing to Adrienne?" His bright, toothy smile grew muted and wistful. "She's been waiting for this for an awfully long time."

"Are you going to propose while you're in Port Quincy?"

He nodded, wincing as he clutched his stomach. "Some type of bug must be going around," he muttered.

"Did you get a flu shot?"

Xavier laughed and waved his hand. "Of course not! I don't believe in vaccines. I only take natural remedies."

I sat back, stunned. I liked non-medicinal remedies, like hot tea with lemon, but when it came down to it, I was invested in science.

"Summer is some kid," Xavier said with a smile as he signed his receipt. "Perhaps you can give me some insight, Mallory. Will Garrett allow her to spend a month with us this summer? I know Adrienne will want to marry quickly. She was also thinking about broaching the subject of shared custody with Garrett."

"In Los Angeles?" My voice ended in a squeak. There was no way Garrett would agree. They'd end up in court. My heart ached for Summer. I remembered the hurtful early days of my parents' divorce and shook my head.

"We'll see." Xavier offered us a friendly parting wave and left the restaurant.

"He's not well," Rachel offered, her eyes following the director from the restaurant.

"He's not the only one." I stood and dragged my sister to the bar.

"What are you doing?" Rachel extricated me from her arm.

"Look again," I hissed and wheeled her around to face the dining room. "It's worse than I thought."

Garrett and Adrienne sat at an intimate table for two, the light soft and dusky. I could barely hear Adrienne's tinkling laughter over the chatter of the other diners, but it was there. Garrett was actually mustering up a smile or two.

Traitor.

I shook my head as if to clear it.

They share a child. It's a normal part of co-parenting since Adrienne happens to be in town.

Adrienne picked up a small velvet box and opened the lid. A winking diamond sat on a bed of velvet.

I yelped, backing into a pillar.

Make that a waiter, carrying a tray of drinks. I fell to the floor, bringing the tray and the glasses with me. The cacophony was deafening, and several patrons in the dining room turned to watch the spectacle. Brown liquid, a rum and Coke from the smell of it, drenched my suede boots.

"I'm so sorry!" I moved to help clean up, but the embarrassed waiter waved me on.

I glanced up to see if Garrett had witnessed my klutziness, but he was nowhere to be seen. Adrienne, however, arched one perfect brow in barely restrained amusement.

"Let's get the heck outta here."

Rachel held out her hand and pulled me up. We made for the side exit, a slow heat crawling up my neck, surely staining my face red.

A hand reached out and grabbed my arm.

"Mallory, I need your help."

Chapter Eight

It was Becca Cunningham. The stress of fulfilling the role of Helene's almost daughter-in-law must have been wearing on her. Up close I could see that her trademark stripe of dark roots stood out against the blond hair in an even bigger swath than usual. She'd lost weight and her left eye twitched with a suspicious tic. The surprising rush of sympathy I'd felt for her in the dining room returned. She may have absconded with my fiancé, but I wouldn't wish her current position under Helene's thumb on anyone.

But I had to get out of Pellegrino's. Garrett would be returning to his dinner with Adrienne any minute now. I was already embarrassed enough, I didn't want him to think I'd been spying on him.

"Um, this isn't the best time." I glanced at my green dress, awash in a pungent, sticky mixture of Shirley Temple, iced tea, and cosmopolitan. It was time to make a graceful exit.

Okay, so the graceful ship has sailed.

"Please." Becca's eyes were wild and frantic. She

glanced furtively at the dining room, where Keith was busy helping Helene into her fur coat. Becca's hand gripped my arm like an eagle's talon. "You're my only hope."

Rachel smirked at Becca's Princess Leia speech and gently removed her grasping hand from my arm. The large ring on her left hand had left an imprint on my skin, the princess-cut diamond biting into my flesh from the force of her pressing fingers.

"Sorry, we've got to scram." Rachel gave Becca a no-nonsense glare and we slipped on our coats.

"I need to meet with you tomorrow. I'm desperate." Becca winced and fingered the ruby pendant around her neck. "I'll forever be in your debt."

I shivered, thinking of how I'd been in Helene's debt, and ended up throwing the disastrous Winter Ball. But Becca seemed to be in dire straits, and part of me was downright curious.

I felt my face soften. "Fine. I'm meeting with the florist at the Petal Shop tomorrow at ten-fifteen. Can we speak right before then?"

A wave of gratitude seemed to crest and break over Becca's shoulders. She sagged with apparent relief, and a tenuous smile quivered on her lips. "Thank you, thank you, thank you! You won't regret it." And with that, she wheeled around to join Keith and Helene in the dining room.

"What in the heck was that all about?" I stared at her retreating form for a few seconds before Rachel and I finally slipped out the side exit. I glanced behind me and caught a glimpse of Garrett helping Adrienne into her coat. I pushed the sight from my mind and let the door shut behind me.

"Becca probably wants some survival tips on making it out alive as Keith's fiancée," Rachel quipped as we reached the Butterscotch Monster.

I put thoughts of Becca out of my head and replayed the scene with Adrienne and Garrett in the restaurant.

"Did you see what I think I saw?" I leaned back in my squeaky seat, the leather worn and cold. I recalled the small diamond ring in its little velvet box and took a few calming breaths. It didn't work.

Did Adrienne just propose to Garrett?

"It wasn't what you think." Rachel waved her shiny acrylic fingertips in a dismissive motion. But her eyes were wide and incredulous, revealing her true thoughts. "Garrett is just being a good co-parent. I bet they're talking about Summer."

"But I saw a ring!" My voice was high pitched and hysterical, and I swallowed hard and jabbed the key into the ignition.

You're not Garrett's keeper or warden. Besides, Rachel is probably right. They're just discussing Summer.

Maybe I'd seen something else on the table. The lighting at Pellegrino's was kept low to create a cozy atmosphere, and it could have been anything glinting on that table.

Right?

I had my doubts but turned the key. The engine coughed and sputtered in the cool night air.

Rachel began her campaign immediately.

"I know what you're thinking, Mallory. You're making a mental pro and con list about why we should or shouldn't do the destination show." Rachel sat back in the worn leather seat and clicked her seat belt with a satisfied smirk.

"You know me well," I grudgingly admitted as we pulled onto Main. "It's an interesting opportunity, but—"

"But what! It's the chance of a lifetime!"

"I don't know if I'm cut out for constant filming." I thought back over the past few days and the ever-present cameras. I was getting used to them at an alarmingly fast rate, and for the last day, I had forgotten they were even there. Still, I wasn't sure if I could deal with the fabricated drama of reality TV on a daily basis.

"I really, really want this for us." Rachel batted her long sable lashes. "Pretty please? I have it all figured out."

I laughed and kept my focus on the road. "Okay, let's hear it."

Rachel beamed and launched into her pitch. "Mom and Doug could run the B and B while we're gone."

"Whoa, whoa, whoa. Mom has plans to un-retire and start a new decorating and staging business after she moves from Florida. I don't know how she'd feel about being recruited to run the B and B."

I thought back to the colossal debates my mother and I had had about decorating Thistle Park and shivered. I wasn't sure I wanted to leave the B and B in my mother's undoubtedly capable hands for half the year. She might be caught by the decorating bug, and I'd come back to a completely different house.

"And we don't even really know what Doug is planning to do," I volleyed. Our stepfather was in agreement about moving back to Pennsylvania soon, but I wasn't sure he'd be keen on running the B and B.

"You just don't want me to succeed." I turned my head away from the road for a split second, in time to catch one of Rachel's maudlin pouts.

We'd advanced on the slalom-like road down the hill leaving the business section of Port Quincy and its rows of pretty but worn art deco office buildings, and crested the hill leading to Sycamore Street. Downtown gave way to a valley of neat saltboxes, cape cods, and cottages before we started our ascent again. Soon, we turned onto Sycamore Street, where Thistle Park rose like a crown jewel, an Italianate mansion holding court over a coterie of painted lady Victorians.

"Oh, good grief! Of course I do." Had my sister forgotten she'd talked me into this B and B and wedding-planning business in the first place?

Rachel slammed the car door behind her and hurried up the herringbone path. I gave a weary sigh and chased after her.

Rachel wheeled around when we reached the front hall. "Maybe if we get out of Port Quincy, I can find someone to date and not have it blow up in my face." Hot tears gathered in the corners of her eyes and threatened to spill over. "Owen is the first guy I've had the guts to go out with in four months. I'm not sure if Port Quincy is a big enough pond for me."

"Oh, Rach." I reached out to give my sister a hug. "We'll talk this over and come to a decision together."

"Promise?" Rachel pulled back, a single tear

streaking down her face. She hastily wiped it away and broke into a tentative, quivering smile.

"I promise. But I wanted to ask one thing. Don't mention this to Mom and Doug yet, okay?"

"Deal." Rachel beamed and held out her hand, her new manicure sparkling under the chandelier. She crooked her smallest finger and we sealed our promises with a pinky swear.

"Excuse me, ladies." Adrienne advanced up the path and hurried through the front door. I breathed a sigh of relief. Her meeting with Garrett was over. Adrienne bustled up the stairs, her spiky heels striking each stair with angry taps. She took a sharp left down the upstairs corridor. A door slammed with surprising force. Rachel and I glanced at each other and headed off in that direction.

We could hear the argument, muffled and intense, from a great distance at the top of the stairs. It was emanating from the blue room, the one I'd given to Adrienne and Xavier. Rachel and I tiptoed over the heavy brocade carpet, our steps muffled and quick.

"We shouldn't be—"

"Shh!" Rachel clapped a hand over my mouth and motioned to the door.

I rolled my eyes and followed my sister to the threshold. I didn't want to admit I was just as curious.

Rachel leaned against the door, her eyes wide.

"Let's get out of here—"

"You promised!" Adrienne's voice was strangled and shrill through the door. I gave up any pretense and leaned against the carved mahogany wood, pressing my ear as close as possible.

"You were going to do everything you could to keep *I Do* on the air."

"It's not up to me, babe." Xavier's cadence was as calm and Zen as usual. If I were Adrienne, it would have been mildly infuriating. "I've made entreaties to the producer and the network, but things aren't looking good."

Rachel's brows arched in surprise and she leaned back against the door.

"This will probably be the last episode of *I Do*." Xavier's voice was reluctant yet firm.

A wail, undoubtedly Adrienne's, resounded through the door. "I need to be gainfully employed if I'm going to try to get more custody. I've fought so hard to make something of myself for her."

A stab of sympathy slipped into my side. So Adrienne was serious about trying to be more present in her daughter's life. I wondered if she'd made her plans known to Garrett tonight or to Summer herself. I heard the muffled sound of sniffles; then Xavier resumed the conversation.

"Don't worry. If Dakota and Beau's wedding continues to be the train wreck it is so far, we'll catapult up the ratings." Xavier's voice was matter of fact without a hint of glee, but I still felt disgusted.

"But even if this episode isn't enough to save the show, I have another plan. I was devastated when Caitlin died and *Silverlake High* was cancelled," Xavier continued. "I promised myself I'd always have something new in the works. The network is scouting for talent for a new destination wedding show. The executive producer asked me to keep an eye out."

"Oh, Xavier! I'd love to do a destination show." Adrienne's voice cracked with relief. Rachel's eyes went wide.

"She's stealing our—"

"Shh!" This time I clapped my hand over my sister's mouth and shamefully continued to listen, my ear pressed so hard to the door I was sure it would be red.

"Actually, I'm going to suggest Mallory and Rachel as hosts." Xavier's voice was not unkind, but it didn't matter how he broached it. The explosion that followed could be heard without pressing our ears to the door.

"What?" Adrienne's voice was a genuine squawk. "That mousy wedding planner and that hussy? What are you thinking? I'd be perfect to host a destination show, but you're considering them?"

"That's it—" A wave of fury washed over Rachel's face and she put her hand on the brass doorknob. "She just called me—"

The door flung open and Rachel and I toppled into the room. Adrienne gasped, then composed herself with startling swiftness.

"Well, excuse *me*." She stepped over the tangle of limbs and red faces that was me and my sister and primly exited down the hall, with nary a backward glance. Her steps were as precise and delicate as usual, but her back was uncomfortably ramrod straight. I felt a rush of embarrassment from openly spying. Adrienne's ring finger was bare, so I guess Xavier hadn't popped the question just yet.

And neither did Garrett.

I peeled myself off the floor for the second time this evening and dared to look Xavier in the eye. His lips were twitching, and his eyes were filled with mirth. I could finally see a few wrinkles in his impossibly smooth face, the laugh lines daring to come out.

Phew.

"We were just, um, checking up on you," I lamely lied. "You didn't look so hot at dinner."

Xavier nodded, giving us an out. "I think I'm coming down with the flu." He rested his hand on his flat stomach and sat down in a striped navy chair with a weary sigh. He drew his warm and luxurious merino wool hoodie closer around him, and shucked off his ever-present Adidas shoes.

"I could get you some cold medicine," I suggested, ticking the options off on my fingers. "We have NyQuil, Robitussin—"

"Oh, *no,* no thank you." Xavier screwed up his face as if the mere suggestion of over-the-counter cold remedies were an invitation to ingest poison. "I never take that dreck. Adrienne's been on me all season to get a flu vaccine as well, but I don't believe in them."

Just what we need. The flu going around.

"I think I'll make a nice, healing smoothie." He winced and cradled his stomach again. "Perhaps lemon, wheatgrass, and mint. A pinch of sea salt. A base of green tea."

His latest concoction actually sounded delicious, not like his usual noxious mixtures.

"The last time I had the genuine flu, I was laid

up for a week." He shuddered and leaned into the striped wingback chair, pulling the hood over his head with a shiver. "It was that awful week when Caitlin Quinn died on set."

I thought back to Ellie and Iris's recounting of that fateful week thirteen years ago and leaned in closer. Xavier closed his eyes as if recalling the incident.

"Caitlin was holding up shooting to try to get more money in her new contract. We couldn't film, so Dakota had her friends from Port Quincy out for a visit. The studio was considering replacing Caitlin, and I got to weigh in on the final decision. I watched a bunch of auditions, and then the flu hit me full force. Knocked me flat on my back." He shivered as he recalled his illness. "I stayed at home for the next two weeks in a NyQuil fugue, and when I came out of it, Caitlin was dead, Dakota's visitors were gone, and the show was cancelled."

"You were incapacitated when Caitlin died?"

"Roxanne took care of me." Xavier's eyes fluttered open and he seemed to stare into the past. He shivered again.

A thought skittered across my brain.

Roxanne used to drug Dakota when she had trouble sleeping. Could she have drugged Xavier when he had the flu?

But all I said was, "Roxanne?"

"We were a couple back then." He offered a rueful and blinding white smile through his evident pain. "I think I shocked the hell out of her when she saw me this week. I guess Dakota didn't tell her I'd be directing, or Roxanne never would have allowed her to take this gig." He chuckled mirthlessly.

Rachel and I held a silent conference over his head.

So Roxanne and Xavier were a thing.

"We'll let you rest." I practically dragged Rachel from the room and we headed down the back stairs to the kitchen.

"The plot thickens." Rachel raised a brow and motioned upstairs. "So Roxanne used to date Xavier."

"And from the looks of it, she never got over it."

We clammed up as we hit the last stair, but we couldn't be heard anyway over the whir of the blender. Adrienne was whipping up a restorative smoothie, and from the looks and smell of it, the ingredients were the ones Xavier had mentioned.

A grain of an idea seeded itself in my head.

"What if we used some of the herbs in Ellie and Iris's greenhouse to craft a signature drink for Dakota?"

Adrienne whirled around, her face genuinely excited and interested. "That's a lovely idea, Mallory." She offered me a small smile and advanced up the back stairs.

"She's not so bad," Rachel sighed. "When she's not giving you the evil eye for being with Garrett, or trying to redo all your wedding plans."

I left my sister in the kitchen and hurried to my office to start brainstorming up a drink. I stopped short at the door, the yellow crime tape still looped over the doorknob. I could picture Ginger slumped over my desk, the enormous bouquet of blue flowers perched in front of her like a sentinel of death. If I closed my eyes and took a deep breath, I swore I could still catch a whiff of the awful, nose-burning chemical smell. I'm sure it had dissipated by now, and my mind was just playing tricks on me, conjuring olfactory hallucinations when the air was really safe to breathe.

I backed away from my office and wondered when I'd ever feel comfortable working there. I dashed off a few emails to vendors in the parlor, trying to find some closer to Pittsburgh who could supply the magenta, crimson, and blush linens for Dakota's secret reception. After half an hour of emailing out queries, I turned to concocting a special drink.

I wandered over to the library, the room rich and warm and light and airy. It was one of my favorite rooms in the house with a massive yet cozy marble fireplace, buttery-yellow walls, and a new, soaring tin ceiling after the original had suffered a mishap while renovating last fall. Soft gray velvet drapes framed sweeping bay windows with fluffy crimson pillows and sweeping views of the grounds. Cozy mysteries, romances, and thrillers nestled next to volumes of Freud and *The History of the Decline and Fall of the Roman Empire*. The books were plentiful and eclectic, with something for every reader. I was proud of this little collection, and guests always said it was one of their favorite things to take advantage of during their stay.

I pulled out a giant encyclopedia about gardening, plants, and herbs. The tome was heavy and elaborate, a gold leaf reference work given to me as a gift by my contractor, Jesse Flowers. He'd

restored the greenhouse, but left it barren. He'd
suggested I leaf through the book to get ideas for
planting. I rested the big book on a low-slung table
in front of the fire. I spent half an hour reading
about edible plants, herbs, and spices. I absent-
mindedly thumbed to the page on bleeding hearts,
and the one on belladonna. I marked my pages
with the gold foil butterfly bookmark that had
come with the book, and thought of Ginger.

Who wanted to kill her, and why?

My mind kept circling back to Helene. She had
the most reasons to want to get Ginger out of the
way, from keeping Dunlap Academy an all girls'
school, to putting the tiara back into rotation. But
then there was the tiara itself. The Port Quincy
Eagle Herald had practically rolled out an invitation
for thieves by quoting Helene about the tiara's use
at the Winter Ball. And then there was Sterling
Jennings, furious at Ginger for missing their meeting and not putting his daughter on the lacrosse
team. But that didn't seem like a dire enough reason
to kill.

A slip of paper caught my eye, peeking out from
behind a claret cushion. I recognized one of Rachel's
notebooks, and my mouth crooked up in a sad
smile. She must be working here too, too distraught to use our joint office. The little book fell
open to the most recently used page. There was a
pros and cons list hastily jotted down, detailing
whether it would be better to pursue the destination wedding show with me or to go it alone. In
the half hour I'd spent emailing vendors from the
parlor, Rachel had already planned to abandon

me to remain on TV. I dropped the notebook back behind the cushion, stung by the realization that Rachel was going to try to get on the show, with or without me.

I buried my hurt over Rachel's plans and wearily sank into bed. I awoke bright and early, fed my two kitties, and served up a buffet breakfast of cinnamon rolls, bacon, and fruit salad. After breakfast, I avoided Rachel and straightened up the rooms. Then I wandered around the first floor to find Dakota for our meeting with the florist. The doorbell clanged its clarion carol, and I opened it to find a beaming Summer and Garrett on the doorstep.

"I'm going bowling with my mom," Summer explained, leaning in to give me a hug. I pulled her close, then did a double take. Summer wasn't wearing her usual weekend garb. She was dressed in head-to-toe pale blue, the kind of pastels Adrienne favored. Just this past July, she'd been a goth princess, complete with inky hair and ripped clothes. She'd settled into comfortable tomboy style as of late, her hair back to its usual blond, cut rather short.

I raised my eyebrows over Summer's shoulder in silent conference with Garrett. He returned my concerned gaze.

She skipped into the parlor, where I could see Roxanne playing with Pixie. The Shih Tzu bounded over to see Summer, and Roxanne gave her a proud-doggie-owner smile.

"And I'm just glad to see you." Garrett leaned in

for a kiss, the beginnings of a five-o'clock shadow tickling my face. I thought of his strange dinner with Adrienne yesterday and held on to him longer than usual. He broke away with an amused look in his laughing dark eyes.

"I feel like it's been forever since I've seen you, too." He broke into a grin, effervescent and warm.

See? You have nothing to worry about.

"Only a few days, but it's been long enough." I brushed a lock of hair from his forehead and was treated to a lightly cleared throat.

"Ahem. Are we ready?" Adrienne materialized at my elbow, a vision in blue, from her skinny jeans to her perfectly figure-hugging sky-blue angora sweater. She held out her hand and Summer took it with a smile. They could have been sisters in their matching outfits, rather than mother and daughter.

"Xavier isn't feeling well." Adrienne's face clouded over for a moment; then it passed. "Could you check in on him in a few hours, see if he needs anything?" I promised I would, and Adrienne started to fix Summer's scarf.

"See you soon?" Garrett leaned in for a rather perfunctory kiss, distracted by Adrienne's fussing over Summer. They were soon out the door, leaving me staring in their wake.

"Mallory?" Dakota broke my reverie and I turned with a start.

"Oh! Sorry."

That was a quick good-bye.

I chastised myself for worrying about Garrett and Adrienne's dinner and settled down across from Dakota. She was knitting, at work on a pretty shawl of some sort in shades of green and yellow. She reminded me of a reverse Penelope, working on her knitting each night before the fire this week, as if to stave off her suitor.

"Penny for your thoughts?" She set down the knitting needles and rested her chin in her hand, her engagement ring winking.

"If you were me, would you do a destination wedding show?" I heard myself blurt the question out before I could stop.

"Ah, Xavier's newest project." Dakota smiled and nodded. "He always has something up his sleeve." She cocked her head in thought. "I love acting, don't get me wrong, but I don't like being on set for too long. It's hard to see your family when you're away shooting. But the offer is for you and Rachel too, right?"

If Rachel doesn't go behind my back and negotiate the show for herself, that is.

"It is," I affirmed, still doubtful.

"I saw you there with Garrett just now. Are you guys serious? Everyone will tell you it doesn't matter if you're gone part of the year, but it does."

I sat for a minute.

How serious are things with Garrett?

It was a damn good question.

"Things are going well. I don't know if they're well enough to withstand being away so much though," I admitted.

Dakota sighed. "If I could do it all over again, I'd stay here and work with Ellie and Iris at their nursery. I let Roxanne convince me to return to

L.A. after I finished school, when all I wanted to do was stay in Port Quincy." She grew wistful and took a sip of tea. "I'd wanted to return to Port Quincy since I was on *Silverlake High*. I was miserable on the show, and Ginger and Ellie and Owen were back here. They got to go to school and be normal and hang out together."

"And then Caitlin died," I mentioned carefully, gauging her reaction. I was still curious as to why it was a taboo subject, remembering Dakota's stern demand in the greenhouse not to mention it.

She nodded gravely. "Do you know why I feel so guilty about Caitlin? I feel like I wished it upon her."

My eyes went wide, but I stayed silent so Dakota would continue.

"I couldn't help thinking when she went on strike that the show would end. My mom liked to think I was the bigger star, but I'm not blind. It was Caitlin. I wished something would happen so the show would be cancelled, and then it came to fruition. Caitlin died on set and the show ended. I feel like I willed it to happen, inadvertently." She shivered, despite the rollicking flames dancing in the fireplace, the peacock tiles reflecting the fire in hues of electric blue, aqua, purple, and green. She set down her knitting needles again.

"I never wanted anything to happen to Caitlin, but I can't say I wasn't glad the show ended." A tiny tear beaded in the corners of Dakota's violet eyes, and she sniffed, seemingly embarrassed.

"It was an accident?" I procured a box of tissues.

"It was gas," Dakota affirmed, nervously twisting

her huge Asscher ring. "All my friends were visiting. Ginger and Ellie and her little sister, Leah, and her mother, Iris. Everyone but Owen."

The big man-in-the-moon grandfather clock in the hall chimed ten times, and I sat up straight with a start.

"We'll be late for the florists. Time to go."

And time to see what it is that Becca Cunningham wants.

We had no more time to dwell on Caitlin Quinn's death from thirteen years ago. We needed to meet with the new florist to put Dakota's secret red and pink Valentine's Day wedding plans into play, as well as Owen's black-tie event.

I pulled the Butterscotch Monster up to the curb and started to giggle.

Becca skulked beneath the eave of the florist's door, dressed like a 1940s detective. She sported big glasses that nearly covered the top half of her face and had a colorful orange Hermes scarf tied around her head and under her chin. She'd completed her look with a long camel trench. Her face swiveled right and left in herky-jerky motions as if she were looking for someone following her.

"You came." She gripped my hands in hers, her fingers cold and clammy.

"Yes," I said guardedly. I wondered if she was going to ask for something impossible, like a kidney or a Rumpelstiltskin-esque favor.

"I need your help planning my elopement."

I relaxed, then broke out into a grin.

"That is an excellent idea."

Why didn't I think of that for myself?

I recalled my aborted nuptials with Keith, now Becca's fiancé. I'd come up with idea after idea for our wedding, only to be shot down by Hurricane Helene. I'd finally acquiesced, worn down by her constant strident objections, and planned the wedding of *her* dreams, not mine. Before I'd discovered Keith's infidelity with Becca, and thankfully called the whole damn thing off.

Could I really help the woman who had stolen my fiancé?

It was his choice, too, I chastised myself. I'd resisted trying to paint Becca as the enemy in the fiasco that had been my engagement. It was Keith who'd decided to break our engagement, not Becca.

I took a deep breath and glanced at Dakota, who wore an amused and quizzical look on her face.

"When were you and Keith planning on escaping—er, getting married?"

The wild look returned to Becca's eyes, and she glanced behind me and shuddered.

"We'd like to leave tomorrow."

I stared at her, stunned. I considered myself a good wedding planner. I'd learned a lot through trial by fire over the last half year, and I could whip up some pretty amazing plans in a pinch. But leaving *tomorrow?*

"That's impossible." I took an inadvertent step away from the increasingly desperate woman before me. But Becca wasn't ready to hear no.

Becca clutched the lapel of my green coat and pulled me closer, a definite streak of madness marring her usually cool and dismissive demeanor.

"Please, I'm begging you."

I carefully removed her hands from my collar and put a foot of space between us.

"Becca—"

"We'll need travel arrangements, and an intimate venue for two. Something far, far away from her. I mean here. I mean far away from her *and* here." Her left eye twitched again, her heavily mascaraed lid doing a jumpy tango. "Preferably the Caribbean. Helene must not know."

She's gone mental.

"It's going to cost you." I jumped as Dakota waded into the fray. "Mallory can't plan a wedding in a few hours' time for nothing."

"Um, Dakota, I haven't agreed . . ."

"Of course I'll pay!" Becca's voice was near hysterical. "Twice your going rate."

Dakota shook her head.

"Triple. Quadruple!"

"All right, all right!" I stopped this madness before it could get out of hand. "Becca, we need to meet with the florist for *Dakota's* wedding, but I'll see what I can do for you."

"Thank you, thank you, thank you!" Becca grabbed me in an impetuous, crushing hug. She pushed her glasses up her nose and disappeared down a narrow alley between the florist's shop and the bakery, pulling her orange scarf tighter around her face.

"What have I done?" I buried my face in my hands, my head swimming with ideas and buzzing with despair.

"I'd want to run off as soon as possible if Helene were my mother-in-law, too," Dakota breathed through her laughter.

We pushed open the door to the Petal Shop, a soft chime announcing our entry. The store was a modern space in pink and black, flowers neatly displayed and chilled behind sleek glass cases. Bright white overhead lights illuminated the hundreds of blooms lining the walls. A giant worktable stood raised in the middle of the store, where the florist, Clarissa Crosby, artfully built a large pink and red arrangement, stem by careful stem.

"You must be Mallory." Clarissa stepped down from the raised platform and gave my hand a hearty shake. "And of course I know who you are. Dakota Craig! I can't believe I'm doing the flowers for your wedding." Twin spots of pink that matched the roses she'd just arranged dotted Clarissa's smooth cheekbones.

"I'm so grateful you could squeeze me in on such short notice." Dakota clasped Clarissa's hands in hers and offered her a warm smile. I couldn't help but think that, much like the favor I was going to try to pull off for Becca, the florist could only attempt to deliver a bounty of red and pink blooms in a mere week because Dakota and Beau were paying through the nose for it.

"I'm sorry about Ginger," Clarissa gushed, dropping Dakota's hands. "I hear you were friends."

"Yes," Dakota breathed, the pain etched in her face anew.

"She received a standing order every Friday," Clarissa said, her eyes far away.

"Excuse me?" I dropped my bag and knelt to retrieve it.

"From a mystery admirer."

"Her secret boyfriend," Dakota muttered. The

hurt was written on her face, clear to see. "I still can't believe she didn't breathe a word of it to me." She cocked her head in thought. "Can you tell us who it was?" Her violet eyes were pleading and bright, innocent and hopeful.

Damn, she really is a great actress.

But Clarissa shook her head, her giant sunflower earrings brushing her shoulders. "I couldn't tell you even if I did want to breach confidentiality. The person was quite careful to protect his or her identity. They mailed in a rather large sum in cash at the beginning of the year to pay for a recurring weekly delivery."

"Where was the money postmarked from?" I broke in.

"Here in Port Quincy, I believe." Clarissa began to look nervous.

"So she got the flowers for a year," I mused. "Does the chief of police know this?"

Clarissa's eyes went wide. "Do you think he needs to know?"

"Of course!" Dakota softened her voice. "I would let him know as soon as possible."

Clarissa seemed unsure, and I made a note to tell Truman myself. The florist disappeared into the back room to bring out a representative arrangement for Dakota, and I turned to her.

"What if she was murdered by her secret lover?"

"It's possible," she said with a frown. "Especially if he was someone she felt the need to keep a secret. Maybe he was dangerous or he was blackmailing her."

Or maybe it was someone who admitted to having

dinner with her weekly. Someone you seem to have a bit of a crush on.

"What are you thinking?" Dakota's eyes narrowed.

Here goes nothing.

"Do you think she was seeing Owen?"

"*No!*" Dakota lowered her voice. "Absolutely not. They were just friends." Her voice was testy and hot, and she swallowed hard. But she seemed to be trying hard to convince herself as much as me.

"Here we are. Ranunculus, roses, tulips, and freesia." Clarissa carried a conical arrangement and set the heavy silver vase before us, the flowers lush and fragrant, a sumptuous mosaic of pink, red, cream, and white.

"Oh, it's gorgeous." Dakota reached out to run her hands over the soft petals and breathed out a sound of delight. I was happy the flowers had arrived to take her mind off my musings about Owen.

"If you come into the back room, I have a few more arrangements to choose from," Clarissa beamed, clearly over the moon at Dakota's reaction. We followed her back to gaze at gorgeous bunches of flowers in monochromatic arrangements of pink and red.

"Excuse me a moment." The tinkling chimes of the door sounded again, and Clarissa disappeared. A heated argument commenced, and I recognized the other party.

Uh-oh. She wouldn't dare.

"Mallory? Dakota?" Clarissa's voice was impossibly small and meek. "I'm so sorry to have wasted your time. I can't do the wedding." The last pronouncement was said so softly I barely heard her.

"I'm sorry?" Dakota didn't understand, but I did.

"Excuse me." I brushed past Clarissa to find the source of the problem.

"Helene."

The reining doyenne of Port Quincy set down the rose she'd been admiring and offered me a chilling smile.

"Mallory. We meet again. I was just letting Clarissa know that it would be advantageous if she remembered the Valentine's Day party for the Daughters of the American Revolution. She is contracted to create quite a few arrangements for us, and she can no longer be of service to you."

"You snake!" I advanced toward Helene, then thought better of it. I stood rooted to the floor, quaking with anger. I didn't need a charge of assault on my plate.

"You would have done well not to cross me regarding the Winter Ball, Mallory, after all I did to put you on the map."

"I don't need you to put me on the map! I'm hosting a celebrity wedding, haven't you heard?" A fleeting thought zinged through my brain. I thought of Helene's face, contorted with anger, when she'd soon realize Keith and Becca had absconded right from under her surgically enhanced nose. I felt my mouth twitch up in an inadvertent smile.

"You dare to mock me?" My smile must have set Helene off. "I helped you renovate your B and B in record time, and you go behind my back?" She drew herself up to her full height, balancing on her kitten heels. "You can't even keep people from expiring at your events."

"How *dare* you speak of Ginger that way." Dakota took a step forward, no longer acting.

"She got what she deserved." Helene clapped a hand over her mouth, even she realizing she'd gone too far. With that, she swept out of the store, and I swore I caught a whiff of brimstone.

"That horrible, horrible woman." Tears coursed down Dakota's face.

Chapter Nine

Helene's grim threats haunted my thoughts as I drove Dakota back to Thistle Park. I had no idea what we were going to do for her flowers in such a short amount of time.

"Don't worry about the flowers. I'd rather catch my best friend's murderer than have a single petal at this cursed wedding." She promptly burst into tears, and I left her at the B and B, nursing a hot cup of tea. I checked on Xavier before I left, and his muffled reply told me he was napping. I headed out to Iris and Ellie's greenhouse to brainstorm solutions for wedding flowers now that our florist connection was blacklisted by dear old Helene, suspect numero uno for Ginger's murder.

"We'll just have to plant more bleeding hearts," Ellie suggested. She held her hand out over the sea of distinctive flowers. We were loading up the plants onto a truck to transport them to Thistle Park. Iris, Ellie, and I were joined by Owen, and we performed the backbreaking work for an hour, the delicate blooms stacked in crates and ready for transport.

"You weren't kidding when you said this was hard work." I wiped the back of my hand across my face, realizing too late I'd probably smeared some dirt.

"It's my favorite kind of work to do," Ellie admitted. She stopped to take a sip of water. "Don't get me wrong, I love being a drama teacher. And becoming headmistress was a dream come true." A dark cloud marred her angular looks. "Not that I ever wanted to become headmistress if it meant Ginger getting killed. But this is what I would do if I had the choice. Just work in the nursery with my mother."

I took a swig of water and set the bottle down. "No offense, but if you want to work in the nursery, then why are you still teaching drama?"

I thought back to my career as an attorney and how I had enjoyed some aspects of it, but ultimately was more fulfilled running my own business at the B and B and planning weddings. I couldn't fault Ellie for not striking out and following her dreams, though. My current gig had been helped along by my surprise inheritance of Thistle Park from Keith's grandmother, Sylvia.

Ellie flushed and glanced around the nursery before answering. We were alone at the moment; Owen and Iris were shoring things up in the truck.

"It's kind of embarrassing that a woman in her early thirties is so beholden to her mother." She let out a gust of air. "I guess I just followed the path my mom laid out for me, but I wasn't too successful at it."

I slung an arm around Ellie's shoulder and gave

it a comforting squeeze. "You're plenty successful. You're a wonderful teacher, your students adore you, and now you're headmistress. Are you still down about not getting the role on *Silverlake High* all those years ago?"

Before we could answer, Owen came back with some empty crates. "Thanks again, Mallory, for planning the benefit for Helping Hands." He stood next to Ellie, offering her a gentle smile. Ellie nervously brushed her hair from her forehead.

"And I haven't had a chance to formally congratulate you on becoming headmistress."

This time, Ellie blushed for real, a scarlet bloom dotting her cheekbones. "Thanks Owen." She stopped playing with her hair and put her hand down, brushing Owen's in the process. She nearly jumped a mile.

Whoa there.

There seemed to be some serious tension in the air. I wondered if Ellie and Owen had ever been a couple, and where Dakota fit into the equation. Ellie seemed nervous enough around Owen, and Dakota seemed rather smitten with him too. But she was about to marry Beau, his almost-kiss with Rachel notwithstanding. And Owen had admitted he had dinner weekly with Ginger. Was it just because they'd been such good friends, or something more? I couldn't discount Owen as Ginger's lover. It made sense. Maybe Ginger hadn't told Ellie the identity of the man she was seeing and hadn't told Dakota at all because she'd known they both had a thing for Owen.

"We keep changing the plans for your black-tie

event," I admitted. I filled Owen in on our new plans to use the fake yellow-themed wedding for his gala, as well as Helene's success in getting me black-listed with one of the town's florists. "But your event is several months away, so I suggest we just work with my usual florist, Lucy at the Bloomery."

Owen shook his head. "Ginger tried not to let Helene bother her, but that woman was obsessed with making her life impossible. It's like Helene had a personal vendetta against Ginger. It went beyond their differences at school."

Ellie nodded and dug her hands into her pockets. "Ginger and Helene had a long-standing feud, ever since Ginger became headmistress a year ago. Helene thought she could walk all over her because Ginger was the youngest person ever to hold the position. They fought about modernizing technology at the school, over merging with the boys' academy, and fundraising. Helene was used to running the board and influencing the members to do her bidding. Ginger put a stop to that, and people actually had a voice." Ellie gave a rueful laugh. "Ginger didn't even want to have the damn Winter Ball. If Helene hadn't strong-armed you into throwing it for free, Mallory, the tradition would have been scrapped."

Interesting.

"Tell me about the vote Helene was talking about before the ball started. She threatened Ginger about the board convening about something."

Ellie grew serious. "The board votes on serious matters that affect the whole school, like the proposed merger with the boys' school. There's an old-guard faction, led by Helene, and a newer faction that usually voted in line with Ginger. It's kind of like congress. If there was a tie, and there usually was, Ginger as headmistress got to break the tie. Kind of like the vice president and the U.S. Senate. Helene couldn't take it anymore, and was rallying alumni against Ginger behind her back." She paused, her face more thoughtful. "Helene won one important battle. That old coot amassed enough support against Ginger to renovate the ballroom that led to the discovery of the time capsule. Ginger didn't want to, but Helene pushed it through."

"So now you're the tiebreaker."

Ellie nodded, then shivered. "I don't want to contemplate whether Ginger was killed because she voted a certain way to break ties from board members."

Owen's eyes went wide, and he took Ellie's hands in his. "Be careful, Ellie. I wouldn't mess with Helene Pierce. Or some of the parents at that school of yours, either."

He blinked when he realized what he'd done and dropped Ellie's hands as if he'd been holding live coals. "I've got to go. I have a meeting with a group of volunteers in an hour."

He offered Ellie a sheepish smile and ducked out of the nursery, leaving her to stare after him.

"Why do you think Ginger hid the identity of her boyfriend?" I thought of the weekly flower delivery Ginger received from the Petal Shop and the lengths the giver had gone to conceal his identity.

Ellie sat down on a worktable, swinging her long legs in thought. "Ginger was a private person in general. I've been wracking my brain to try to

figure out who it could be. Believe me, Chief Truman
has asked me enough times."

"Could it have been a student from the boys'
school?"

Ellie cocked her head. "It's possible, but I
wouldn't bet on it."

"Could it be Owen?"

Ellie sat up and swung off the table in a flash.
"No!" She realized her overreaction too late and
toned down her outburst. "Ginger and Owen were
just friends." Her voice went flat. "I'm sure of it."

Iris, Ellie, and I performed another hour of gru-
eling work unloading the bleeding hearts to be
planted in a few days. I took a shower and noticed
I had the slight rash Iris had warned us we could
get from handling the blooms.

I brought Xavier some rooibos tea, which he
gratefully accepted. He appeared to be on the
mend, and I was cheered that he probably didn't
have the flu. I was just about to settle into making
plans for Becca's lightning-quick nuptials to my ex
Keith when the doorbell rang.

"You can use your office again." Truman stood
before me with a smile. "I bet you'll be glad to get
back to normal."

I shook my head and motioned him in.

"I'm not sure if I can use that desk, let alone the
room, ever again."

"Make that two of us." Rachel sauntered over,
and the three of us stared at the office and the
yellow crime tape cordoning off the door.

"I'll do the honors." Truman turned the handle and gave the door a gentle push. The crime scene techs had returned the room to its normal state. There wasn't a single trace of fingerprint powder, broken glass, or even a whiff of the chemical smell. Still, I didn't want to enter the room. It was too soon after Ginger had perished at my desk, and I could picture the scene all too vividly.

"Let's go somewhere else." Rachel gulped, and Truman and I followed her to the parlor.

"Do you have any leads on Ginger?"

Truman sighed and ran his hand through his salt-and-pepper hair. "No one seems to know a single thing about Ginger's mystery man. Now I'm not saying that's who I think did it, but it's an important piece of the puzzle."

"Can you get DNA from the wineglass at her house?"

Truman chuckled. "DNA evidence takes months to process in the real world. This isn't some TV show. We ran the glasses, but we won't know for a while and I doubt it'll hit someone in the system."

"Ginger got a weekly flower delivery, probably from the secret guy in question," I rushed on, hoping Truman wouldn't be annoyed.

"Dammit, why don't people tell me these things?" He thumped the table in front of him, the glass candy dish jumping. "How did you find this out?"

I filled him in on my and Dakota's unsuccessful meeting with Clarissa at the Petal Shop. Truman shook his head ruefully. "You'd think with a murder that people would want to share any pertinent detail. I can understand though why she might not have thought it had any bearing."

"I still think it's Helene," Rachel mused, unwrapping a strawberry candy from the now-settled cut-glass dish and popping it in her mouth.

"She's the most obvious candidate. She actually did threaten Ginger mere hours before we discovered her in my office."

"I know all this." Truman selected a mandarin-orange candy for himself and viciously bit into it, cracking it in two. Ginger's case must have really been getting to him.

"I have another hunch," I said with a small voice, selecting a butter-rum candy for myself. Rachel wasn't going to be happy. "Owen had dinner with Ginger weekly. He admitted it himself. He didn't say they were an item, but he seems to know so much about her."

Rachel cocked her hip and sent me a death glare. "Are you saying you think Owen Holloway, Port Quincy's most eligible bachelor, is a suspect in the murder of Ginger Crevecoeur?"

"I'm not saying anything," I stammered. I felt my face heating under the glare of Rachel's penetrating and miffed gaze. "But I think you should be careful."

"And why is that?" Truman crunched his candy and went digging for another in the fancy glass dish.

"Because she has a date with him tomorrow night."

"You just don't want me to get back in the saddle again!" Rachel flung a candy back into the dish in apparent disgust and crossed her arms.

"I want you to be happy, but with someone nice who isn't involved in a murder investigation!"

Rachel shook her head, her tresses flying. "Owen isn't involved, Mallory. He just happened to be best friends with Ginger." She frowned. "I think."

Truman unwrapped a licorice candy. "I'll look into Owen, and I want you two to be careful. No deputizing yourselves as amateur detectives, like you usually do, either."

We'd had our fair share of weird events and crimes taking place at Thistle Park, and I'd prided myself in helping Truman out a time or two.

"We promise," Rachel and I said in unison as we walked Truman to the door.

Rachel rolled her eyes at me after Truman was safely down the walk. "I don't appreciate you trying to find some reason for me not to be happy again." She shrugged. "Not that it even matters—we won't be in Port Quincy for long."

"You mean *you* won't be in Port Quincy for long." I couldn't resist. I was still smarting from finding my sister's pro and con list about doing the destination wedding show with or without me.

"What do you mean?" Rachel took a step back, but I saw worry hiding in her green eyes.

"Rach, I found your list. I know you're considering doing the show without me."

My sister suddenly became very interested in examining a cuticle. When she looked up, her green eyes were wide and a little chagrined.

"So it's true, you'd really leave here? After you wanted to launch this wedding-planning business with me?"

We both jumped as the front door swung open, an exuberant Summer and Adrienne piling in.

"We're back!"

"Saved by the bell," I told my sister.

Summer went off to play with Pixie again. She wanted to be a veterinarian when she grew up, and she loved all animals. At home she had a cat, Jeeves, who was Whiskey's kitten and brother to Soda. But I knew she was lobbying Garrett for a dog as well. Adrienne and I headed off to the kitchen, where Xavier was bent over, his head stuck in the refrigerator.

"Who moved my smoothie ingredients?" He rifled through the drawers, getting more and more agitated. His usual patchouli and Zen affect had dissipated in a cloud of annoyance. Adrienne moved to help him. But Roxanne was quicker on the draw and reached him first.

"I moved them to the crisper," she soothed, gently placing her hands on Xavier's back to get him to move from the refrigerator. I thought Adrienne's eyes were going to bug out of her head. "Here, allow me."

Roxanne was wearing another teenybopper getup, this time some painted-on jean leggings and a midriff-baring pink sweatshirt. She must work out like crazy, as her body was taut and gravity defying for her fifty-some odd years. She sashayed through the kitchen and amassed a pile of leafy greens on the counter, rifling through my cabinets until she found a cutting board. "I'll do it," she simpered and threw a glance at Adrienne. "I remember how you like them, Xavier."

"That's okay," Adrienne said quickly. She moved to take over the smoothie-making duties. "Xavier isn't feeling well, and I know just how to make his drinks the right way."

"I can handle it." Roxanne dismissed Adrienne with a flick of her wrist and a jangle of her bangle bracelets. She set to making a green concoction. Xavier looked so ill he probably didn't care who made the drink for him. Adrienne stalked from the kitchen in disgust, and for once my heart went out to her. I followed her to the dining room, where she paced around the table.

"The nerve of that woman!" She picked up a glass animal from the credenza and palmed it. "She thinks she can hover over Xavier because they once dated, oh, a bajillion years ago."

I gently removed the pink elephant from her hands lest she break it and motioned for her to sit down.

"I guess they broke up when all that stuff went down with the death of Caitlin Quinn."

Adrienne blinked, probably wondering where I'd gotten that information. "They wouldn't have lasted anyway. They have nothing in common." She sniffed and stared at her naked left hand. "If I'm so good at planning weddings, why am I not engaged?" Twin tracks of tears traced down her beautiful face and I found myself consoling Adrienne. I wished I could tell her about the ring Xavier was planning on giving her, but I didn't want to ruin the surprise.

"I'm sure it'll happen very, very soon," I counseled, secretly elated. If Adrienne was expecting an engagement from Xavier imminently, then the box I had seen on the table at Pellegrino's with Garrett truly had been nothing. I even began to doubt that I'd seen anything at all. Perhaps it had just been a trick of the light.

Adrienne must have felt better, because she turned back into planner mode. "How was your flower meeting? Is everything full steam ahead for Dakota?" Her tears dried at an alarmingly fast rate, and she was all perfectionist business again.

"Er, about that. The flowers are a no-go, but—"

"Oh, Mallory." Adrienne stood, a condescending smirk marring her face. "You needed to have a backup! The first rule of wedding planning is to have ready and willing vendors at your disposal." She sighed and placed her hands on her hips. "I'm personally worried about you and whether you can handle this wedding. You look so tired. This all should have been done ages ago. It really shouldn't be this hard."

I regretted falling into this trap consoling Adrienne.

"I'm tired because—" I stopped, about to spill the beans on Dakota's secret wedding and Keith and Becca's elopement. "Because you've been changing things at the last minute!"

I regretted snapping. My nerves were brittle and jangly, what with being bathed in a steady flow of coffee.

"May I ask a question?" Adrienne's icy blue eyes narrowed in pretend concern.

"I'm not sure I could stop you if I tried," I blurted out.

"How long have you been dating Garrett?"

I stood up, ready to end this conversation. "I'm not sure why that's any of your business."

"Just since last summer, right?" Adrienne answered the question for herself. "Then it's not that serious," she mused, studying her flawless manicure. She stopped, suddenly more serious. "Summer seems quite attached to you. I wanted to suggest you not get too close."

I stared her down, imaginary laser beams shooting from my eyes. "I beg your pardon?" I asked in my quietest voice possible.

Adrienne stood, easily besting me in the height department by half a foot. "Summer only has one mother, and that's me."

I swallowed and stared up at her, gathering my thoughts for a response.

Adrienne moved in for the kill. "Garrett and I were engaged, you know."

For some reason, this hit me in the stomach like a swift kick. I'd known about Adrienne's existence, but not that Garrett had asked her to marry him. "So make no mistake. I know him quite well." Adrienne filled the silence and offered me a small smile. "Take this advice however you see fit. I'm not really sure if you and Garrett are right for one another." And with that, she flounced off, leaving me to set the glass elephant carefully back into place with shaking hands.

Chapter Ten

The next morning, the weather turned cold again. The sky was a canvas of leaden clouds, the sun nowhere to be seen. The air smelled faintly metallic, the way it did before it snowed. The early spring the groundhog had predicted and that we'd all been enjoying for several days seemed like a fluke that was about to be viciously snatched away.

My emotions mirrored the freakishly erratic weather. My will to stay calm was plummeting like the mercury in the antique brass thermometer on the kitchen window. I'd stomped off after Adrienne's little advice session, vowing not to let her verbal smack down get to me. I hadn't succeeded.

Adrienne's dress-down plagued my thoughts as I burned the midnight oil in the library making travel arrangements and booking a ceremony for Keith and Becca in St. Kitts. I'd talked to five incredulous travel agents before I was able to cobble together a posh honeymoon suite, dinner for two, and a beachside ceremony complete with minister, flowers and a tiny reception. I'd finally lucked out and found an all-inclusive luxury resort that had an opening due to another couple's cancellation.

I'd trudged up to my third-floor apartment by 4 AM. I tossed and turned for what was left of the night as the winds from the west whipped against Thistle Park, bringing a cold front and the promise of snow.

And I wasn't the only one affected by the weather.

I arrived in the kitchen to make breakfast for my guests to find Owen straddling a kitchen chair, his laptop in front of him, and a mug of coffee beside it. Dakota sat beside him, their heads bent together in conference, planning Ginger's memorial service, which was to take place the morning of Dakota's wedding day. Whiskey, my beggar calico, meowed and pawed at my jeans when she realized I'd be making breakfast. I bent down to scratch her pretty mottled orange and black ears and promised her a piece of bacon later.

"It's too cold to release butterflies," Dakota mused, nearly brushing Owen's ear with her hair. "But we could put them on the program."

"Consider it done." Owen typed up a few sentences and stroked his auburn beard. Today he wore red suspenders over his Campbell plaid shirt and a cozy knit cap. I realized with a start that it was a piece Dakota had been knitting just last night, a mixed yarn beanie of red and navy and green. "I can't believe Ginger's really gone."

I heard the distinctive clop of cowboy boots on the back stairs.

Uh-oh.

"Oh, what a beautiful morning, oh what a beautiful day," crooned Beau, nearly skipping off the last step. "What do we have here? Oh."

He stopped short as he observed his fiancée sitting next to Owen.

"We're planning Ginger's memorial," Dakota explained, motioning to the chair next to her. "Have a seat, darling. Help us come up with ideas." Dakota's face was pleading and nervous. Beau stared at Owen with a dueling look in his bright blue eyes and made no moves.

"Has anyone seen my—oh." Rachel padded into the kitchen in her silky robe and stopped short when she saw Beau. She tied the knot around her waist tighter in a wary and defensive stance. "Why hello, there." She lit up when she saw Owen. "Are you ready for our date tonight?"

"I'll pick you up at seven. I'm looking forward to it." Owen offered my sister a warm smile. He stood with a wistful look at Dakota, a lock of hair falling over his thick-framed glasses.

"I should actually be going now. Nice to see you, Beau." He shouldered on his corduroy coat and slipped out the back door before Dakota could even protest.

Beau snorted and moved to get a cup of coffee.

Dakota looked stricken, at Owen's leaving, his reminder of his date with Rachel, and Beau's angst.

"I didn't really believe you two used to knock boots until now." Beau turned around, an annoyed look marring his good looks. His countrified voice rang false in his anger, and it modulated back to New Jersey.

Dakota said nothing, her silence speaking volumes.

"You lied to me." Beau's bright blue eyes darkened and he set down the mug of coffee.

That's rich, since you're a cheating lothario.

I could see Rachel agreed with my sentiment. She rolled her eyes and moved to get her own cup of coffee.

"Rach, let's go."

"But—"

I nearly pulled my sister from the kitchen and together we huddled in the breakfast room.

"Looks like the old karma boomerang has made its return trip to smack Beau upside the head," she gleefully sang, holding up her coffee cup in salute.

"Shh," I counseled, leaning closer to the swinging door. But I couldn't help privately agreeing.

"I don't even want to do this show anymore, Dakota," Beau's voice rang out. "This was just supposed to help our careers."

"Maybe this marriage is just to help your career," was her icy rejoinder.

I had to press my ear to the door to get the next bit. "And just so you know, I was never officially an item with Owen."

I raised my brows at my sister, who let out a sigh of relief.

"That's just because your mom wouldn't let you," Beau spat back at her.

That's interesting.

We heard the kitchen door slam again, and

Beau was off on a walk in the back garden, the snow spiraling around him like a passel of angry white honeybees. He stomped off toddler style, little puffs of ice crystals swirling in the air with each crash down of his cowboy boots. Dakota chased after him in the swirling snow, neither one wearing coats or hats in their haste.

"He's right, you know."

"Argh!"

Rachel and I jumped a mile when we realized someone had caught us listening in on Beau and Dakota. We whirled around to face Roxanne sheepishly.

She sighed and sat down at the breakfast room table. She patted her lap and Pixie made an impressive leap up. Roxanne and Pixie were wearing matching outfits today, both in little cream crochet sweaters. Roxanne wore a red headband in her platinum-dyed hair, and Pixie sported a similar crimson bow. "I kept Dakota and Owen apart," Roxanne admitted. "And I'd do it again. That boy was going to ruin her career. She would have given it all up to be with him."

My disgust for Roxanne curdled in my stomach.

"What happened to Caitlin Quinn on set was awful. But it freed my daughter to come back to Port Quincy." Roxanne shuddered, causing the Shih Tzu to gaze up at her in alarm. "I don't want her falling under Owen's spell again. I can't have that happen." And with that, Roxanne set off after her daughter and future son-in-law into the blizzard. At least she'd donned her leather coat before she'd left the B and B. She slid and righted herself on the slick brick herringbone walkway, determined to follow her daughter.

"What an awful woman." I turned from the window. "She kept her daughter from the one she loves just so Dakota could be a star and Roxanne could ride her coattails."

Pixie whined, pawing at the window seat as her mistress set off in the snow. I picked the Shih Tzu up and held her under my chin, earning a dark glare from Soda the kitten.

Rachel was strangely silent.

"What if Dakota did something to Caitlin?" Her voice was high and thin.

"Oh, come on, Rach, Caitlin's death was an accident. Something about a gas leak."

"Yes, but what if Dakota made it happen? You heard Adrienne." Rachel was insistent. "It sounds like Dakota would have done anything to get off that show—she was miserable."

"Are you suggesting an eighteen-year-old Dakota climbed into the bowels of the set with a wrench and created a gas leak?" I chuckled. "That's preposterous."

"You're just taking the bride's side because she's famous."

"No, I just don't think Dakota is capable of murder."

And you might just want to accuse Dakota because Owen is still interested in her, despite your date, and despite the fact Dakota is engaged.

I let the matter drop. My sister and I went about our day, straightening up the guest rooms and attending to business matters. As the sun set, Rachel sighed and glanced at her watch. "I've got to find a suitable outfit. I want to look perfect for my date with Owen."

I raised my eyebrows in surprise. "You're not going out with him in this weather, are you?" The snow had continued, off and on throughout the day.

She shrugged. "Why not? He said his Subaru is all-wheel drive. We'll be fine."

I followed my sister to help her get ready for her date, Pixie trotting close behind. The little Shih Tzu made herself at home in the apartment portion of Thistle Park, and promptly commandeered a little cat bed Whiskey usually dozed in in our living room.

Rachel flipped through her large closet with increasingly frantic movements, taking out shirts and sweaters and dresses and rejecting each article of clothing. Her normal femme fatale wardrobe didn't seem to cut it for her date with the young philanthropist Owen. He didn't seem the type that would go for her usual come-hither getups.

"I need something a little more . . . understated," Rachel mused, fingering a celadon sequined miniskirt and ultimately rejecting it. "Something safe so as not to come on too strong." She frowned and twisted a lock of honey-kissed brown hair around her sparkly nails. "Frankly, I need something a little bit safe and *boring*." She perked up. "Can I raid your closet?"

I rolled my eyes at the backhanded compliment only my sister could give and marched down the hall to my bedroom.

"Have at it." I flung open my closet doors and waited in amusement while Rachel went digging.

Ten minutes later, she'd assembled her outfit. She wore dark blue skinny jeans, boots trimmed in faux white fur, and my white sweater that reached my waist, but on my sister, exposed a healthy swath of inexplicably tanned midriff. She completed the outfit by snatching my snowflake earrings from my dresser drawer with promises to return them.

"You look perfect." My sister did look wonderful. I think I was more excited for her return to the dating world than she was.

Except I don't quite trust Owen.

Rachel skillfully applied quite a bit of makeup that somehow made her look like she wasn't wearing any at all. Her most arresting feature was the hungry praying mantis look in her pretty green eyes. It had been over three months since my sister had sworn off men, and she looked eager to start dating again.

Watch out, Owen. She's a man eater.

Maybe it was Owen I had to worry about, rather than my sister

"How do I look?" Rachel executed a neat twirl, her wavy caramel hair fanning out around her.

"Wonderful, per usual." I frowned as I took in her minuscule purse. "You still have that mace you're saving up for Beau, right?"

Rachel rolled her eyes and applied another coat of mascara to her sable lashes. "I have something even better." She whirled around and opened the small handbag, extracting a long, coiled strip of leather.

"And just what is that?" I moved to unroll what looked like a rope, when Rachel flicked her wrist, and a long whip unfurled. She snapped it against the claw-foot tub, snaring a bottle of shampoo in the process, like an Amazonian, female Indiana Jones.

My mouth opened in a little o and Rachel left me in the bathroom, laughing and running down the steps to answer the newly rung front door.

Okay, I definitely don't have to worry about my sister. She can hold her own, and then some.

"You look amazing." Owen picked Rachel up promptly at seven, carrying a small spray of pink roses. He'd dressed up for the occasion, wearing skinny wool gray pants, a tightly checked navy gingham shirt, and a little polka-dot bow tie. He'd swapped out his cloth suspenders for leather ones, and the hat Dakota must have knitted for him was gone, his glossy auburn locks now under a jaunty felt newsy hat. He took in my sister with a warm and appreciative glance, and I chastised myself for worrying about his motives.

"Mallory, please put these in some water." Rachel beamed and nearly skipped out the door, hand in hand with Owen, her boots crunching in the newest layer of freshly fallen snow.

"Call me if you have any trouble!" My voice rang out into the blizzard before I could stop myself, and Rachel turned around and stuck out her tongue at me.

Oh, real mature.

Then she turned back around and offered me a wink.

But as I watched my sister advance down the walk under the increasingly heavier snowfall, my trepidation returned. Owen opened the door of his dark green Subaru and tucked my sister inside, a gallant philanthropist hipster if there ever was one. But what if he was Ginger's killer? I'd be counting down the hours until my sister returned from her date.

I turned in the direction of the muted sniffles I heard emanating from the parlor, where Dakota was watching Owen help Rachel into his car. I was about to offer her a cup of tea when a navy BMW struggled to advance down the drive.

I couldn't get over the irony of planning my once-cheating fiancé Keith's nuptials to the woman he'd stepped out on me with. Keith helped Becca up the increasingly icy walk and onto the porch. Becca slipped through the front door with a panicked look cast over her left shoulder.

"I think she's on to us," she breathed, her left eyelid displaying an impressive tic.

"Who?" Keith shook off a flock of snow onto the marble floor and stepped back to take a look at the renovated B and B. His mouth fell open in apparent surprise when he saw the delicate yet massive glass chandelier fashioned from peach, blush, and yellow bird figurines. The last time he'd been in the house, he'd let himself in with his grandmother's key and tried to find and pilfer some valuable paintings. He hadn't yet seen the masterful renovation pulled off by my contractor, Jesse Flowers, and the gorgeous decorating job my mother had achieved just this October.

"Your mother, of course!" Becca whirled around to stare out the keyhole. She performed a jittery jump when Keith moved to take off her long, snow-dotted overcoat.

"I love what you've done with the place," Keith muttered, insincerity lacing each word. "I'm not so sure Grandma Sylvia would approve, though." Sylvia had passed away a few weeks before I was to marry Keith last July, and had left me Thistle Park in a surprise move, disinheriting Keith and Helene.

"Sylvia would adore the fact that her house is being used to host people and offer them a wonderful time while they're in Port Quincy." I spoke with firm conviction. I sometimes thought I'd been fulfilling Sylvia's secret plans for me to a T. "Besides"—I couldn't resist getting in a jab—"she left me the house to do what I see fit with it." I offered an annoyed Keith a sweet smile and motioned for him and Becca to follow me to the library. He wiped now dripping snow from his receding hairline and followed me with a huff. I still wasn't ready to host couples in my office, or the scene of the crime, as I liked to think of it now.

"Here we are." I spread their itinerary papers on the low-slung coffee table and beamed. Keith and Becca certainly were not my favorite people, but I was proud of the work I'd done whipping them up a tropical elopement in the span of a mere twenty-four hours.

"You'll need to leave right away to get to the Pittsburgh airport on time. Check-in is in two hours, and the roads must be pretty bad. Your flight leaves at nine with a connection in La Guardia. I booked you the nicest honeymoon suite at the Paradise Gardens resort. Becca, you'll have a white strapless silk gown, size two, waiting in the room. Keith, your tux will be there as well. Tomorrow you'll marry at five p.m., just before sunset, on the beach. I've arranged for dinner in the private dining room, and dancing with the other guests at the resort if you so choose."

I waited expectantly for their adulation, but Keith just nodded as if this were all a matter of course.

Figures.

I hadn't realized it until our engagement dissolved, but growing up as Port Quincy's most wealthy and favored son had given Keith an air of expectancy that everyone would do his bidding. He blinked his gray eyes impassively and waited for me to wrap up this meeting.

Becca was more grateful.

"I can't believe you pulled this off. Helene will be *furious.*" Her nervousness seemed to melt away, and a giant, cheek-splitting grin lit up her face. I sat on my hands to avoid impetuously high-fiving Becca.

"Are you more interested in marrying me or getting back at my mother?" Keith turned to Becca with a sour look on his face, and she rolled her eyes.

"We'd better get going—" Becca stood.

"Where are they? If I find out you're hiding them—" Helene's shrill voice bounced off the marble floors in the great front hall and alerted the two would-be honeymooners in front of me.

"Oh, dear God." Becca turned as white as the

newly fallen snow and clutched Keith's arm. "We have to get out of here."

"Use the back door. Head through the back hall and the butler's pantry, through the dining room and breakfast room and kitchen. You can skirt the porch and get back to your car." I flinched. "Provided Helene hasn't blocked you in."

I felt like General Patton giving marching orders as I shooed Keith and Becca off on their mission. And not a moment too soon.

"Mallory! Where is my son, and that wretched girl?"

"I don't know what you're talking about," I answered sweetly, my arms crossed.

"Don't you lie to me, missy." She shook her crooked index finger at me, her large sapphire ring flashing. "Their car is in the driveway."

She'll find out soon enough.

"I don't divulge any information about my clients." I felt a warm brush of fur at my legs and glanced down at Whiskey and Pixie. The kitty and pup had shown up for the fireworks. Whiskey let out a low growl and paced in front of me.

A horrible flash of recognition stole over Helene's papery face.

"*Clients?* You don't mean . . ."

"Yup. They're going to the chapel, and they're gonna get married!" I couldn't resist, and Pixie got into the act, barking and turning around in an exuberant circle.

"You won't get away with this!" Helene shook her fist in the air and wheeled around on her kitten heels, mincing back through the front hall with surprising speed. I followed her, Pixie trotting in my wake. Helene slipped down the front walk and threw herself behind the wheel of her Cadillac, driving off in pursuit of Keith and Becca without scraping the snow from her front window.

I laughed and cradled Pixie in my arms.

"Good luck, Keith and Becca."

Just as Helene's gold Cadillac advanced down the driveway, Garrett pulled in. His Accord was a welcome sight.

He leaned in for a kiss as I stood in the doorway and I brushed snowflakes from his broad shoulders. He glanced at his watch when he came in, worry clouding his hazel eyes.

"Adrienne took Summer to the orthodontist," he murmured, shaking his head. "Some mother-daughter bonding time while she's here. They were supposed to be back half an hour ago."

"I'm sure they're fine," I breathed. But I was also worried about Summer being out and about in this snowy weather.

I filled him in on my elopement plans for Keith and Becca and Helene's subsequent meltdown. We had a good laugh as we waited for Summer to return.

Garrett breathed a sigh of relief as the rental SUV Adrienne was using turned into the driveway and slowly advanced up through the several inches of wet and clinging snow.

"They're back. See? Nothing to worry about." I let out a breath I hadn't known I'd been holding in and felt cheered as Summer advanced up the front walk. Adrienne followed, a serene smile on her face. They entered the front hall, brushing snow from their shoulders.

"Look, Dad!" Summer grinned, her smile whiter and pearlier than ever.

Wait a minute. Where are her braces?

Her trademark magenta braces were gone. Her teeth were unencumbered and she looked ecstatic. I felt Garrett tense up next to me and reflexively grabbed his hand.

"Mom said if I want to audition this summer, I'd need to have my braces taken off. I can get special clear retainers when I'm out visiting her. They'll straighten my teeth without the braces!" Summer was nearly jumping for joy, her teeth liberated. Adrienne stood behind her, a look of triumph and defiance heightening her icy cold beauty.

Garrett squeezed my hand, released it, and took a deep breath.

"Summer, sweetheart, why don't you head into the kitchen and fix a snack?"

Summer's face fell as she seemed to pick up on the frisson of tension in her father's voice that I knew he was trying hard to conceal.

"But, Dad, I can get these new retainers, and they'll be the same as my braces! Mom said—"

"Listen to your father, Summer," Adrienne said softly. She seemed ready to have her showdown with Garrett. Summer headed for the kitchen in the back of the house, her slender shoulders slumping.

"It's interesting," Garrett said, his voice deadly calm. "The last time I spoke with Summer's orthodontist, he figured she had at least one more year in braces. How is it that you were able to get them removed, and you're not even the custodial parent?"

"Listen, for just a minute, Garrett." Adrienne placed her hand on Garrett's chest and he gently removed it. "Summer is a natural. She could go so far as an actress." Her face was pleading and intense. "But it's almost too late. She'll need to get an agent when she comes to visit me. I thought we could get a head start on headshots while I'm in Port Quincy."

Garrett took a step back from Adrienne, his face a mask of anger. "She's going to be a veterinarian, not an actress. That's your dream, Adrienne. It always has been, and it ruined your chance to parent. That was your choice. Don't make Summer's for her."

The door flung open and Dakota and Beau returned, the tips of their noses and their cheeks a deep rosy red from a recent evening walk in the snow. They'd spent much of the day sulking in opposite corners of the house, but now they looked delighted to be together. They laughed and shook snow from their damp coat sleeves and stamped their boots on the front porch before coming in.

So they're back on.

I guessed I'd still have a secret wedding to plan after all.

"Things seem a little tense here," Beau remarked, his smile fading.

"You don't know the half of it," Garrett spat.

"Everybody calm down." Xavier appeared at the bottom of the front hall stairs to defend Adrienne's honor. He was her knight in shining black tracksuit. Roxanne fluttered into the front hall, carrying his smoothie in his wake. Xavier wasn't looking so great from his bout with whatever cold he had. His face rivaled the green concoction Roxanne handed him, a light olive hue flecked with something red.

"Kale, spirulina, broccoli, and goji berries," Roxanne announced.

Yuck.

Xavier clutched the Lucite mug of smoothie, as ubiquitous and ever present as a toddler's sippy cup.

Adrienne looked furious to realize that Roxanne had been ministering to her boyfriend while she took Summer to the orthodontist.

"I'd like it if you didn't speak to Adrienne that way." Xavier took a cautious step toward Garrett and stepped in between him and his girlfriend.

"Oh, give me a break." Garrett ran a weary hand through his dark hair, mirroring his father's exasperated pose to a T. "I'm just trying to figure out why she had Summer's braces removed."

"I'm sure she had her reasons." Xavier cleared his throat, suddenly serious.

"Adrienne." He sank to one knee, his stance wobbly and uncertain. "I've waited too long to do this. You're the one who has stood by me through thick and thin, richer and poorer. You're a patient woman. I'd give anything for you to be my wife." He reached into his tracksuit pocket and pulled out a ring, an enormous round diamond flanked by sapphires.

"Oh!" Adrienne shrieked and held out her hand, her long slender fingers seeming to itch for the ring. Her argument with Garrett was forgotten.

Xavier moved to slide the bauble over her finger, his hand trembling. But before he could complete the act, he moaned, clasping his stomach. His smoothie toppled from his hand and careened onto the marble floor. The Lucite mug shattered and splintered. Goopy green goo covered Adrienne and Xavier. The ring bounced down the hallway, forgotten. The smoothie mixture spread out around Xavier in a circle, sending up a heady fume of herbs and greens.

Chapter Eleven

Several frightening and frantic minutes ticked by as the ambulance struggled to climb Sycamore Street. I could see the flashing red lights from the front porch, zigging and zagging up the hill, the tires struggling for purchase in the half foot of snow. The wailing siren compounded the maddening slowness.

"Hurry, he's not breathing!" Adrienne shouted with a hoarse voice over her would-be fiancé as Garrett performed CPR. "Stay with us, Xavier." A stream of tears raced down her face, and she held the director's hand as Garrett pressed on his chest. "Don't you dare leave me now!"

Roxanne sat on the bottom stair, her face sullen and stricken. Her emotions were visible for once, even through her mask of Botox. Pixie sat in her lap, whining and licking Roxanne's face in commiseration, her little red doggie bow shaking in her black and white ponytail.

The paramedics worked to stabilize the director and hoisted him onto a stretcher. Adrienne followed close behind. Her slender frame was wracked with sobs. She climbed into the ambulance and her slim blue form disappeared. The ambulance skated into the void, the snow whirling white and confetti-like against the inky black sky, the world a nightscape snow globe.

Summer had been in the kitchen and thankfully hadn't seen Xavier's collapse. Garrett whisked her away and explained what had happened as they carefully circumnavigated the mess in the hallway.

I started to clean up the smoothie, when it hit me.

It might be evidence.

Xavier had been consuming smoothies every day, and had grown sicker and sicker, culminating in his collapse. I eyed the green mixture puddled on the marble and carefully entombed the kitchen towel I used to wipe it up in a plastic bag. A pinging sound alerted me to the presence of my cats.

Whiskey batted Adrienne's large diamond and sapphire ring with her mottled orange and black paw, as deft and skillful as any hockey center. Her calico tail swished in delight, and she gamboled after the ring on clattering claws. The metal and stone skittered down the hallway, whacking into the wall with a loud *plink*. Soda, not to be outdone, picked up where her mama cat left off and delicately retrieved the ring in her mouth. She headed for the stairs with her prize. Whiskey gave chase down the hall and batted at Soda's tail.

"Oh no, you don't, little kitty." I scooped up the little orange ball of fluff as Soda started her ascent and delicately extracted the ring from her jaws. "I think Adrienne will want this back." I pocketed the ring and a wave of sadness crescendoed and crashed. Adrienne Larson was no longer my professional idol, but it wasn't lost on me how unfair this evening had been. Xavier had fallen ill just as he'd delivered on his long-promised proposal.

"Shoo, kitties. I'm not so sure it's safe to touch that."

Now that I'd confiscated their engagement ring toy, Whiskey and Soda turned their attention to the green goo from the shattered smoothie glass. Their curious kitty-cat noses twitched and their whiskers quivered. They advanced toward the kitchen towel and I scooped them up, the vision of Xavier crumpled on the floor fresh in my head. "I'm afraid that's evidence, little ones." I headed to my third-floor apartment, taking solace in the purring cats I held in my arms.

I texted Rachel three times, then stopped myself from sending a fourth message.

She's probably just having a great time with Owen. You're not her mother.

But when the snow didn't abate, neither did my blood pressure. I couldn't keep myself from ringing Truman about my sister.

"I have more important things to do than fetch your sister from her date, Mallory," he chastised before hanging up.

I fell into a fitful sleep, stringing together fretful and unfulfilling bouts of shut-eye as I tossed and turned. Whiskey and Soda curled together in two little balls of fluff at my feet, the better to conserve heat. The wind howled and the sky continued to dump snow like salt from a fast-flow shaker. All I

could think of was my sister out on treacherous,
slippery roads with Owen.

Owen, who could be Ginger's secret lover. And murderer.

I flung off the heavy comforter and flannel sheets
as soon as the sun rose and grabbed my phone.

Be home soon.

Phew. Rachel had answered my neurotic texts
and appeared to be alive and well. I padded down
the back stairs and began whipping up breakfast,
a feast of fruit salad, cranberry sunflower muffins,
hash browns, turkey sausage, and pancakes. Health
food be damned after our rough night. I thought
everyone could use some real food.

"He's in a coma."

By midday Truman delivered the news to Garrett
and me, as well as my guests Dakota, Beau, and
Roxanne. We were assembled in the breakfast
room around the old octagonal oak table. I'd made
a third pot of strong black coffee. My guests nursed
the brew as they sullenly stared out the bay window.
The blizzard had finally ceased. The grounds were
a dazzling expanse of crystalline white powder as
far as the eye could see. Delicate daggers in the
form of icicles hung from the barren deciduous
trees, and the sun glinted off the sugary snow.
What was a gorgeous scene was wasted on us as we
pondered Xavier's fate and what it meant.

A sagging Adrienne stood next to Truman, who
had driven her back to Thistle Park. Adrienne had
spent the night in the hospital with Xavier, and she
still wore the same blue angora getup from yesterday. Silvery streaks of eye makeup traced a track to

her cheekbones, and she'd fashioned her pale hair into a messy ponytail. It was the first time she'd appeared anything less than utterly unflappable. My heart did a little flutter of commiseration. The fiery light had gone from her blue eyes. She sank into a chair and accepted the strong cup of coffee I proffered without a word.

"I'm just glad Summer was in the kitchen and didn't see it happen," Garrett muttered, taking a swig of bitter black coffee. Summer had appeared with her snack from the kitchen as the ambulance pulled away, none the wiser until Garrett explained on their way home.

"We won't have the toxicology report back for a few days," Truman cautioned, "but the doctors think he was poisoned by some kind of plant or herb based on the contents of his pumped stomach."

Adrienne lost it then. She'd already known, but she crumpled onto the table and rested her head on folded arms. In a second, Garrett was holding her up, supporting her as she sobbed. I stood motionless. The coffeepot dangled from my hand as he comforted his ex-flame. She fit perfectly in the crook of his arm, a little shaking blue bird, occupying the space I normally did. A ribbon of panic wended its way around my heart and gave a sharp tug as he tentatively patted her on the back.

Um, hello! She almost lost her fiancé. Take a chill pill.

I shook off the green monster perched on my shoulder and counseled myself to be kind. I placed the hot coffeepot on the credenza lest I spill its contents and sat down. Adrienne looked at Garrett with a gaze of gratefulness. She raked her forget-me-not blue eyes over him and her tears dissipated to mere sniffles. Garrett carefully helped her into her chair and returned to his seat next to me. He grabbed my hand from under the table and gave it a comforting squeeze.

See? Nothing to worry about.

"You're lucky your ex-husband didn't get ill when he performed CPR," Faith Hendricks, Truman's partner, soothed Adrienne. She motioned to Garrett and flipped open her notebook, ready to start questioning us.

Ex-husband?!

"Oh, they were never married," I piped up. The correction flew out before I could clap an embarrassed hand over my mouth.

Nice one.

I grimaced and gave Garrett a sheepish shrug when he raised one dark brow. I dropped his hand like a hot potato and laced my fingers together in front of me on the scarred table.

"I'd like everyone to stay here at the B and B," Truman counseled, mercifully taking attention away from my embarrassing gaffe.

"You mean for the day." Roxanne stared sullenly out the window, a veritable apparition of herself. Her blingy jewelry and teenybopper wear were gone, replaced by an oversized black sweater and plain black pants. She appeared to be in mourning for her former love Xavier, her anguish rivaled only by Adrienne's.

"No, I mean for the indefinite future. We're treating Xavier's collapse as attempted murder."

"But what about our honeymoon in the Maldives? You'll be done with your investigation by then, right?" Beau stuck out a petulant bee-stung lower lip, his countrified accent forgotten, the New Jersey out in full force.

Truman narrowed his hazel eyes, reducing them to seemingly annoyed slits. "Son, we have a murderer on the loose, and no one's going anywhere until we figure it out."

"And just when will y'all get around to that?" Beau had remembered to temper his emotions this time, and his folksy twang was back. "When" came out as "way-en." His accent switcheroos were highly disconcerting. I felt like Dakota was dating a male country star version of Sybil. "Ginger up and died almost a week ago, and you've made no headway, I reckon."

Truman drew himself up to his full six foot four inches of height and opened his mouth to rejoinder. His big belly strained the belt of his uniform. Faith cut in before he could start.

"Believe me, we're doing everything possible to find and prosecute Ginger Crevecoeur's killer." Beau's face darkened with sadness at the reminder of Ginger, duly chastened. "Now," Faith continued, "would you all rather be questioned here or down at the station?" She smiled her sweetest smile, her milkmaid countenance dimmed slightly by the long night she'd undoubtedly just pulled.

The answer was resoundingly to stay at the B and B. My guests started collecting more coffee for their questioning in their rooms when my sister and Owen trudged through the snow on their way to the back kitchen door. They appeared seconds later in the breakfast room, their cheeks rosy and their faces exhilarated. Owen caught sight of Dakota's open mouth and his smile took on a slightly sheepish cast.

"It's gorgeous out there," Rachel crowed. She gave everyone a dazzling grin as she unwrapped a turquoise scarf threaded with silver from around her neck. She wore her clothes from last night, the skinny jeans nearly painted on. I had to hand it to my sister; there was no shame in her game.

"What happened?" Owen picked up on the sullen faces all around the table and lasered in on Dakota. Beau tightened his jaw and wrapped his arm around Dakota's shoulders in a possessive stance.

"Xavier collapsed. The hospital thinks someone put something in his smoothie." I kept my recounting of what Rachel had missed short and simple.

Rachel clapped a hand to her mouth as the table erupted with hurtled accusations.

"You never got over him," Adrienne spat, pointing a French tip in Roxanne's direction. "You've been mooning over *my* fiancé all week, and now you're here wearing all black, like you're so upset, when I know you were the one who poisoned him!" Gone was her weepy willowiness, replaced by the fiery Adrienne I knew from TV spats with brides and wedding planners. Adrienne appeared crazed and feverish in her rumpled outfit, her makeup from last night spread beneath her eyes in shiny silver half moons.

"How *dare* you!" Roxanne stood, her chair falling behind her with a crash. "I know Xavier better than you, you interloper! We were together much longer than you've been, and as I recall, he didn't finish proposing last night. So you're not technically his fiancée." Roxanne delivered her speech with Oscar-worthy aplomb, giving her daughter a run for her money.

"Mother—" Dakota stood and placed a tentative hand on Roxanne's arm, but her mother shook her off.

"You and Xavier used to date?" Truman stopped writing in his little notebook and directed his question to Roxanne.

She colored and collected her chair, righting it and sitting down with a dejected huff. "For ten years," Roxanne spat. "I know him better than *anyone*, and I would never, ever harm him." She wore her love and admiration for the fallen director on her black mourning wear sleeve, and it was painful to behold. "Perhaps you should be focusing your attention on those who would wish Xavier harm."

"And who might that be?" Faith tightened her swinging ponytail and picked up her pen, poised and ready to go.

"Iris and Ellie. Duh!" Roxanne's voice rose an octave as she slammed the saltshaker for emphasis. Little grains few out and dusted the table. I longed to toss some over my left shoulder, thinking we didn't need any more bad luck.

"Mother, how could you?" Dakota rocketed up, knocking Beau's arm from her shoulders. "That's the most ridiculous thing I've ever heard." But Dakota didn't act every second of her life. There was a kernel of concern in her wide violet eyes as she digested what her mother had just declared.

"Iris is the worst stage mother imaginable," Roxanne continued. She'd definitely gotten Truman and Faith's attention.

Um, pot, meet kettle.

"Iris would stop at nothing to make Ellie a star just like Dakota," Roxanne went on, her voice now weary and ponderous. She traced a pattern in the spilled salt with one red fingernail. "Ellie is a nice enough girl, but she doesn't stand up to her mother and always did what she wanted. And Ellie isn't that bad of an actress, either. Dakota, being a good friend, too good in my opinion, arranged for Ellie to have an audition to replace Caitlin Quinn when Caitlin was on strike."

"Who in the devil is Caitlin Quinn?" Truman put down his pen.

"She was only the biggest star of *Silverlake High*," Faith answered him, her incredulity plain. "Go on."

Truman frowned and allowed Roxanne to continue. "Ellie's screen test was wonderful, even I'll admit it. But the producer didn't think she'd be a good fit. Neither did Xavier. He was the director, but he had a lot of sway with casting. Ellie was crushed she didn't get the part, and Iris was furious. It was embarrassing how she ranted and raved that week."

"When was this?" Truman continued to scratch in his notepad, taking time to observe Roxanne as she shared her hunch.

"Thirteen years ago, to the month."

"That's a long time to hold a grudge," Faith mused.

"I'm telling you, I know they're behind it." Roxanne's eyes were wild and rimmed with red from lack of sleep.

"I think I'll be going now. You guys be careful." Owen had stood in silence, listening to Roxanne's accusations while my sister got filled in. He sent a fleeting glance Dakota's way, and then dropped a perfunctory kiss on my sister's forehead. She beamed and walked Owen out through the kitchen, nearly skipping.

A cup shattered on the wooden breakfast room table. Dakota gasped as hot coffee drenched her lap.

"S-sorry," she muttered.

Four hours later, Truman and Faith were willing to call it a day. After Roxanne's impromptu sharing of her theories, they'd broken up the group for separate questioning in each guest's room. It was nearly dinnertime. The sun had crawled low in the sky, eager to dip below the white blanket of the horizon for its evening rest. The sunset scape sent rose-gold rays over the snowy landscape, the clouds tinged purple and pink. I leaned against Garrett on a chaise lounge in the library, listening to the gentle cadence of his heartbeat. It felt good to rest in companionable silence after the turmoil of the day. I savored my time with Garrett before he would leave to have dinner with Summer.

Truman and Faith stopped to get my and Garrett's takes before they headed out.

"Can we meet somewhere more private?" Truman scoped out the library with its two curved, open doorways. His eyes strayed down the hall.

Uh-oh.

"You want to use the office." My heart began to beat like a caged hummingbird at the mere thought of entering the room where Ginger had died. I'd ignored the small vestibule Rachel and I shared for the past week and sincerely wondered if I'd ever be able to work there again. It was a light and airy space, painted a soft sage green, with warm maple wood, plump striped sofas where brides and grooms sat for consultations, and a pleasing mix of nineteenth-century watercolors and modern photographs from the grounds of Thistle Park. But now the bright and cozy space felt utterly ruined.

"We don't have to—" Faith began, peeking her blond head out the doorway.

"No, it's okay. I'm willing to try it."

Truman and Faith followed me and Garrett down the hall. I paused before the office, the door handle mercilessly free of crime tape. I pushed the door and took a fortifying breath before plunging into the room.

Garrett gave my hand a squeeze and led me to a green and yellow chintz sofa.

Good call.

I could stomach being in the room, but it would take an even longer while before I'd chance sitting at the wide maple desk. It stood on one side of the office, a big block of honeyed wood, and its twin, Rachel's desk, mirrored it at the other end.

Truman and Faith seated themselves in two cozy mustard wingback chairs and pulled out their notepads.

"This B and B is brimming with shifty characters," Truman announced. He rubbed the bridge of his nose with thumb and forefinger. Ginger's investigation probably weighed heavily on him, and now he had another attempted murder added to the mix.

"What do you mean?" I was excited Truman was making me privy to his investigation. He usually told me, in not so many words, to butt out of his cases.

"Your guests were awfully quick to point fingers at each other," Faith chimed in with a shake of her ponytail. "It makes them look a tad guilty."

Truman held up one finger, then another. "First Ginger, now Xavier. And both crimes used plants as a weapon of delivery, although in different ways." The chief leaned forward in his chair. "Ginger was murdered by a mixture of bleach and ammonia, forming chloramine vapor, but the killer used a blue floral arrangement to deliver the fatal fumes. And our toxicologist thinks the bits of plant matter in Xavier's stomach are some kind of flower, ground in a blender."

"He's addicted to smoothies," I piped up, shuddering at the thought of the noxious concoctions he always had on hand. "And I love me a good smoothie, but these were kind of pungent. It would have been easy for his would-be killer to chop up something poisonous and slip it in his drink." Easy enough, that is, now that we'd transported a bunch of live plants from Ellie and Iris's nursery to Thistle Park's greenhouse. I shared that thought with Truman and Faith.

"We've gathered the contents of your crisper and the spilled drink from yesterday, of course," Faith explained.

"But do you think Ginger's murder and Xavier's attempted murder are linked?" It was the sixty-four-thousand-dollar question.

"There were so many people in this house the

night of the Winter Ball," Garrett mused, his arm around my shoulder. "But every person who was present when Xavier collapsed was also present at the dance." He had his defense attorney thinking cap on, and his brow was furrowed in thought.

Truman gave his son an appraising look. "Ah, but the doctors think Xavier had been poisoned for a while, possibly starting when he arrived at Thistle Park. It probably wasn't a one-off, but a slow accumulation of toxins."

"He's been ill all week," I said. "We thought it was the flu. It's going around Port Quincy. And Xavier doesn't believe in vaccines." I wracked my brain, trying to pinpoint the day Xavier became sick. A chilling thought flitted through my brain.

"What if Helene did Ginger in, then tried to poison me for daring to defy her Winter Ball plans?"

I tried to eat some greens each day, and usually used the crisper for my own salads. I'd just been abstaining this week while Xavier filled the fridge with his exotic herbs. But Helene wouldn't know that.

Truman and Faith exchanged a weighted glance. "It's possible," Truman began, skepticism lacing his words, "but how would she have gained access to Thistle Park?"

He had me there. But what Helene wanted, Helene got. Whether she carried out her nefarious plans herself or, more likely, hired some henchmen, I could easily imagine her poisoning me if that were her goal.

"We shouldn't make assumptions," Garrett said, "but let's just say the poison was meant for Xavier because it's obvious the smoothies would be the perfect medium to hide a toxic plant. Why would someone kill Ginger, then Xavier?"

"Maybe to sabotage Dakota and Beau's wedding," I suggested, latching on to the idea. "Or to ruin this particular episode of *I Do*."

"Then why not just go after Dakota and Beau themselves?" Truman asked. "They weren't too happy when I broached that line of questioning," he added drily.

"Adrienne claims Roxanne made the smoothie Xavier consumed right before he collapsed," Faith stated, changing course. "Can you confirm that?"

I cocked my head and then nodded. "She did make it, and she had access to the crisper all week. You heard her today—she used to date Xavier, albeit over a decade ago. She's been mooning over him since she arrived here. She almost had a cow the first day of filming. Dakota didn't tell her he was directing this episode. Maybe she never got over him and if she can't have him, no one can."

Truman and Faith exchanged another ponderous glance, and this time I was asking the questions.

"Okay, you two, spill it."

"Their relationship didn't end well, according to Dakota," Truman mused. "She said that Xavier was the love of her mother's life. We're definitely looking into Roxanne."

"And what about Beau?" Garrett asked. "He's been grumbling to anyone who'll listen that he doesn't want to do this show. What if he took matters into his own hands and tried to end it prematurely?"

"That's a possibility," Truman admitted. "But

why would he have anything to do with Ginger's death?"

"They could be unrelated," Faith suggested. "And several people have said to us today that Dakota doesn't really want to do this reality show episode either. She was just doing it as a favor to Xavier. Maybe she was tired of helping him out."

"So you know the show is going to fold soon," I said.

Truman sat up. "No, that's new information."

I bit my lip and sent Garrett a fleeting glance. I was about to tread into dangerous waters.

"I overheard Adrienne and Xavier arguing." A heat started at the base of my neck, and I felt it climb upward, an outward sign of my embarrassment over snooping. "Xavier mentioned the producer and network are thinking of canning *I Do*. This episode is basically their last shot."

I chanced another glance at my boyfriend before I plunged on. "Adrienne was . . . *furious*. She accused Xavier of not taking care of her." Garrett's hand tightened in mine.

I paused then and did something I'm not proud of. I committed a teeny, tiny lie of omission and left out a detail that may or may not have been pertinent. I held back the fact that Adrienne was upset Rachel and I had been offered our own destination wedding show. I wasn't ready to broach the topic with Garrett.

"I just have to wonder . . ." I trailed off and tried to broach the delicate subject in the least confrontational manner possible. "If Adrienne might not be the culprit."

Garrett dropped my hand and turned so fast his

head seemed to bobble on his neck. "You can't be serious, Mallory."

I prattled on in a rush, eager to unload my theory before it slipped out of my head. And before Garrett slipped out the door.

"She mentioned to me just yesterday how upset she was that Xavier hadn't proposed yet. Maybe she was getting antsy and she thought a life-threatening illness would speed things along. She makes most of his smoothies," I continued, "except for the one time Roxanne did."

"This is outrageous." Garrett stood and paced in front of the low glass table we'd been convening around, his long legs churning up the carpet. "We just went over all of the other people who could have poisoned Xavier, and you fixated on Adrienne."

I gulped and sent Truman and Faith a *help me* look.

"She's right, Garrett," Truman broke in, his voice steady and even. "We have to look at the significant other. I'm sorry."

"But what about Iris and Ellie?" Garrett spat. "You heard Roxanne. Iris's never gotten over Xavier not recommending her daughter for that role. They run a nursery, for goodness's sake—they're the prime suspects for poisoning via plants."

"But Iris and Ellie all but announced to everyone who's been working in the greenhouse this week that bleeding hearts are poisonous in large doses. Maybe someone took them up on that little tidbit. It didn't have to be them." My voice sounded petulant. I was hurt Garrett had rushed in to defend Adrienne so quickly.

Maybe there is something still there, a wheedling little voice whispered in my head. I pushed the thought away.

Truman gritted his teeth and stood. "And why am I just learning this now, that Ellie and Iris told people bleeding hearts were poisonous?"

I flushed for the second time this meeting. "I just recalled."

"This changes things. We'd been thinking anyone other than Iris or Ellie would have needed to search for plants and poison online. But they were just handed that information."

"There is one other way they could have known. . . ." I stood and exited the door, Truman and Faith and Garrett hot on my heels. I skidded to a stop in the library and made a beeline for the largest coffee table.

"It's gone!" The large tome on herbs and perennials was missing from the table. I skimmed the shelves for a few minutes in case one of my guests had helpfully re-shelved the encyclopedia, but it appeared to be missing.

"My big book about plants, which had an entry on bleeding hearts and their use as poison, is missing. I even turned down the page for that entry. Everyone but Adrienne and Roxanne knows we're planning a secret wedding using bleeding hearts in the greenhouse. So even if someone hasn't helped us plant, they'd know they're poisonous from the book."

Garrett seized on what I'd just said with a triumphant smile. "You just exonerated Adrienne, Mallory. She doesn't know there's a secret wedding plan for Dakota, ergo she has no knowledge there are bleeding hearts in the greenhouse."

I felt myself deflate, and then chastised myself.

Why do you want Adrienne to be the culprit so badly?

I held my hands out, palms up, another thought percolating. "Bleeding hearts can give you a slight rash. I have one, but I was planting in the greenhouse. Not everyone else was. Maybe you should check out each guest."

"Will do. Thanks for the information." Truman and Faith exchanged another significant glance. I wondered if they'd already noticed rashes while questioning each of my guests this afternoon.

Garrett glanced at his watch, his earlier annoyance forgotten. "I'm going home to see Summer." He cupped my face in his hands and set a gentle kiss on my brow, for which I was grateful.

Phew.

I was glad I'd spoken my mind about Adrienne. Garrett may not have wanted to hear it, but she was suspect numero uno in my book.

And I wasn't the only one. As soon as Garrett had left, Truman and Faith and I returned to the quiet confines of the office. I was beginning to think I could use the space again after all.

"I have one last request, Mallory."

"I'll do whatever it takes to help you close this case."

"I need you to snoop."

My stomach plummeted somewhere in the vicinity of my knees.

"Um, anything but that."

As a former card-carrying member of the ACLU, I wasn't keen on wading into the murky and nebulous waters of hotel searches. I'd prefer it if Truman and Faith came back with official warrants, all above board, in keeping with the Fourth Amendment.

"Just hear me out." Truman held up his hand. "You know as well as I do I don't have enough evidence to go through the rooms. *Yet*," he added with a rueful smile. "Just the fridge for now. I know your guests have a reasonable expectation of privacy, but I'm unofficially deputizing you to do a search."

I squirmed in my chair, torn. On one hand, I was delighted Truman trusted me to help him with his investigation. And I yearned to find the person who had murdered Ginger and tried to do the same to Xavier.

But I wasn't sure I could do it. "What did you have in mind?" I asked in a small voice.

"You have a lot of leeway when you're straightening up rooms. You do occasionally open drawers and peek under beds as part of your cleaning, correct?"

"Oh, no way, Jose." I shook my head. "Tell you what. I'll compromise. I'll be on the lookout while I'm cleaning for anything suspicious or interesting *in plain sight*. But that's it. No looking under beds, no rifling through drawers. I'm not above the law."

Truman nodded, pleased.

I've been had, I realized with a start. Truman thought I'd refuse altogether, so he pitched a slightly illegal version of the search he wanted me to perform, knowing I'd settle somewhere in the middle, straddling the line between legality and not.

"You're good." I sighed, shaking my head. "Really

good." I worried for the criminals who had killed Ginger and tried to do Xavier in. In the end, they'd have no chance against Truman Davies.

Truman offered me a triumphant smile, and he and Faith swept out of Thistle Park.

Chapter Twelve

The next day stretched on, cold and clear, but the sun didn't make a dent in the icy cap of snow reaching for the horizon. I wondered if Adrienne would want to ditch the newer yellow, early spring wedding plans and revert to Dakota's original black and white affair. But she had bigger fish to fry. She spent the rest of the day in silent vigil next to Xavier's bedside at the Port Quincy McGavitt-Pierce Memorial Hospital, named after the family that had built Thistle Park, and Helene's late husband.

Truman's plea to walk the tightrope of criminal procedure rules and perform a soft search of the rooms weighed on me. But for now I could ignore his proposed snooping and focus on wedding-planning tasks. Dakota and sisters Leah and Ellie had a dress-fitting appointment to try on their new gowns for the secret pink and red wedding scheme. Bev Mitchell, proprietor of the Silver Bells dress shop, had offered to do the fitting in Thistle Park, rather than requiring Dakota to brave the onslaught of nosy fans following her around town. Dakota had gratefully accepted Bev's offer. Now we huddled in the parlor drinking tea as the bride and her maids tried on their gowns, and Bev bustled around them with pins in her mouth. Iris sat on a chair observing the fitting, accompanying her two daughters. Roxanne was nowhere to be seen. I'd overheard her arguing with her bank, pacing on the front porch. Now she'd retired to her room with Pixie the Shih Tzu to mourn Xavier's continued coma. It was just as well, since we couldn't have her observing the new gowns. She still didn't know about the new pink and red wedding plans.

"It won't be the same without Ginger," Dakota breathed. She looked gorgeous and sullen and exhausted in her satin ball gown. She stood on a chair as Bev pinned her faux fur hemline. Bev's voluminous beehive sparkled, dotted with crystal snowflake pins.

Uh-oh.

Bev was the biggest gossip in town, and whatever Dakota discussed with her friends would be shared with all of Port Quincy posthaste.

"Things are happening again," Leah glumly reported from the couch. She sat with a calculus text on her lap, half listening to the conversation, half studying. Her purple hair was scraped into an artfully sculptural bun, strands pointing out in jagged lines, Edward Scissorhands-style, defying gravity. The tresses clashed magnificently with the fire-engine-red brocade gowns Dakota had selected. Leah pushed her black glasses up her angular nose and rested her hand on her chin, her eyebrows raised.

"What do you mean, again?" Bev shamelessly asked, taking a pin out of her mouth. "There, dear, you're all hemmed. You can step out of your dress now." She smiled at Dakota, who was shooting Leah a warning glare in silent conference.

"Caitlin Quinn died thirteen years ago almost to the day Ginger did," Leah continued, her calculus book forgotten. She seemed to defy Dakota's panicked eyes. "I was the one who found her," she added. Her young face was awfully somber and pensive.

"How terrible," I breathed. "You were what, just a little girl?"

"She was five," Iris cut in crisply from her perch on the fainting couch. "Imagine trying to explain what happened to a child, finding that girl locked in her dressing room." She shuddered and came to sit next to Leah. "Why must you bring up Caitlin's accident, dear?"

Leah stared at her lap, chagrined. "I'm just trying to make sense of things, Mom." A single tear slipped beneath the rim of her glasses and dribbled down to the tip of her nose. "Ginger was my mentor, and now she's gone."

"There, there." Iris drew Leah to her and handed her a tissue from her purse. She'd dropped her tiger mama routine and was comforting and sweet. "We have enough on our plate with that odious little director's illness without dredging up the past."

Okay, the tiger mama is back.

"Iris!" Dakota peeked her head from behind the antique cherry blossom screen where she was changing and shook her head in anger. "Do not speak of Xavier that way. He's a personal friend, and he may never wake again."

"If it weren't for him, I wouldn't be under suspicion for murder!" Iris twisted the tissue in her lap and reduced it to shreds. "Ellie and I spent most of this afternoon at the police station going over how plants from our nursery could have ended up in Xavier's smoothie." She shook her head, the corona of soft gray and brown hair bobbing around her rounded cheekbones. "Someone is trying to frame us." Gone was her warm, earth-mother demeanor. Her voice was high pitched and histrionic. "The man is a fool, not picking my Ellie for *Silverlake High*. But I don't want him *dead*, for goodness's sake."

"Oh, Mother, it's time you got over my not having an acting career," Ellie piped up, her voice clear and low. "It's been thirteen years since I lost that role. It's time to move on." Ellie stood statue still as Bev fluttered behind her, pinning and folding fabric.

"Fair enough," Iris replied. She finally stilled her busy hands and gave the tissue a break. "We all know who tried to kill Xavier anyway. I'm sure Ellie and I will be exonerated in due course." She sniffed and held her head high again. Her serene demeanor was back in full force.

"And who is that?" Bev stopped drawing in Ellie's red gown and eagerly leaned around.

"Why, Roxanne, of course!" Iris stood and ticked off reasons on her plump fingers. "She was with

Xavier when we visited thirteen years ago, and just like Adrienne, she couldn't pin him down. She was pining for marriage and it never came to fruition. And now he's with Adrienne. If Roxanne can't have Xavier, no one will." Iris sat down and avoided Dakota's red-hot gaze.

"Then why not just do away with Adrienne?" Leah piped up. She set aside her calculus textbook for good.

"Because it isn't my mother!" Dakota exploded, finally back in her jeans and sweater. "She's not a killer. Maybe she isn't over Xavier. So what? That doesn't mean she'd ever poison him." She dug her shaking hands in her pockets and paced in front of the roaring fire. "My money's on Adrienne herself. Tell them what you told me, Mallory." She sent me a pleading gaze, and I choked and sputtered on a gulp of tea.

"Me? Tell them what?"

Okay, so I personally agree that Adrienne is the number-one suspect. But I can't let my guests turn on each other. I will not allow my B and B to devolve into a pit of vipers.

"Tell them about the show."

I sighed and shared the news of the destination wedding show.

"I'm so excited for you," Ellie squealed. She jumped up and down in her voluminous red gown, appearing like an inverted, buoyant hot-air balloon. Iris cast hot, jealous eyes my way.

"I'm not sure if we'll even agree to do it, and it's not a sure thing," I cautioned. "But I do know Adrienne wasn't happy about Xavier pulling strings to get us our own show. Especially"—I glanced at

Dakota—"since *I Do* will probably be cancelled, and Adrienne will be out of a job."

Dakota nodded. "I'm only doing this show as a favor to Xavier. If this Hail Mary episode doesn't work, the show's off the air." She twisted her ring from Beau around and around her finger and sighed. "I wish I'd never done this episode. First, my best and oldest friend is murdered, and now my colleague and mentor Xavier is poisoned by his fiancée, Adrienne."

A gasp echoed through the front hall. We all swiveled our heads to see Adrienne staring in horror at Dakota.

"Wait!" Dakota ran after Adrienne, her dress fitting forgotten.

Bev left with the gowns and some juicy tidbits of information. Adrienne refused to leave her room, and Dakota stood outside her door. She dithered for a while before she offered a long and fumbling apology. I put on my sleuthing cap and gathered my cleaning supplies, ready to grudgingly do Truman's bidding.

Weird things were afoot in my B and B, and though I didn't approve of snooping, even I couldn't deny it was time to do some investigation. I smirked as I gathered my cleaning supplies and glanced at my watch. Rachel was nowhere to be seen. More often than not, she'd find a way to shirk the scullery maid aspects of running the B and B. I didn't mind cleaning though, and was okay going solo. I found straightening up the rooms to be therapeutic. I'd usually don my headphones and clean on autopilot, gathering my thoughts for the day. But this afternoon I'd be eagle-eyed and questing, on the lookout for anything unusual—within constitutional limits, of course.

Rachel did have a special kind of radar for fun, since she showed up right before I entered Roxanne's room.

"Truman called me to help you search the rooms," she breathed, her cheeks still rosy from a jaunt outside.

Nice one, Truman.

My sister would have no compunction about sifting through people's belongings and landing on the illegal side of search and seizure law.

"We can't look through drawers, or peek under beds or open closed wardrobe doors," I cautioned. I caught a glimpse of my face in the large gilt mirror at the top of the stairs. I was stern and brooked no wiggle room.

Rachel pouted, her heart-shaped mouth turning down in a frown. "That's so *boring*."

"That's *the law*," I shot back, then stuck out my tongue.

Rachel laughed and shook her head. "Fine. We'll be boring. And legal."

We made hasty plans to search most of the rooms separately, and then join forces for Dakota and Beau's room, as well as Adrienne and Xavier's and finally Roxanne's room.

"What have you been up to?" Dakota's wedding had proved to be a somewhat lonely endeavor ever since Beau tried to kiss my sister and she'd exiled herself. I was used to running my ideas past Rachel and getting her input.

"I just went sledding with Owen," she breathed, her green eyes sparkling.

"So you spent the night with him during the blizzard?" It slipped out before I could stop myself.

Rachel grabbed a dust mop and headed down the hall, ignoring my query. "A lady never kisses and tells," she said with a smirk. She inserted her master key into the lock of the room occupied by the lighting technician for *I Do* and gave the door a hearty push.

"Rachel Marie Shepard, don't you dare hold out on me! We're sisters, remember?" I'd never known Rachel not to share the juicy details of her latest conquest. She'd been on her self-imposed dating moratorium for three months, and her date with Owen had lasted all night, whether due to the weather or something else.

Rachel turned, her face suddenly serious. "Owen is something special." She looked close to tears. She whisked herself into the room and shut the door behind her with a soft *click*.

I shook my head and entered the camerawoman's pink bedroom. Most of the guests cleared out of their rooms by early afternoon, as they understood that was when I straightened up. The room was empty, and nothing stood out. I made quick work of the gaffer's room and met Rachel back in the hall to go over Roxanne's room.

"Ready?" Rachel nodded, and I turned the key.

Roxanne's yellow bedroom was neat and tidy, the bed made and all of her clothes put away. Pixie's doggie bed stood near the electric fireplace, as well as a collection of canine toys. Rachel and I stood in silence in the middle of the big room, willing our eyes to pick up a clue worthy of Agatha Christie and Hercule Poirot.

"This is harder than it looks," Rachel mused. She set down her dust mop and turned in a slow circle.

"Nothing's jumping out, but what did we expect? A big pile of chopped-up leaves and stems? Maybe a confession note?"

Rachel drew in a sharp breath and advanced to the small teak vanity, her eyes wide in the antique mirror.

"What did you find?"

She picked up a small jar and squealed. "Crème de la Mer! I've always wanted to try some." She unscrewed the small ceramic container and dipped her sparkly nails into the face cream, patting a dab under her eyes.

"Rachel, you can't sample our guests' toiletries!" I pulled her from the vanity and marched us out the door.

"Oh, lighten up, Mallory. I only took a dab." Rachel locked the door behind her and rolled her eyes.

"I wonder what Truman would say if he found out you were sampling suspects' beauty products instead of snooping," I mumbled.

Next up was Dakota and Beau's room, the sumptuous purple honeymoon suite. Dakota's belongings were neatly placed on luggage racks on the right side of the room, while Beau's things spilled out of a prodigious amount of luggage on the left. The bride had brought way less things than her groom, besides the two garment bags holding her gowns. Beau's side of the room was a little messy, but there was nothing out of the ordinary. We made their bed and fluffed their pillows, wiped down their bathroom, and opened the drapes.

"Well, well, well, what do we have here?"

I came out of the bathroom to find my sister flat on her stomach, her arm elbow deep under the cherry wardrobe.

"Rach, that's not in plain view!" I dropped my duster and hustled over to pull her out.

"But a scrap of silk was peeking out from under the wardrobe," Rachel argued, emerging with a small satin box. "See?"

A thin strand of shiny red material hung from the edge of the box, a ribbon of some sort.

"So what?" I murmured. "Put it back."

"Uh-uh." Rachel held the box over my head, using her height to her advantage. "Why put a present under the wardrobe?"

"It's probably some wedding-night lingerie or something. Put it away. You just engaged in an illegal search."

"Let's just see—" Rachel executed a neat pirouette away from me and whisked the top of the box off.

"Huh."

"What?"

"What size does Dakota wear?"

"A zero, I believe." Yes, that was it. I'd heard her discuss her dress size with Bev as the seamstress had unbelievably had to take in the waist of her size-zero dress another half inch. I'd never make it in Hollywood. I glanced down at my size-eight jeans and snorted.

"So definitely not a six?" Rachel cocked one brow and held up the lingerie, a spicy red and lace number obviously too big for the bride.

"Holy tamale. Who is that for?" My visceral dislike of Beau grew tenfold.

"And you didn't want me to look," Rachel tsked, folding the scarlet-letter lingerie and neatly placing it in the box. "We're definitely telling Truman about that."

My heart hurt for Dakota. I'd been cheated on by my fiancé, and while I was ultimately glad that the discovery had led to the dissolution of our engagement, there was a small part of me I wasn't sure would ever get over the initial betrayal.

"I'll have to tell Dakota," I whispered, staring at the satin box as Rachel pushed it back into hiding under the wardrobe.

Rachel let out a bitter laugh. "We already told her he tried to kiss me, and she reasoned her way out of that truth." She blinked. "Some people just see what they want to see."

We locked up and headed to the last room, Adrienne and Xavier's blue suite. She was thankfully out again, no doubt perched beside a slumbering Xavier at the hospital. I let out a breath I hadn't known I'd been holding in. The last time I'd straightened up her room, before her fiancé had been poisoned, she'd given me some unsolicited advice.

"Are you a wedding planner, or a B and B purveyor? You spend an awful lot of time fluffing pillows and changing sheets. Perhaps you should reassess your priorities and hire out more." Her icy blue eyes had drilled into mine. As usual, her criticism was correct.

I'd grudgingly admitted she had a point. I'd been meaning to hire more help. When I held weddings at the B and B on weekends it was nearly impossible to pull off the ceremony and keep the B and B running like a well-oiled machine.

Rachel and I got to work straightening up the room as we kept our eyes out for anything unusual.

"I thought Xavier didn't believe in medicine," Rachel mused, a bottle in her hands. I plucked it from her fingers and read the label.

"Melatonin. I think this would be right up his alley. It's a natural sleep aid."

Rachel snatched the bottle back and unscrewed the top.

"Okay, that's totally outside the bounds of this search," I warned. My sister scattered the contents of the bottle into her outstretched palm. Little blue, triangular pills rained into her hand.

"Those don't look too natural."

Huh.

She had a point. They looked pharmaceutical grade, not like some kind of health supplement pill as I'd been expecting.

"We'll have to tell Truman," she said, dumping the little pills back into the melatonin bottle. She shook the bottle like a castanet and raised her brow.

"Tell him the fruits of our *illegal search*," I muttered bitterly. "Maybe those are sleeping pills. Xavier must have been all jacked up on the natural high from the green tea and smoothies and needed something to come down to sleep each night."

A thought skittered through my head. Dakota had revealed that Roxanne used to drug her with sleeping pills on the set of *Silverlake High*. I tucked away that tidbit for later and vowed to clue Truman in.

"I guess that's it," I said as we headed for the door.

A little orange paw darted from under the bed.

"Oh no! Soda, how did you sneak in here?" I crouched down and coaxed my naughty kitty from under the bed. "Adrienne will go insane if she finds you in her room."

My cat had a blue feather dangling from her jaws. I recognized it as the jaunty decoration from Adrienne's cloche felt hat and shook my head.

"Come on, sweetie. Adrienne could be back any minute. We need to get you out of here." I finally succeeded in getting the bedraggled feather from my kitty, but she remained under the bed, batting around a small ball. She knocked it out from under the bed and it skittered across the delft carpet and rolled under a small desk.

"What the heck is that?" Rachel bent to scoop up the ball, which proved to be a small sachet of netting tied with a ribbon.

"It smells like Adrienne, all right." Rachel handed the parcel to me. I gave it a tentative whiff. My sister was right. Adrienne left a trail of lavender and dew in her wake, her presence redolent of a Provençal meadow, all heather and poppies and cool blue light. The sachet was filled with crushed, dried flowers, leaves and stems in shades of purple, green, and olive.

And red.

The ribbon of the sachet was loose, as if it had been opened and retied. I pulled the satin with trembling fingers to get a closer look at the contents. There, amidst the fragrant herbs and petals, were fresh but wilted bleeding heart blooms.

Rachel snapped a picture of the smoking gun sachet with her cell phone. I shoved the perhaps lethal ball of herbs and fragrant flowers back under the bed. Together we hightailed it out of Adrienne's room with Soda purring in my arms.

"Ohmigod, she did it," Rachel breathed. She placed a hand over her heart and rested against Adrienne's now-shut door. "She tried to off Xavier!"

"It does look bad," I admitted. "We have to let Truman know what we found."

We carried Soda back to our third-floor apartment and called Truman, breathless from running up the back staircase.

"He's not in," the police secretary said in a bored voice. "Do you want me to give him a message?"

"Tell him we may have found the means to kill Xavier Morris," I breathed. That got her attention, and she promised to pass the message along.

"Let's send him an email," I suggested. I opened my laptop, and Rachel and I sat down on our couch in our light and airy crow's-nest perch of an apartment, a cat on each of our laps. I marveled at how different it was in the quiet, soothing confines of the space our stager mother had decorated this fall. The apartment was fashioned as a Gulf Coast getaway, in shades of aqua, sunny yellow, melon, and lime. It was a welcome respite at the end of a long day to leave the lower levels of Thistle Park and retreat to my and Rachel's own private space. Not for the first time this week, I regretted taking on Dakota and Beau's wedding.

My sister and I crafted a succinct email to Truman, admitting where we'd strayed and gone beyond the confines of a plain-sight search.

"I feel better now it's all in writing," I said as I hit send. "Now there's no wiggle room and twisting the facts to get something into evidence that we shouldn't have really found."

"But we found the real goods thanks to you, cutie pie." Rachel patted a sleeping Soda on the head. The Creamsicle-colored kitty cat earned scratches behind the ears for her role in uncovering Adrienne's hidden stash of bleeding hearts.

"I'm meeting Garrett for dinner tonight." I glanced at my watch and headed off to get ready.

"I'd love to be a fly on the wall when you tell him about Adrienne." Rachel smiled drolly. "I wonder what he'll do."

So do I.

An hour later, Garrett picked me up and we entered the Greasy Spoon, a Port Quincy institution. The old-fashioned diner was decorated in black and gold with a checkered floor, squeaky, cracked vinyl booths, and enough chrome to outfit a fleet of 1957 Chevys. It was comfortably threadbare but sparkly clean, and the air was laden with the smells of delicious comfort foods.

"What a day." I leaned into Garrett as he helped me out of my coat. I rested my head on his broad chest for a moment and felt a few coils of stress release as he held me close. I wanted this wedding and the impending hubbub with Adrienne to all go away.

"Mallory, Garrett. So nice to see you here." The owner of the diner stopped at our booth with a grin and a fresh pot of fragrant coffee. "Thanks for giving us a call the morning after the Winter Ball. We were wondering why no one had shown up, and we'd prepared a breakfast feast for the girls and their dates. We were glad not to let it go to waste." She poured two cups of the smooth, steaming brew and set down two menus.

"It was a crazy morning, and you saved us with your breakfast delivery." I shook my head ruefully. "I'll never forget finding Ginger."

"They haven't found her killer yet, I've heard." The owner left us to our perusal of the menu with a sad shake of her head.

"I'm worried about that investigation," Garrett mused, closing his menu. I bet he'd be getting his usual, a Reuben sandwich and a cup of French onion soup. I pushed my menu to the side, having decided on a grilled cheese sandwich and tomato soup. I needed something hot and gooey and comforting to combat the cold outside and my growing sense of trepidation about revealing to Garrett that Rachel and I had found something that would likely implicate Adrienne in her fiancé's attempted murder.

"The longer time passes, the less likely they'll find Ginger's killer."

"What I can't understand," I pondered after we'd put in our orders, "is how the two crimes could be linked."

"They might not be." Garrett sighed and took a gulp of coffee. "It's looking more like Ginger's murder had something to do with her role as headmistress of the school. Perhaps it was that parent whose meeting she missed, Sterling Jennings. Or Helene."

"Or a random thief," I chimed in. "The tiara is long gone, and everyone in town knew it would be at the Winter Ball."

"Whereas Xavier has his own set of enemies. There's Iris, although Ellie herself seems to not care that he didn't cast her all those years ago. And Dakota and Beau, who might not want this episode to air after all."

I thought of the lingerie in a size suspiciously not Dakota's and renewed my interest in Beau as a possible suspect. But I couldn't ignore the sachet filled with fresh bleeding hearts.

"And then there's Adrienne." I blinked, gauging Garrett's reaction.

"Mallory—" Garrett's face immediately took on an annoyed cast. But we were blessedly interrupted by the arrival of our food, fragrant and steaming and delicious looking. I used the opportunity to take a big, gooey bite of grilled cheese rather than defend myself.

"It's been a long time since I was with Adrienne—" I started to choke and sputter on my sandwich.

"—but I know for sure she didn't try to murder him. I'd bet my life on it." Garrett sat back, satisfied, and took a vicious bite of his sandwich. A chill ran down my back. I didn't want him betting his life now that Adrienne was the prime suspect.

"I'll never forgive Adrienne for walking out on

Summer then waltzing back into her life once a year and breaking her heart." He sighed and took another swig of diner coffee. "But she's tried to turn her life around and make something of herself for Summer's benefit. I'm considering giving her a chance."

I felt my eyes grow wide and threaten to fall out of my head.

"A chance to spend some more time with Summer," he quickly amended, a sheepish grin on his face. "What on earth did you think I meant?"

My heart began to decelerate from the rapid rat-a-tat-tat his misunderstood pronouncement had elicited. I thought of Garrett and Adrienne's dinner together with the mystery ring. I felt my fear curdling to annoyance. I took a deep breath and launched in.

"You probably should hear this from me first. Your dad asked me and Rachel to keep our eyes open when we straightened up the guests' rooms this afternoon."

"You snooped on behalf of Truman?" Garrett shook his head in disgust and threw down his napkin. "Did you do anything illegal?"

"I resent that!" I tossed my napkin as well, the corner landing in my tomato soup. An orange stain quickly crept up the cloth, spreading through the white fabric. "Of course I was above board, and I resent you'd think otherwise."

I won't tell him about Rachel's questionable tactics or the help we got from a certain adorable orange kitten.

"I thought you were on the right side of the law." Garrett's eyes narrowed slightly, and he tore into a roll.

"I just want to find out who put Xavier in a coma, and maybe who killed Ginger too. I used to defend people for a living, don't forget."

"You were a corporate attorney, Mallory. It's different from defending people's criminal rights."

I had practiced some white-collar law when I'd worked at a big law firm, but I knew he was right. Still, it stung. I wasn't trying to implicate anyone unfairly. I just wanted justice to be done, and for Truman to catch the killer.

Or killers.

My phone buzzed to announce a text.

I reached for my phone, barely able to read the text from Truman before I fumbled it. The slim case clattered to the diner floor, skittering under the booth near Garrett's foot. He retrieved my cell, a look of horror marring his craggy good looks.

"Let's go." He tossed some twenties on the table and pulled me along after him. I barely had time to grab my coat.

Chapter Thirteen

Truman had pulled out all the stops to arrest his granddaughter's mother. Two cop cars blared their sirens and flashed their strobe lights in front of Thistle Park, sending red and blue patterns dancing across the snow like a demented aurora borealis.

Garrett screeched to a halt. His Accord hit a patch of black ice and we spun in a circle in the driveway, coming to a halt just inches from the police vehicle.

"Calm down," I nearly shouted. My heart beat somewhere in the vicinity of my throat. "What's done is done."

"I know my father, Mallory. And he's letting his personal feelings cloud his judgment."

Truman's personal feelings didn't chop up a passel of bleeding hearts and hide them in a lavender sachet.

Truman led Adrienne, weary and battle proud, down the steps from the porch. Maybe she'd known the arrest was coming. She'd showered and changed into another gorgeous blue outfit, this

time an azure wool turtleneck and striped navy
pants. She carried a small valise in powder-blue
leather with her, as if she were about to jaunt off
on a short weekend getaway, not languish in the
Port Quincy jail.

Garrett left his car turned catty-corner in the
drive and nearly leapt from the driver's side. He
slipped on the ice in his haste to make it to the
porch and gripped the sides of the flashing
police car to steady himself. I slowly unlatched my
seat belt and crept up the drive, my arms out for
balance, apparently forgotten.

"She didn't do it." Garrett arrived at the bottom
stair panting and out of breath. A look of gratitude
flashed in Adrienne's eyes, and I saw the tight line
of her shoulders relax a smidgen. "You have a half
dozen other viable suspects, yet you've zeroed in
on Adrienne."

"We have incontrovertible evidence," Truman
snorted, his breath creating a jet of white steam
visible in the frigid night air. He glanced at me for
a split second.

"You shouldn't have made Mallory part of your
scheme to get back at Adrienne." Garrett narrowed
his eyes at his father and refused to glance my way.
My breath caught in my throat. I resented Garrett
thinking I'd been had by Truman just to find evidence implicating Adrienne.

"Faith, bring Ms. Larson to the station for booking," Truman commanded. Faith gently took Adrienne's arm, which I noticed wasn't cuffed, and led
her to the back of a police car. Faith carefully ma-
neuvered around Garrett's abandoned Accord

and drove away from Thistle Park, her lights still flashing.

"It could have been Iris or Ellie," Garrett began. He seemed eager to start exonerating Adrienne. "They've never gotten over Xavier not casting Ellie on that silly show. Or it could be Dakota. She agreed to be on this reality episode as a favor, but it's been a disaster. Maybe she wanted to end things prematurely. And what about Roxanne? She's in love with Xavier and now he's engaged to Adrienne. Perhaps—"

"You can stop playing defense attorney," Truman snapped at his son. "You aren't defending Adrienne."

Garrett let out a snort of derision. "I'm not representing her *yet*."

Truman took a step from the porch and met Garrett eye-to-nearly-identical-eye. His voice was low and quiet and serious as a grave. "I'll tell you once, son. Stay out of it."

"And if I don't?" Garrett took a step closer to Truman, a dangerous look in his hazel eyes. I wanted to scream, *Stop it, you two!* But some sixth sense cautioned me not to get involved.

"You always let her twist you around your finger," Truman muttered. "This is just like old times."

I gulped, my throat dropping to my stomach like a leaden ball.

Garrett mercilessly diffused the situation, letting out a genuine, if not bitter, laugh.

"Cut it out, Dad. If there's one finger I can't be twisted around, it's hers." He sighed and ran a hand through his thick dark hair. "I just don't think she did it."

A ribbon of relief threaded its way through my nerves.

"And while you've arrested Adrienne, the real killer is on the loose somewhere in Port Quincy, maybe right here in this house." Garrett looked up and up the front of the edifice to the widow's walk and the thistle weather vane at the tippy top of the attic and back down to his father.

I shivered and held my arms close around my middle, the cold suddenly cutting through my wool pea coat.

"And I don't want anyone to get hurt." Garrett suddenly seemed to remember me. He advanced down the stairs and pulled me close to him.

"Adrienne is the mother of my child," he continued. His voice dropped lower still and his hazel eyes reduced to slits. "But she's also the woman who abandoned my daughter. And that I'll never forget."

"Then you don't need to represent her," Truman gruffly announced, case closed.

"Oh, I'll be her defense attorney," Garrett retorted, and I felt myself stiffen in his arms.

"You haven't been retained by her," Truman sputtered. His face turned an angry tomato red.

"I'll offer my services." Garrett flashed his father a triumphant smile. I usually loved Garrett's chivalry and modern gallantry, but I didn't appreciate those qualities tonight.

Garrett gave me a rather perfunctory kiss on the

cheek and headed back to his car, eager to start working on Adrienne's defense.

"The producer called. They need a new host." I sat stunned and stared at my cell phone. One day had passed since the host's arrest. Adrienne had kept the network apprised about Xavier's poisoning and coma. She'd been assigned to direct and host the rest of the episode despite being traumatized to the point of catatonia. I'd thought the episode would gently go away into that good night, but instead it was like a zombie that couldn't be squashed for good.

"The show must go on," Rachel dryly quipped.

"But this is outrageous! Who will they find to fill in on such short notice?"

A hungry gleam glinted in Rachel's pretty green eyes.

"Oh, no. Don't even think about it."

"But why can't I host?" Rachel was petulant. "Xavier said I was a natural. Besides"—she filled her eyes with maudlin sadness designed to pull my sisterly heartstrings—"you probably won't agree for us to have our own destination show, so this is my last chance."

"Oh, good grief." I hadn't yet explored my own feelings about leaving Port Quincy half the year to jet around the world planning weddings for the Wedding Channel. Part of me was excited for the opportunity; the other part would miss Port Quincy dearly. I had looked forward to spending more time with my mother and stepfather, Doug, now that they were moving back to Pennsylvania, and I'd thought things were heating up between Garrett and me before Adrienne had arrived in town and clouded my view. And the choice wasn't mine to make alone. Since the show offer so far was for Rachel and me we'd have to agree to go all in together or not at all.

Unless Rachel succeeds in convincing the network to give her her own show.

Nothing was ever simple. Including Rachel angling to host the rest of this episode of the cursed train wreck *I Do.*

But the network had other ideas. They discovered one professional actress in the vicinity who'd starred in a few bit parts for television.

"I knew this day would come! This is your big break, kiddo." A mere hour later and Iris was strutting around the parlor like a peacock while Ellie sat in a chair getting her makeup done.

Rachel pouted in the background after she grudgingly congratulated Ellie on landing the role as temporary host for the rest of this episode.

"I'm not sure if this is the best idea," Ellie mused as the makeup artists applied thick foundation to her already flawless complexion. "I won't take time off from school to be on the show."

"We already worked it out with the producer," Iris simpered, beside herself with excitement. "You'll film each day after school is out." She clasped her dimpled fingers together and two gushes of tears sprang from her lively close-set eyes. "It's finally happened—you've been discovered at last!" It was more likely that Ellie had landed the part due to the continuing inclement weather, and the spotty flights from Los Angeles to Pittsburgh. The network didn't want to risk sending out another actor or actress, and had settled on Ellie, who was already in town.

I watched Ellie get made up with a growing sense of trepidation bathing my nerves in an icy bath.

"It's awfully convenient that Adrienne was arrested for having bleeding hearts in her room," I murmured to Rachel in what I hoped was a barely audible whisper. "Especially because, as far as we know, Adrienne doesn't even know we planted the bleeding hearts in the greenhouse for Dakota's secret wedding."

"What are you saying?" Rachel keenly observed Ellie's star treatment, the green-eyed monster out in full force.

"What if Ellie—or Iris—planted the bleeding hearts in Adrienne's room to implicate her?"

Rachel's eyes went wide. "What if it's even worse than that?"

"What could be worse than framing an innocent woman?" Not that I was entirely sure Adrienne was innocent. It wasn't looking good for her. But I couldn't get it out of my mind how neatly things were falling into place for Ellie.

"Maybe Ellie killed Ginger to get the headmistress position just to get Iris off her back," Rachel suggested. She dropped her voice when Iris glanced in our direction.

"And then she poisoned Xavier and planted the bleeding hearts in Adrienne's room to get the host position."

It fit.

"Or it could have been Iris," Rachel hissed.

"She does seem more likely to orchestrate it so her daughter could be more esteemed in her eyes." A pang of pathos rippled through me as I thought of Ellie and Leah growing up with a mother for whom nothing was ever good enough.

"Let's go tell Truman."

My sister and I slipped from the room to pay a visit to the chief just as Ellie started filming her first monologue.

"That's not a bad theory."

Truman rubbed his hand on the stubble that had sprouted on his chin after a long day trying to untie the Gordian knot that was the nexus, or lack thereof, of Ginger's death and Xavier's coma.

"Iris Barnes was always the worst kind of stage mother imaginable." He shook his head and leaned back in his easy chair. "I remember being called to the Methodist church one December, long ago, to break up an altercation." He chuckled mirthlessly. "Iris had started to go after another mother when Ellie didn't get the part of baby Jesus in the nativity play."

"She'd do anything to make Ellie a star, or get the headmistress position, or get Leah into Harvard," I said. My own mother had decreed that either Rachel or me had to become a doctor or a lawyer, and I'd fulfilled her edict. But I don't think she would have killed to make it happen. I shivered despite the cozy warmth of the Davies family's living room.

Truman left us to change into civilian clothes, and Rachel and I idly leafed through the voluminous collection of photo albums sitting on the bottom row of bookshelves flanking the fireplace. Photo albums were a rare commodity these days, since everyone, yours included, seemed to keep digital copies of their pictures on computers or in the cloud. I enjoyed looking at photographs of Garrett as a child.

"Check this out." Rachel laughed with glee at a photo from the mid 1980s, of Garrett dressed as the Cookie Monster for some long-ago Halloween.

I giggled and wondered what Garrett would think of us perusing his own personal memory lane. I selected a newer-looking album and the book fell open down the middle, the selection of photos from Garrett's college days. There were pictures from the debate team and track meets and one from a dance.

I stared in wonder at a photograph of Garrett, his arm around a laughing and beautiful Adrienne Larson. They were dressed for a school dance in formal wear, Garrett in a dark suit, and Adrienne in a cool blue sequined gown. The banner behind them announced it was Quincy College's homecoming weekend.

"They looked so happy," Rachel mused. She took in what must have been a mixed look of wonder and upset on my face and amended her comment. "They looked so *young*."

They did look young. Young and happy, carefree and in love.

"Will you take me to the orthodontist, Mallory?" Summer appeared at my elbow and I dropped the book like a molten potato.

"Ouch!" It fell on my toe, causing some damage even through my heavy snow boots.

That's what you get for snooping.

"Sure, sweetie. But don't you usually go with your dad or grandparents?"

Summer shook her head, the short blond hair flying out around her ears. "Dad's busy at the office trying to get Mom out of jail. Grandma's grocery shopping. And I won't go with Grandpa, since I'm boycotting him."

Rachel raised a perfectly plucked eyebrow. "Boycotting?"

"Since he unfairly arrested my mother." A wave of hurt crested and crashed in her hazel eyes.

Oh, boy.

"Sure, we'll take you. Let me just see your grandpa for a minute."

I got the all-clear from Truman, who was sad about Summer's boycott, but understanding. "It's for the best," he grumbled. He settled back into his easy chair, now clad in his West Virginia University sweatpants. "I can understand why she's mad at me, but she'll know the truth someday."

Summer, Rachel, and I climbed into the Butterscotch Monster. I caught a glimpse of Summer's outfit under her coat. She was still wearing light blue, in what must have been solidarity with her mother. Gone were her hoodies and sweaters in bright colors.

"I just want my mom and dad to be friends," Summer blurted out. Her teeth were still startlingly bare. I wasn't used to seeing her without braces, something that would be rectified momentarily. "Dad's just defending her because he believes in civil rights, not because he even likes her."

It was a big speech for such a young girl, and I was at a loss for words. Rachel adjusted my rearview mirror and used it to look Summer in the eye.

"Your parents are trying hard to do what's best for you," Rachel soothed. "Even if that means different things."

It was a diplomatic thing to say, and I smiled at my sister's wisdom.

"Mom wants me to get into acting and live with her for half the year."

"She *what?!*" The tires screeched as I steadied the giant boat of a station wagon. I'd carelessly pulled the wheel in response to Summer's announcement, and I righted the course now. "That's big news," I amended, my heart pounding in my chest.

Summer nodded, somewhat miserably.

"What do *you* want, sweetie?" I adjusted the rearview mirror back into place.

"I used to want to be a veterinarian," she began, her heart-shaped face confused and gloomy. "But Mom says I can't pass this up."

I groaned inwardly and kept my eyes on the road.

"You don't always have to do something just

because you can," I counseled as we pulled into the orthodontist's office for the last appointment of the day. "There are so many doors open to you. You're only thirteen."

"You can do anything you want," Rachel added. "Why, I've been a hairdresser, dental assistant, dog walker, baker, and now assistant wedding planner!" She beamed at her spoken resume and swung her long legs out of the car.

Summer disappeared into an examination room to get her braces put back on, and Rachel and I talked in low tones in the waiting room.

"Do you think Garrett knows Summer is considering spending time in L.A. with her mom?" I knew at one time in his life, Garrett would have been keen to have Adrienne take more of an interest in their daughter, and for Summer to seek out more time with her mother. Now I wasn't so sure.

Rachel bit her plump frosted lip. "There's no way." She brightened, abandoning a glossy magazine on a side table. "You should tell him—that'll get him back on your side again."

"He's not taking sides!" I said this a little too loudly, earning a glare from the receptionist. "Garrett and I are doing just fine."

Aren't we?

"I'm going to stay out of it," I announced.

"I'm ready." Summer nearly skipped out of the examination room, her trademark magenta braces firmly in place. She flashed a smile in the mirror behind the reception desk and let out a satisfied sigh. "It was fun having my braces off for a few days, but I feel like me again."

"And that's a great thing to be. Come on, sweetie. Let's go home."

The next morning, I awoke from a troubling dream. Summer and Garrett were moving to Los Angeles to accommodate Summer's budding career as an actress. Garrett gave me a cursory hug goodbye, and I watched him and his daughter disappear through airport security. I implicitly understood they weren't coming back to Port Quincy.

I sat up from the dream with sweat pouring down my back. Whiskey stared at me in alarm, her calico tail swishing. She crept up the comforter and nuzzled my nose with hers, trying to offer comfort.

I picked her up and cuddled her close and called my stepfather for a bit of advice about whether to spill the beans of Summer's wishes to spend more time with her mother to Garrett.

"It's a delicate balance," Doug counseled, his voice steady and measured. "I know your mother wanted you girls to have access to your father, even if that wasn't his intent."

My father and mother had gone through a brutal divorce and custody battle, before he'd eventually disappeared. Unlike Summer's yearly visits with Adrienne, Rachel and I had never seen our father again.

"Your mother worked so hard for you and Rachel not to feel your father's absence," Doug continued. "And I think she did a great job."

"I agree," I murmured, a lump of gratitude making

my throat froggy. "Thank you," I whispered, glad I'd called.

"Hello, darling! Why didn't you tell me you're getting your own show?" My parents were two of the three human beings on the planet who still had a landline, and I'd heard the loud click of the phone being picked up somewhere in their house down in the Florida panhandle to announce my mother joining the call. Her voice boomed over the line.

"You weren't supposed to know about that," I grumbled, ready to kill Rachel. "Not *yet*," I amended.

"Don't you worry about a thing," my mother prattled on, gaining a head of steam. "Doug and I got some promising leads at our open house yesterday. It's only a matter of time before we sell and move to Port Quincy." She took a deep breath, her excitement radiating through the phone. "I will run the B and B for you while you're filming your show!"

Truman is about to get even busier. I really will kill Rachel.

Didn't pinky swears mean anything these days? I couldn't believe my sister had tattled. Actually, it was probably inevitable, but I at least thought I'd get a few more days before Rachel revealed the tantalizing possibility of our very own reality show.

"I don't think that's necessary, Mom." I gritted my teeth.

"Nonsense."

An annoyed frisson ran through my nerves. Rachel hadn't just accidentally spilled the beans; she'd done it on purpose. She'd told our mom about the show to bring in the big guns. My mother was no lawyer, but she was highly persuasive. She'd wear me down until I acquiesced and handed over the keys to the B and B and my book of business. Adrienne could take lessons on getting her way from the master, my mother, Carole Shepard.

"I have to go," I announced, my voice curt. "Thanks, Doug."

"Think about my offer. It will be marvelous!" my mother trilled into my ear as I hung up.

I set off on a mission to find Rachel and give her a piece of my mind. I found her shivering on the front porch, mail in hand.

"Lots of fan mail for Dakota and Beau." She rifled through the thick pile, her shiny, sparkly nails dancing by the light of the cold, high sun. "This one feels like it has a rock inside." She palpated a thin, plain white envelope and examined the letter. "No return address, but postmarked Port Quincy."

"Don't worry about Dakota's mail." I plucked the letter from her grasp and placed a hand on my hip.

"What were you doing, telling Mom about our show offer?"

The blood drained from my sister's face, then returned a few seconds later, staining her cheekbones.

"*Someone* needs to be on my side." She rolled her green eyes and mirrored my motions, her hand on her hip. "I thought Mom could point out what a great idea it would be to do the show."

"You mean you thought she could browbeat me into it," I seethed. "We pinky swore!"

"Pinky swore about what?"

In my haste to dress down my sister, I failed to see Garrett advancing up the walk. He offered me a weary but sexy smile, and I colored, my face warm and hot and probably as red as my sister's.

"Nothing."

Smooth.

My sister and I clammed up and joined Garrett in the breakfast room for a cup of coffee. Dakota was nursing a cup of her own and offered us a smile just as tired and distracted as Garrett's.

"These are for you." Rachel pushed the envelopes across the table and I added the one with the mystery item inside to the top of the pile.

"It's a shame the show is still filming," Dakota said. I handed her a letter opener. "Although it wouldn't have been good for you guys not to have the episode air."

"Oh, I don't know about that." I still wasn't sure if the producers would try and lobby to show the disastrous, deadly Winter Ball. It would take some tricky editing to cobble together a presentable episode for *I Do*. I was ready to call the whole thing off.

"Well, you always have your destination wedding show offer to fall back on," Dakota mused as she opened the top letter.

"Your what?" Garrett stopped, his coffee cup aloft and frozen in midair halfway to his mouth.

Uh-oh.

"Mallory and I have been offered our own show!"

Rachel crowed, now that the cat was out of the bag. "We'll film half the year in vacation spots. It'll really help our business grow back home, too."

A queer look stole over Garrett's face. One of recognition, disappointment, and resolve.

"Garrett—"

"Oh my God." Dakota jumped back as if she'd just been bitten. A delicate snowflake fashioned from platinum and old mine-cut diamonds fell out of the plain envelope and skittered onto the table. "A piece of the tiara."

Chapter Fourteen

The breakfast room was utterly still. Dakota broke the silence as she pushed back her chair with a spine-tingling screech. Her teeth began to chatter, though it was quite warm in the room.

"Ginger's murderer sent that."

"Don't touch it," I warned, mindful of fingerprints.

"I'll call Truman." Rachel seemed to have realized she shouldn't have so gleefully crowed about our show offer and lowered her eyes to the table.

"Can we talk?" Garrett practically pulled me from the breakfast room to the dining room.

"The tiara—"

"The tiara can wait." Storm clouds gathered in Garrett's hazel eyes. I felt as if the people in the painting above the fireplace were watching me in censure.

The jig is up.

"I was going to tell you—"

"That you're leaving." His voice was flat and somehow derisive all at once.

"I—I haven't decided." I dragged my smarting eyes from the blinding white landscape outside the big bay window to meet his hurt ones. "It would only be for half the year. Rachel wants this so badly, Garrett. I don't feel right entertaining this offer, but I can't just say no, either."

He stared at me, his jaw working and his eyes wide.

"I can't have Summer hurt twice by women walking out of her life."

"But Adrienne's back in Summer's life," I said, my voice infinitesimally small.

"Adrienne is languishing in jail," he reminded me. His concentration was broken. He dragged his fingers through his hair and began to pace around the long dining room table. "Perhaps it's best I get back to her defense."

I stared at his retreating form, mad about this tiff. I didn't want him to leave angry. I still wasn't sure if I even wanted to be on a destination wedding show. But I knew this argument wasn't fair, even though I'd kept my secret too long.

"Isn't it a conflict of interest, defending the mother of your child for murder?"

Garrett froze and wheeled around. "No one else wants to defend her," he said simply. "I'm all she has here in Port Quincy."

I figured it was time for all the secrets to come out, now that mine may have ruined us.

"I saw the ring," I whispered, tracing the pattern of leaves and berries in the deep red tablecloth. "At Pellegrino's."

A red flush started at Garrett's Adam's apple

and crept up to his face, tingeing the five o'clock shadow I normally loved to run my fingers over.

"I don't have anything to hide." Garrett spoke clearly and plainly. "That was the ring I gave Adrienne that she never deigned to wear. I thought she'd used it to fund her trip out to L.A., but I guess she kept it all these years. She didn't return it until now. She thought Summer might like to have it. Not that she should have kept it. We were never compatible."

He swept back into the room and took my hands in his. He tipped my chin up so he could look directly into my eyes. "Adrienne and I never should have been together, but I do thank my stars every day that I have Summer. You have nothing to worry about, Mallory. I just wish you'd have told me you're considering leaving Port Quincy."

He ran his finger down the side of my jaw, sending shivers up my spine. He turned to go, without a word, and walked out the door.

"Don't worry. He'll be back." Rachel bustled around the kitchen with a Valentine's Day apron tied around her minuscule waist. She was putting the finishing touches on Dakota's comfort food menu. Her words were clear and convincing, but her eyes told a different story.

"He was pretty pissed, Rach." I stopped chopping onions and wiped an itch on my nose with the back of my hand. "Not that I blame him." The dull ache in my stomach that had appeared as Garrett strode out the door sharpened to a stab I felt each time my heart beat.

"Well, at least now we can go to L.A."

"Rachel! How could you?" I put down my knife and turned to my sister. "I don't want to break up with Garrett."

"And I don't want to pass up this opportunity because you're unsure what to do!" Rachel sighed and wiped her hands on the pretty heart and cupid apron.

"Let's make a pro and con list and decide once and for all." Her eyes narrowed. "Together."

We washed up and put away the makings of a comfort food feast and settled into the parlor. I nestled a legal pad in my lap and stared into the licking flames of the fire. The bedrooms upstairs for our guests featured realistic electric inserts to provide warmth and ambiance. They were insurance-friendly, as there was no chance of a guest dozing off and creating a fire hazard. But downstairs, in the public part of the B and B, several original fireplaces remained. They'd been carefully reappointed and lovingly restored by my contractor, Jesse Flowers. Most days of the week guests could be found lingering in front of the real fireplaces in the parlor, library, and dining room.

The parlor held the most impressive specimen, a floor-to-ceiling tiled wonder of a hearth with a peacock mosaic in a rainbow of colors. Real flames reflected off the minute glass tiles in pleasing shades of iridescent violet, turquoise, and electric blue. Wood hissed and popped. A single page fluttered out of the fire, like a bird with flaming wings alight, the edges curling.

"What is that?" Rachel jumped up and I stamped it out.

I picked·up the brittle page, desiccated and singed around the edges from its time in the hearth.

"It's the plant encyclopedia." I held up the page, a lump forming in my throat.

"The bleeding heart entry." Rachel gingerly took the page from me and turned as the doorbell rang.

"That'll be Truman, here for the piece of the tiara."

"Not a moment too soon."

Truman collected the two pieces of evidence and ferreted them away in brown paper evidence bags. He refused to make either heads or tails of the items, but the grim set of his jaw told me everything.

"How's the investigation going?" I asked with a tentative lilt to my query.

"It's going," was his gruff answer.

Not so hot, then.

Truman swept from the B and B, and I readied myself for filming to start. Rachel and I resumed our ministrations in the kitchen. Ellie arrived and sat for makeup, Iris in tow.

"You seem rather pensive, dear." Iris cocked her fuzzy head and took a seat in the kitchen while I put the finishing touches on the salmon mac and cheese. I sprinkled parmesan and herbed breadcrumbs atop the pasta and fish.

"I'm trying to decide what to do with my life in the midst of a murder investigation," I blurted out.

"Follow your heart, Mallory. That's the best advice I can give." Iris taste-tested our batch of bacon green beans and sighed with pleasure. "Are you having man trouble?"

I choked on the sip of water I'd just taken and sputtered. "Um, er, yes," I finally admitted. "Rachel and I have been offered an opportunity to film a destination reality show," I reminded her.

A jealous gleam lit up Iris's dark brown eyes.

"Well, you should take the offer, then. It's nearly impossible to break into show business."

"But I'd have to leave Port Quincy and the B and B for half the year." I glanced around the kitchen I'd grown to love and out at the snow-capped grounds of the strange old mansion I'd made my home.

"And your fellow, Garrett, wasn't too happy with the proposition."

I smiled at Iris's labeling of Garrett as my fellow and nodded. "I kind of hid the offer from him." I felt a warm flush spread across my face, no doubt obliterating my freckles. "And he eventually found out from Dakota, not me. I should have told him first."

Iris nodded sagely. "You should swallow your pride and chase after him, Mallory. Don't let him get away."

I smiled again at her advice and sprinkled chopped rosemary atop the fancy mac and cheese. "It's not that simple."

"No, love never is."

I looked up, startled.

Was this love?

My relationship with Garrett had certainly been progressing, and I adored spending time with him. Was I ready to declare I was in love?

Iris broke into my thoughts with another sigh. "Ellie shouldn't have let Owen get away, but it is what it is."

"Excuse me?" I dusted the rest of the breadcrumbs and rosemary from my hands and wheeled around.

"My Ellie and Owen were engaged once, you know. Two years ago." Her face curdled and her mouth twisted down in a grade-A frown. "But Owen couldn't get over Dakota, and he called it off."

So this confirmed the weird tension and chemistry I'd felt coursing between Owen and Ellie in the nursery greenhouse like an invisible charge. It also confirmed that Owen had still recently held a candle for Dakota.

"But," Iris continued brightly, her face now a mask of false cheeriness, "that doesn't matter now. Ellie is headmistress at Dunlap, and the interim host of *I Do*. I'm sure she'll wow them and be offered a permanent spot, and then she'll have two amazing opportunities to choose from."

I kind of doubted *I Do* would make it past this bizarre episode, but I didn't share my thoughts with Iris.

Her face faltered for a moment. "Dakota better not ruin it this time."

A chill shivered down my vertebrae as I caught an unadulterated flash of hate in Iris's eyes. I figured it was now or never to ask one thing that had been bothering me.

"Do you think there's a chance Ginger and Owen were an item?" I kept quiet about my sister's unconfirmed fling with Owen.

A cunning look of realization stole over Iris's face. She didn't look surprised. She'd opened her mouth to reply when the camerawoman entered the room. She began filming, and I momentarily forgot my question. And maybe I was wrong about *I Do* getting cancelled. Ellie was very good. We wrapped up, and Ellie and Iris left Thistle Park on foot, clad in high snow boots.

Rachel and I cleaned the kitchen. We worked for half an hour in companionable silence.

"What were you and Iris talking about?" Rachel finally said as we hung up our dishtowels. "It looked pretty intense."

"Did you know Ellie and Owen were engaged?"

Rachel leaned against the counter and frowned. She shook her head slowly, her caramel-colored bun coming undone. "No, he didn't mention it."

"Iris said it didn't work out because he's still in love with Dakota." I clapped a hand on my mouth too late. Rachel's gaze was hot and petulant.

"That's news to me," she bristled.

"It's just that it could be motive," I rushed on, eager to move past my gaffe. "What if Owen is Ginger's secret lover? We didn't get a chance to talk about it, but Iris had a knowing look when I mentioned it. Maybe she killed Ginger to pave the way for Ellie to get back with Owen. Or maybe Owen did Ginger in over a lovers' quarrel."

"Owen did not murder Ginger!" Rachel flung

her dishtowel in the sink and stomped up the back stairs.

Awesome. You just alienated your boyfriend and now your sister. Could this day get any better?

I was beginning to feel the claustrophobic effects of staying cooped up in the B and B, like living in one of the antique snow globes we'd used to decorate for the Winter Ball. It was time to get some fresh air.

I shoveled a path out of the driveway and headed downtown in the Butterscotch Monster. I made my way to the historical society to pay a visit to my good friend Tabitha Battles. The roads were mercifully clear, though some sidewalks still sported a considerable amount of snow.

"How's the celebrity wedding going?" She ushered me into her office, where several space heaters gamely chugged along, trying in vain to heat the room in a building constructed in the late 1700s.

I settled into a chair before her desk and gratefully wrapped my frigid fingers around the mug of tea she offered, my hands trying to absorb warmth from the china.

"It's going," I offered miserably.

"That well, huh?" Tabitha laughed, her gimlet eyes shining. "If anyone can fix it though, I know you can."

I offered my friend a relieved smile. She was dressed for February in a loden green sweater set, electric blue woolen skirt, and high burgundy boots. Her preternaturally red hair was a vivid contrast to the likes of Dakota's more muted red, and she'd draped a yellow shawl over her shoulders for extra warmth.

"I wanted to ask you about the tiara that got stolen."

"Let's see." Tabitha crossed the charming small office and dug through a set of filing cabinets, humming as she went. "Here we are." She returned to her desk with a thin manila file.

"The tiara belonged to the daughter of a coal baron. Her name was Violet McGill. She attended Dunlap Academy soon after it was founded. It seems like tiaras were all the rage. It was the end of the Edwardian era. Wealthy American girls longed to emulate their English counterparts and act like duchesses or princesses, hence the tiara." Tabitha licked her finger and turned another page in the tiara dossier.

"Here, look." She showed me some grainy pictures of the snowflake crown.

"Yup, that's it. The Winter Ball tiara."

"It was rumored to be composed of diamonds." Tabitha frowned. "But just as many suspected it was cut glass or rhinestones. Violet McGill donated it to the school to be used for each Belle of the Winter Ball after she was crowned the first. The tiara was entombed in the time capsule at Dunlap in 1910."

I nodded. This was in line with what Ginger had told us before she'd met her fateful end.

"Ginger told us," I gulped, "before she died that it had been appraised at fifty thousand dollars."

Tabitha shook her head. "Oh, that may be the starting price, but I'm sure it would fetch way more if it actually reached auction. There would be a lot of wealthy, sentimental Dunlap alumni willing to bid for it."

So the tiara could definitely be a motive in Ginger's death.

"Oh look! It's your dearest friend." Tabitha smirked and dug out some pictures from Dunlap. "These pictures are from Winter Balls of past. Check out 1969." She swiveled a pile of photographs around to face me.

There was Helene Pierce, Belle of the Winter Ball. She sported gumball-sized Mamie Eisenhower pearls, just as she did today, and a snowy satin bell skirt embroidered with daisies. Her youth-softened face was quite pretty. But a harsh, imperious gleam resided in her eyes and there was a cunning lilt to her smile. A man stood by her side, one I knew to be Keith's father, who was long deceased.

"So Helene wasn't crowned with the tiara?"

"No, they would have used a replica, I believe."

I laughed. There was no way Helene would have consented to have costume jewelry placed on her head, even at the tender age of eighteen. I pushed the photographs back across the desk, and Tabitha filed them away.

I gulped. "I came here for another reason, actually."

Tabitha cocked her head, her Ariel-the-mermaid hair sliding over her shoulder. "Adrienne Larson?"

I nodded weakly. "What was the story with her and Garrett?"

Tabitha sat back in her chair, no doubt thinking back to her days as a student at Quincy College.

"We were all so excited that Garrett got into Harvard for law school. Everyone but Keith, that is," she mused. "Adrienne and Garrett broke up that summer he headed off to Cambridge. By then, I bet she was already pregnant, but I don't think she knew it yet."

She took a delicate sip of tea. "Garrett dropped out after his first semester and transferred to Pitt. He commuted and took care of Adrienne, and they tentatively got back together, but we could all tell her heart wasn't in it." She paused and looked out the window, then at me. "And his wasn't either. Summer was born, and Adrienne left. And that's all there is to it."

"But he did ask her to marry him," I blurted out.

Tabitha blushed. "He did, out of a misguided sense of duty." She clasped my hands in hers across the desk. "Mallory, believe me when I say you have nothing to worry about."

Chapter Fifteen

I wasn't so sure I had nothing to worry about.

I left Tabitha at the historical society and headed home, the Butterscotch Monster gamely chugging along and slipping on the now slushy, yellow brick streets. Rivulets of melting snow had run across the once-clear roads and frozen again in certain patches with the sun newly gone, making the trip home a dicey affair.

Garrett called, and I answered the phone in a rush. I was hot and bothered to make amends given Iris's straightforward advice and Tabitha's reassurances. I wasn't sure what the future would bring, but I didn't want to lose him.

"I'm sorry about the way—"

"Summer's missing."

"*What?*" My heart leapt to my throat. "Since when? Where do you think she is?" So many questions raced through my brain.

"She didn't come home from school today. She wasn't on the bus, and she didn't show up at home. Dad is going to put out a bulletin in half an hour if we don't find her. My mother is beside herself." His words sounded strangely hollow, yet tinged with pure primal fear.

It wasn't like Summer to wander off without telling anyone.

Scratch that.

The first time I'd met her she'd been fetching her kitten, Jeeves, from under my back porch, her dad and grandparents none the wiser. She'd been sneaking over to Thistle Park all last summer to feed Whiskey and Soda and Jeeves. She'd even almost witnessed a murder in the dead of night as she unflaggingly tended to the kitties.

"I'll search the grounds."

"I'll join you." He hung up, his voice clipped and tight.

I gathered a flashlight and headed out into the dark late afternoon. The sun had crept toward the horizon an hour ago, and a silvery wafer moon hung from the sky, barely illuminating the sugary smooth ground. Shadows from evergreen trees laden with snow cast their long reach across the lawn, their silhouettes reminding me of monsters.

I crunched through the top layer of ice along-side tracks from deer, raccoon, and rabbits. I called out for Summer until my throat went hoarse. A cursory look through the carriage house proved she wasn't there, the mural of old-time cars we'd had painted in December standing eerie sentinel in the big space. She wasn't in the shed either, and I saw no footprints.

I finally made my way to the greenhouse. A

small light glowed within, the tiniest orb bouncing up and down through the rows of plants.

Footprints.

The crisp top layer of snow had been marred by boots recently. I took a deep breath and pushed open the door to the large glass labyrinth and flicked on the light with shaking hands.

"Summer!"

She stood with her backpack still on. She was holding her cell phone aloft in front of her as a makeshift flashlight.

"Mallory." Her face fell. "You found me."

"Oh, sweetie." I ran down the row. In my haste, I knocked over a planter and spilled a bag of potting soil. "Don't ever not tell your dad where you're going again." I nearly knocked her over from the force of my hug and she hugged me back, fiercely.

"What are you doing here?" I whipped out my phone and texted Garrett as I awaited her explanation.

"I'm taking pictures." Twin beads of tears pooled in her wide eyes and spilled over to stain her cheeks. "I'm trying to do it how Grandpa would if he were investigating. I heard him say they'll be combing the greenhouse tomorrow, and I wanted to get here first." Her voice got progressively higher and thinner as she explained her presence here. She'd taken off her hat and gloves in the nearly tropical air and appeared to be sweating in her heavy purple coat, whether because of the thermostat, or because she'd gotten caught. "I thought maybe I could find something to prove my mom didn't hurt Xavier."

"Honey, you have to let the police do their job." I held her at arm's length and searched her face. "They'll be fair, I promise."

I think they'll be fair.

I couldn't help but recall Truman's convincing me to do a borderline illegal search but pushed the thought from my mind.

"Grandpa is trying to frame my mom!" Summer's voice was full-on shrill this time, and she broke away from my arms and gestured to the bleeding hearts.

"Oh, Summer. I won't let him." Garrett closed the door to the greenhouse behind him and gathered Summer up in a colossal hug.

"I'm sorry I didn't come home on time, Dad." Summer pulled back and stared up at her father, her tears flowing freely.

"I'm just glad you're all right. But don't ever do it again."

She nodded as he held her close.

"Everything is ruined." Summer sniffled and dug a worn tissue from her pocket. She dabbed at her eyes and blew her red nose. "Mom has been promising that we'll spend more time together for so long, and now it's not ever going to happen."

A strange look stole over Garrett's face. "What do you mean, Summer?"

Summer realized she'd spilled some beans and glanced at me. "Mom wants me to come live with her in L.A. for part of the year."

"My sweetheart!" Lorraine Davies came running into the greenhouse and swept Summer into an embrace. "Don't you go scaring your old grandma like this!"

Summer laughed and held Garrett's mom close. She let her grandmother fuss over her and gathered her things to go.

"Good night, Mallory." Summer offered me a small sheepish smile and left the greenhouse with Lorraine, her investigation forgotten.

Garrett's jaw worked up and down, but he said nothing. He dug his hands in his overcoat pocket and waited for Summer to advance across the lawn with her grandmother.

"I never should have represented her." His voice was cold and hard. I couldn't recall having ever seen him angrier.

"Do you really think Adrienne tried to kill her fiancé?" I wasn't sure I wanted to know the answer.

Garrett shook his head, his eyes murderous. "I don't know what to think of her anymore. But one thing's for certain. I'm done helping Adrienne."

He dropped a quick kiss on my forehead and stole out of the greenhouse, his long legs whipping across the snow to catch up to his daughter.

The next morning, I watched as Truman, Faith, and some cadets from the towns and municipalities around Port Quincy destroyed all the hard work we'd put in for Dakota and Beau's secret red and pink wedding.

I stared with a lump forming in my throat as all my late-night ministrations and planning went up in smoke, or rather, churned-up dirt and upended flowers.

I was pretty sure Dakota and Beau wouldn't want to feature bleeding hearts as the focal point of their decor now that Xavier was still languishing in a coma, but it was hard to watch the police ruin every bloom we'd lovingly planted.

"What are they looking for?" I asked Truman in a sullen tone as he observed the men and women combing through clippings and sifting through dirt.

"Any stray item that might help us identify who clipped a bleeding heart plant, ground it up, and put it among Xavier's smoothie ingredients."

"But this place is probably filled with hair and fibers from everyone who worked in here."

"And we're not discounting any of those people," Truman assured me.

I closed my eyes at the ruined greenhouse and tried to brainstorm a final plan for Dakota and Beau's nuptials, but my mind drew a blank.

"Maybe they should try to elope like Keith and Becca," I muttered.

"What was that?"

"Nothing."

Nothing, just like my plans for the moment. It would be nearly impossible to come up with *another* plant or flower to serve as the focal point for a red and pink explosion. All of the florists were spoken for with their normal Valentine's Day orders. A tiny kernel of an idea germinated in my head. I pictured a sea of silk and paper flowers, in every shade imaginable of red and pink. It might work.

I was about to head back to the house to share my idea with my sister when they found it.

"Chief! Over here." The cadets stopped their sifting and shifting of soil when one of their own shouted for Truman. A tall black woman in uniform solemnly held out her hand, a treasure nestled there. It was the snowflake tiara, one prong missing, the mine-cut diamonds still winking and blinking, despite being covered in dirt and grime.

"Truman thinks the killer may have buried the tiara in a bag of potting soil to frame me." I shivered and gripped Garrett's hand tighter. We stood outside the greenhouse watching the technicians take pictures of the bag where the tiara was found.

"It kills me to think the person who did this to Ginger is still at large." Garrett brought my gloved hands to his lips and brushed them with a kiss. "Promise me you'll be more careful."

I laughed a bitter note and lowered my hand. "I'll be as careful as I can, all while I whip up another wedding plan from the smoldering ashes of this latest botched attempt to give Dakota and Beau a beautiful day." I gestured to the destroyed greenhouse that was to be a glittering and cozy party venue to celebrate their marriage. I was having as many problems planning this wedding as the bride and groom seemed to be having in their relationship.

Maybe this is the first wedding that won't go off. And it'll all be captured on film.

I shook the thought out of my head and vowed to come up with an alternate plan for Dakota and

Beau. We could always go back to their black and white Pixie–the–Shih Tzu–inspired wedding, or take back the yellow springtime affair from Owen's foundation.

"I really came to say I'm sorry."

Garrett's apology snapped me out of my feverish plans and I gazed at him. "You what?"

"I reacted badly when I found out you're considering the destination show. It would be quite a coup for you and your sister." He took a deep breath and traced the line of my jaw. He exhaled, a jet of steam leaving his mouth as the hot air collided with the frigid atmosphere. "I even understand why you decided not to tell me right away. You have every right to figure out what it is you want before you include me in your decision, if at all."

I stood back, stunned.

"Thanks," I whispered. I'm eloquent like that.

"I care so much about you," Garrett whispered. His eyes took a faraway cast. "Maybe if I'd been more flexible with Adrienne after Summer was born, she wouldn't have felt the need to run away."

"You can't blame yourself for what she did." I placed a gloved finger over his mouth, but he went on.

"I do blame myself. I wonder if I smothered her."

I must have looked as worried as I felt then, because Garrett gathered me in his arms anew. "I'm completely over her, by the way. She's the woman who handed over Summer when she was two weeks old and walked out the door. Summer's seen her half a dozen times since. She waltzes in and breaks my daughter's heart. Over and over again." He winced, the blinding light of the cold sun glancing off the snow. "I started dating Adrienne in college. She had stars in her eyes even then, and she was determined to go to Hollywood. I stayed with her out of inertia. I'm not proud of that, and we parted when I went away to law school. But by then she'd discovered she was pregnant." He shook his head a little ruefully, unknowingly echoing what Tabitha had told me. "Adrienne was my greatest mistake, and my best mistake. I wouldn't trade anything that happened if it meant I wouldn't have Summer."

"You're the best dad she could ever have." I took a deep breath, not sure if I should broach the topic now. "And I think, in her own strange way, Adrienne is trying to be a better mom. Now, at least."

Garrett cocked his head to the side and finally nodded.

"No matter what happens with this show offer, we should try to work something out." I stepped closer into his orbit and he ruffled his gloved hands through my hair.

"I'll cherish you for now, Mallory. But I won't stifle you."

"You never have, and you never will."

I left him to fix the debacle of Dakota and Beau's plans, as unsure what to do with my life as I had been before. But one thing was for certain; I wanted to give Garrett and me a fighting chance.

Imagine my surprise when my cell phone showed a missed call from the Port Quincy jail. I called the number back and was informed that Adrienne Larson had dialed me as her one phone call recipient.

"It's a trap," Rachel breathed on her newly lavender colored nails, the quicker to dry the polish. "She's just desperate to find out what the police have dug up on her, now that Garrett's let her go as his client."

"Maybe so. But my interest is piqued." The jail wouldn't put my call through to her, but they had let me know she'd called. They informed me that visitors' hours were over today within the hour. I paced in front of the aqua and turquoise couch in the third-floor apartment and discussed the pros and cons with my sister.

"I could just go and see what she was calling me for," I wheedled.

"Don't do it! She tried to murder her fiancé, and Truman will murder you if he finds out you're talking to her." Rachel put down the minuscule nail polish brush and stared at me as if I'd gone crazy. She resumed blowing on her fingers, the sharp smell of acetone and formaldehyde stinking up the room.

She's right.

But curiosity got the better of me.

"I'll just have to make sure Truman doesn't find out."

Fifteen minutes later, I was staring at the Port Quincy jail, a marvel of architecture for a place that housed criminals. It was a small limestone castle befitting some minor British duke or earl. The jail structure towered over the Pepto-pink palace of a courthouse and the hulking, ugly brutalist slab of a municipal building. The tallest tower featured hanging gallows, which, according to

Tabitha, had actually been used in the late 1800s. I shivered at the thought of such rough justice and entered the building.

A few minutes later, after an obligatory trip through the metal detector and relinquishing of my phone, I was face-to-face with Adrienne. She smiled a cat-got-the-cream Cheshire special when she saw me advance toward the bare-bones table in the visiting lounge.

Damn it, Rachel was right. I've been had.

I sighed and sat down, eager to hear what she had to say despite the fact that I felt she'd gotten one over on me.

"Thanks for showing up." She wore the same blindingly bright orange jumpsuit as the other inmates visiting in the room. But somehow she made the standard-issue garb look like haute couture. She'd cinched the material around her waist to highlight its smallness, and the jumpsuit didn't hang in a baggy fashion like those adorning the other two women prisoners present. Her makeup was artfully done, if a bit muted, and her flaxen hair was as flawless as usual. I stared at my dark jeans and kelly green sweater and vowed to try to look a little more glamorous if jailbird Adrienne made me feel so self-conscious. On closer inspection, however, I realized her cool eyes were not as keen and imperious as usual, and her hands shook in a barely perceptible manner.

Adrienne took a deep breath, shifting into pitch mode.

"I need to get out of here." Her perfectly calm, collected visage faltered a bit, and her right brow twitched. "I need your help. You're a lawyer, too, right?"

"Whoa, let's get one thing straight. I'm not here in my capacity as a lawyer." I still had my law license, but I wasn't planning on using it anytime soon. Especially not to help spring Adrienne from the slammer.

"Garrett won't represent me now that he thinks I'm trying to take Summer." Her voice was just panicked enough to draw the attention of a guard, who looked over sharply. Adrienne dropped her voice, finally rattled.

"Um, weren't you encouraging Summer to make an extended visit happen?" I gently removed Adrienne's grasping hand from my wrist.

She sat back, dejected and deflated. "I wanted to arrange to see more of my daughter. Perhaps have her visit for a month in August. I knew Garrett would never go for it."

He has his reasons.

Adrienne bit her lip and looked down at her perfectly preserved French manicure. "I don't expect you to feel sorry for me." She looked up, her icy blue gaze compassionate for once. "My parents were gone before I started college. I didn't know anyone at Quincy College. And then I met Garrett." Her eyes warmed, then shut down. "We were so happy at first. We weren't meant to last beyond college, though, and we should have ended things when he went away to law school." She drew herself up tall in her metal chair and looked me in the eye. "I'm not proud of what I did. He left Harvard for me, to come back to Port Quincy and to take care of me and Summer. But I wasn't in love with him anymore." She winced. "It was overwhelming. I didn't know if I was cut out to be a mother. And then I got a call."

"A call?"

"An invitation to audition for *Silverlake High*. They were looking for an actress to replace Caitlin Quinn. I never told anyone that's why I left. Garrett just thought I flaked out, but I had a plan." Her blue eyes pleaded with me.

A shiver ran down my spine.

How does Adrienne fit in with the show Dakota was on? And Caitlin Quinn died on? Is there a connection?

"It was going to be my big break. I planned to get the part, and it wasn't wishful thinking. Xavier was the director. He later told me I was casting's front-runner. The pay would have been more than enough for me and Summer. I planned to petition for custody." A wistful look graced her lovely face. "I would have gotten it, too."

I shook my head, annoyed. "Judges don't just award custody to the mother because of her gender. You left your daughter, and Garrett was taking care of her."

Adrienne winced at the reminder but went on.

"Strange things are happening again, Mallory. Did you know Caitlin Quinn died on the set of *Silverlake High* in early February? Ginger died on the precise thirteenth anniversary of Caitlin's death."

A cold, clammy chill spread between my shoulder blades.

"After Caitlin died, *Silverlake High* was cancelled. I had no money to get back to Port Quincy, plus my pride was in shambles. I decided to make a go of it in L.A., because if I was invited to try out for a popular show, I banked on there being other roles. But I didn't get anything for a long, long time. I worked on bit jobs, saving up for Summer, and the years slipped by. I'd make it back to Port Quincy to see her for a few days, but it was never enough."

A silver sliver of a tear ran down Adrienne's cheek and she impatiently brushed it away. I felt a frisson of sympathy for Adrienne. And it made me nervous.

The guard came over to collect Adrienne and take her back to her cell.

"I'll see what I can do." I rose from my chair, our already short meeting over.

I was as confused as ever. I hadn't known Adrienne had a connection to Dakota's past. Maybe Adrienne hadn't killed Xavier, but she could have been involved in Caitlin's accident to get the part, desperately doing whatever she could to get a chance for custody of Summer. Adrienne may have been in jail for the wrong crime, but I was glad she was behind bars for now.

Chapter Sixteen

It was time to delve into what had really happened in Los Angeles all those years ago on the set of *Silverlake High*. It shouldn't have mattered, but all roads seemed to lead back to a sound studio in Studio City. It no longer seemed like a coincidence that Dakota's oldest friends had visited her that fateful week thirteen years ago and witnessed a horrific accident. I pictured Leah's round eyes, myopic and scared behind her glasses, as she recounted finding Caitlin Quinn. Something sinister had gone down in L.A., and the repercussions were being felt thirteen years later.

I raced home and brushed past Rachel in my haste to get to my laptop.

"You have to tell me what happened," she sighed, hot on my heels. "What did Adrienne get you to do?"

"I'll tell you when you tell me how your date went with Owen the other day," I needled, earning an exasperated guffaw from my sister.

"I'll never kiss and tell," she airily announced.

I filled her in while my fingers danced across the keys.

"So you think Adrienne murdered Caitlin Quinn to make sure she got the new part on the show?" Rachel's mouth hung open in a little o after she voiced her theory.

"It's possible. She desperately wanted to make more money so she could be secure enough to petition for custody of Summer. But"—I typed in one more search and skimmed some obituaries of Caitlin—"there are other people who had just as good a motive to want Caitlin to go away."

Rachel leaned over my shoulder and we perused several articles about Caitlin's demise. The *Los Angeles Times* article mentioned she'd died from inhaling gas. The article was short and laconic, and it didn't mention whether her death had definitively been caused by an accident, or if foul play had been involved.

"Maybe the police didn't want anyone to know either way," Rachel mused.

"I think you're on to something."

One thing was for sure. The days matched exactly. Ginger Crevecoeur had been murdered at my desk on February fourth, and Caitlin had died on the set of *Silverlake High* precisely thirteen years prior.

"And almost all the same actors were present for both crimes, or at least in town."

"Dakota and Roxanne and Xavier," Rachel said.

"And Ginger, Ellie, Iris, and Leah," I finished. "Though Leah was five years old, so we can count her out as a suspect. But we can add Adrienne to the list."

A stray thought pranced through my brain and I closed my eyes to try to catch it. "Iris said something during the bridesmaid fittings about Caitlin. Something about her being *locked* in a dressing room."

Rachel's eyes went wide. "It's time to call Truman."

We left a message on his voicemail and continued to peruse any and all articles related to Caitlin Quinn's death, and Dakota and Xavier's careers. I added Beau for good measure. The newest articles about Dakota discussed how her star was ascending after over a decade since her rise to fame on *Silverlake High*. She hadn't had many roles in between her critically acclaimed indie films and the teen soap, and I wondered if that was why Roxanne was so desperate to cling to any fame her daughter could get. She probably feared it drying up again, leaving her to become a cleaner once more.

An old *Tennessean* article revealed that Beau was born in Parsippany, New Jersey. His given name was Brian Wright, and he'd eventually changed it to Beau.

"That explains his accent discrepancy," I said with a chuckle. He'd begun his career as a jazz singer, but his first album made at the tender age of sixteen had flopped. He'd moved to Nashville soon after and, with his gorgeous good looks, remade himself as a country star.

We perused Xavier's career next. He'd also made a comeback, far more quickly than Dakota. He'd developed a specialty directing reality shows, most hits, if not somewhat skeevy. He'd worked on

several projects with Adrienne over the years, and
I wondered how long they'd been an item.

Truman finally called back. I gave him the capsule synopsis in a rush of breath.

"Get down here, now." He gruffly hung up and
I raced to the police station adjacent to the jail.
The administrative police quarters were hewn
from similar limestone as the castle jail, but more
staid and traditional. I entered the low-slung
cream building stained with soot from the 1970s
when the glass factory was still running in Port
Quincy and was directed to Truman's office. For
the first time, I stared at the walls, covered in
plaques and pictures of his family. There was his
wife Lorraine on their wedding day, as well as
photographs of Garrett and Summer spanning
the years.

"Spill it, girl detective."

"I can tell you're mad I visited Adrienne," I
stammered. Mad was an understatement. Truman
breathed in and out like a bull ready to charge, so
I rushed on. "But I did get some information that
I think will help your case."

I relayed everything Adrienne had told me. She
hadn't told me to keep the information under
wraps, and I hadn't been meeting in my capacity
as an attorney. It could only help her.

*As long as she didn't murder Caitlin Quinn or attempt
to murder Xavier.*

Truman let out a low whistle when I'd finished.

"Iris's slip of the tongue about that actress being
locked in the dressing room doesn't sound quite
so much like an accident," he mused.

His face turned cloudy again. "Why do people

confide in you?" He shook his head and dragged a hand tiredly through his salt-and-pepper hair. "Don't answer that."

"It's time to call L.A., isn't it." It was a statement, not a question.

"It's time for *me* to call L.A.," Truman corrected, standing up.

"Oh, c'mon. I cracked this case wide open for you!" I stood up too, suddenly indignant.

"What you've done is muddy the waters again." He sighed, relenting. "Fine. You can stay. But not a peep."

He shut his door and called the Los Angeles Police Department. But it was a fruitless mission as he couldn't get ahold of anyone ready to discuss a thirteen-year-old murder, even that of a rising star.

Truman slammed down the phone, frustration rolling from his bearish shoulders in almost palpable waves.

"There is one person we really should be talking to," I said, my voice small.

"Go on."

"One night when she was knitting, Dakota said she thought the show might just end if Caitlin went away."

It was looking like my bride might be the key to the murders, both past and present, finished and attempted.

"I'll have Faith pick her up."

"You have a lot of explaining to do."

Dakota sat pale yet composed in front of Truman. "Am I under arrest?"

I squirmed in my seat, still incredulous that Truman had let me stay for his informal interview.

"If you were under arrest, you'd know it."

Dakota relaxed for a nanosecond, her shoulders sagging in her red cardigan.

"That doesn't mean I'm letting you off the hook."

Dakota sat up sharply again, her metal chair letting out a screech against the old floor tiles as she shimmied closer to the table.

"Caitlin Quinn." Truman let the name hang in the air and said nothing more.

"What about her?" Dakota's voice was a mere whisper.

"I want it all."

Dakota gulped and steadied her hands before her. She was silent for what seemed an eternity but was probably no longer than sixty interminable seconds. Truman waited her out.

"It wasn't an accident. It wasn't a gas leak." Dakota looked down in her lap. "The police didn't release that information." When she raised her violet eyes, they were quivering with tears. "Ginger's murder wasn't original."

"Excuse me?" Truman leaned forward, not understanding.

"Someone borrowed the method." Dakota let out a hysterical yelp that sounded like a stifled sneeze. "Caitlin was locked in a dressing room. With a blue flower arrangement. The vase was filled with bleach and ammonia."

"Murder borrowed, murder blue," Truman muttered.

"Blue was *my* favorite color," Dakota mused. "Used to be, anyway. My fans knew it. Everyone knew it." She wrapped her arms tightly around her middle. "Caitlin was locked in *my* dressing room, not hers." She unceremoniously wiped her nose with the back of her hand before I fetched her a box of tissues. "The flowers were anonymous, not even from a florist. The note with them was addressed to me, too. That chloramine vapor special arrangement was supposed to be for me, not Caitlin." She shivered, the trembling in her shoulders not stopping. "I've lived with the guilt for thirteen long years. I was supposed to be in that dressing room. Caitlin should be alive, not me."

"Who was there that day on the set?"

Truman's voice was calm and monotone. I began to think he was just as good an actor as Dakota, because I could barely detect the fury buried within. But he kept it under wraps, encouraging her to go on. To incriminate herself.

"It was a big mess." Dakota blew her nose and balled up the tissue. "The show was on hiatus while Caitlin held out for more money. She was the undisputed star, though you wouldn't think so if you listened to my mother." She stopped and involuntarily made a face. "The show was behind filming two weeks while Caitlin held her own personal strike. But they opened the set so I could show my friends around and give them a tour." She took a deep breath and threw the tissue in the trash. "Iris brought Ellie and Leah out to visit me, and Ginger came with them too. My mom and Xavier were together then, and they both had the flu."

"What about tryouts to replace Caitlin?" I butted

in. Truman gave me a death glare, but I couldn't help myself.

Dakota screwed up her face as if trying to remember.

"There was one frontrunner, and she'd just tried out the day before. Caitlin was getting nervous they might actually replace her and go on with the show. Ellie had tried out too, but Xavier, the producer, and casting thought this woman was better. Her name was . . ."

"Adrienne."

A look of clarity washed over Dakota and her mouth dropped open. "That's right. I hadn't realized. Adrienne was there too that week, then."

She gathered her thoughts and went on. "Caitlin wasn't supposed to be on set that day. She just swung by as a favor to me to meet my friends. She stayed on while I showed everyone around. I went back to my dressing room to get something, and it was locked. We got maintenance to unlock the door." She shuddered. "Little Leah pushed through first, eager to see Caitlin again. But we were hit with this awful chemical smell and Iris had to drag Leah back out."

The tears had begun anew, coursing down Dakota's face. "There was the most beautiful arrangement of blue flowers you've ever seen, and Caitlin, dead, on the floor. In my dressing room."

Truman asked one more question, not bothering to comfort Dakota. "Who was the last person to see Caitlin alive?"

"Ginger." It came out as a whisper. "I paid for her to go to Dunlap. My mother was against it. Ginger felt she owed me, and I wanted nothing more than to leave the show and just go to school with my friends. I always wondered if Ginger murdered Caitlin to grant my wish of coming home. She felt indebted to me."

Truman's anger finally bubbled over, ash from Mt. Vesuvius before the lava. "Why didn't you say a word of this when we found Ginger?"

"They never found out who killed Caitlin," Dakota sighed. "I didn't want to implicate any of my friends then, and I don't want to implicate them now." She picked at her cuticles, and then looked up, anguish marring her beautiful looks. "I'm so sorry."

I left a stricken Dakota with Truman while he awaited a call from the Los Angeles Police Department. I was anxious to learn whether they'd corroborate her story, but I didn't think Truman would allow me to butt in on his investigation again anytime soon.

At least I know why she hates blue flowers.

Her reaction to Ginger's death now made sense. I hadn't thought Dakota's reaction had been over the top at the time. I couldn't imagine losing someone so close to me in such a bizarre and horrific way. But the added coincidence of Ginger's murder mirroring Caitlin's had obviously resonated with Dakota.

I was torn about her innocence. I drove home on autopilot, while outside my window the dazzling display of Port Quincy's winter wonderland went unappreciated. I wanted to believe Dakota was telling the truth after all these years. But why had she hidden that Ginger died in the same manner as Caitlin, exactly thirteen years ago to the day? And why had Ellie, Iris, Leah, and Roxanne kept quiet, for that matter? I could think of no reason, unless they were somehow complicit in Caitlin Quinn's death. Something terrible had happened in L.A., and they were covering for each other. And now whatever unfinished business had begun thirteen years ago was playing out in present-day Port Quincy.

First, Caitlin was murdered in Dakota's dressing room via chloramine vapor in a blue flower arrangement. Then the modus operandi was borrowed and replicated last week, killing Ginger. And how did poisoning Xavier with bleeding hearts fit in, other than the fact that he was the director for both *Silverlake High* and *I Do*? Maybe he knew something and had realized it, and one of the women had poisoned him.

And we may never know.

Each day I asked for an update on Xavier's condition, and each day was the same. He still languished in a coma, with no promise or hint of awakening. Whoever had wanted to silence Xavier had succeeded.

I didn't want to believe Dakota was guilty, but she seemed to be at the heart of it all. Yet just now with Truman, Dakota's tears had seemed genuine.

She's also an accomplished actress.

I didn't want to admit it, but it was looking more and more like my bride was responsible for her costar Caitlin's death. She'd desperately wanted off *Silverlake High,* and thought the show would end if the lead star Caitlin went away. The question was how far Dakota had been willing to go to make that happen.

Or how badly Adrienne had wanted to get custody of the daughter she'd just abandoned. I didn't want to believe Adrienne could have killed Caitlin to secure her role on *Silverlake High*. But her ambition knew no bounds, and I'd already witnessed her questionable ethics when she wanted to get her way.

And then there was Ellie. She'd wanted to get her mother off her back and had agreed to audition for a role on the teenage soap. Iris was an inveterate nag when it came to pushing her daughters to grab higher and further brass rings. I wondered if the pressure had gotten too intense for Ellie, and she'd gotten rid of Caitlin to improve her chances of landing a role. And Iris herself could have been complicit. I hated to admit it, but it wasn't a stretch to picture Iris locking Caitlin in Dakota's dressing room to improve her daughter's chances. The wild gleam that showed up in her normally soft eyes when she spoke of her daughters' successes wasn't new, and she'd already gone pretty far to make things happen for them.

And Iris wasn't the only crazed stage mother on the scene. Roxanne had been obsessed with Dakota eclipsing Caitlin's fame. She needed *Silverlake High* to go on and may have killed Caitlin to grab the limelight for her daughter and to end Caitlin's strike so the show could resume filming.

And where did Ginger fit in? She'd felt beholden to Dakota since the starlet had paid her tuition fees to the prestigious and expensive Dunlap Academy. She knew her best friend was deeply unhappy and wanted to quit the show and return to Port Quincy. Had Ginger taken her indebtedness too far and helped Dakota out by getting rid of Caitlin?

I shivered as I recalled Ginger's take-charge attitude and unflappability. But just being a confident woman who had gone after what she'd wanted in life didn't make her a killer.

Or did it?

Maybe she had known something, just like Xavier, and that's why she'd been murdered in my office. Or someone had figured out she'd killed Caitlin and murdered Ginger as payback.

The clues were disparate and varied, and they were stacking up quickly. But I couldn't make heads or tails of all the threads. It was like viewing a pointillist painting up too close. I saw each minute piece of evidence, but they all swam together in a jumbled mess of dots. I hoped Truman and Faith could make sense of things before another murder took place.

But it was time to put the sleuthing on the back burner. I shivered as I left downtown and headed east toward Dunlap Academy. I had a wedding to put on—that was, if my bride didn't end up in jail next to Adrienne. A tiny smile ticked up the corner of my mouth as I pictured throwing my first jailhouse wedding, Beau kissing Dakota through the iron bars.

"I can't wait to see what my sister came up with." Ellie shut the door to her new office, once Ginger's, and locked the door firmly behind her. I followed her with frank curiosity through the labyrinth maze of stone hallways and peered into rooms and vestibules.

The medieval fortress motif from the outside continued inside Dunlap Academy. The girls gathered around floor-to-ceiling fireplaces, the rooms we passed alive with chitchat and laughter. We headed up a wide stone stairway toward the dormitories, which appeared more modern than the main structure.

"This wing was added in the 1990s," Ellie explained as the cold stone floor gave way to cushy carpet. "The school has a lot of history, but parents wouldn't send their daughters here without modern amenities." The rooms looked a little posher than the average college dorms with high ceilings, fireplaces, plump upholstered chairs, and rich, dark furniture.

"Leah made a slideshow of memories to play at Dakota and Beau's wedding. She pored over hundreds of photos and selected music to go along with a video." Ellie's face dimmed. "Ginger was going to put it together before the accident."

Interesting choice of words.

Ginger's death had been no accident, and neither had Caitlin's. Yet that's how Ellie seemed to frame the incidents in her mind. I'd kept quiet about my recent whereabouts with Truman and Dakota. I didn't want to tip off Ellie or Iris or anyone else to the fact that they'd probably be hauled in for questioning soon.

We arrived at Leah's door and Ellie called in for her sister. "Mallory's here to see the video," Ellie announced as she pushed open the door to the dorm. Leah must have been hard at work, since she didn't turn around. She wore huge headphones over her ears, and her purple hair was tied up in a jaunty genie ponytail, the bangs spiked and jagged as usual.

Ellie gave me a shrug as Leah continued to feverishly bang away on her keyboard, lost in her own world. I squinted and caught some text about the Italian renaissance.

"Earth to Leah!" Ellie's voice rang out through the small room.

"Oh!" Leah shut her laptop with a loud clap and whirled around in her desk chair. "You two scared me." She placed a hand on her chest and took in a deep breath. "I thought I locked the door, but I guess I forgot. With all the crazy things happening around here, I'm trying to be extra careful."

I don't blame you.

Leah was the only person I was sure wasn't involved in the attempted poisoning and murders of Caitlin, Ginger, and Xavier. Sure, she'd been the first person to discover Caitlin in the dressing room, but she'd only been five at the time. I felt better knowing there was one bridesmaid whom I didn't suspect of murder.

"Tell me what you think. I know Ginger would have done a better job selecting photos, but I did the best I could to honor her." Leah bit her lower lip, a bead of a tear forming in each eye, and held out an iPad.

The slideshow was lovely. Leah had selected photos of both Dakota and Beau from when they were infants all the way up to their courtship. The music complemented the slideshow of photos, several of the songs featuring Beau's greatest hits.

I felt determined to pull off a wonderful day for Dakota and Beau no matter what had happened.

"This is amazing. You did a great job." Ellie pulled her little sister into an impetuous hug. The two women's faces were so similar they could have been twins, not just sisters, had it not been for Ellie's sensible shoulder-length chestnut hair and Leah's punky purple tresses.

"I'll email you a copy," Leah promised as she walked us to the door of her dorm room. We exited and turned to leave when I heard a soft moan emanating from the left.

"What was that?"

Ellie frowned and cocked her head to the side. "The wind does odd things in this building. Sometimes it sounds like sighing. It's probably nothing." She gently nudged me along and we started down the hall.

"No, it sounds like a person." I stopped and held my arm out so Ellie was forced to wait. "Listen."

Ellie ceased walking and frowned, her brows furrowed. "I can't—"

"There it is again!"

The sound was barely perceptible, and it was coming from the door to our right. Ellie's eyes grew wide and she rapped on the door with increasingly panicked knocks.

"Open up—this is the headmistress," she commanded. When no one complied, she withdrew a large master key from her pocket and inserted it in the lock.

She pushed the door open, and there lay Nora Jennings, the daughter of the heart surgeon who'd argued with Ginger, sprawled on the floor. She was facedown, her limbs all akimbo, a syringe at her side.

"Call nine-one-one." Ellie sprang into action, rolling the student onto her back and feeling for a pulse.

"She's still with us, but just barely."

Chapter Seventeen

Ellie performed CPR while I held Nora's hand and spoke in low and urgent tones.

"Stay with us. Don't leave now." An extra shiver ran down my spine as I recalled Adrienne saying the same thing to a prostrate Xavier. People around me were dropping like flies and there was nothing I could do.

The ambulance soon wailed up the long, curving drive to the boarding school, and by the time the paramedics reached us, there was a horde of girls crowding around the door to watch Ellie's frantic ministrations. Leah stood at the front, a stream of tears coursing down her face.

"Get back! Everyone out of the way." The paramedics shoved into the room with a stretcher and worked for a few harried minutes trying to stabilize the increasingly lifeless Nora. She moaned as they loaded her limp body onto the stretcher, her arms dangling off the sides.

The sea of girls parted like a school of minnows

to let the emergency responders take away their fellow student. Leah was beside herself. "It's happening again. First Caitlin, then Ginger and Xavier, and now Nora." She sobbed in Ellie's arms as stricken students stood motionless in the hall, dazed and shocked for the second time in two weeks. Only this time they weren't wearing their Winter Ball gowns, just their Dunlap Academy plaid uniforms.

"It's not time to jump to conclusions," Ellie said in a stricken tone, "but this doesn't look like murder." She gestured with her pointy heel to the syringe on the floor. "I didn't know Nora had a drug problem, but this could be an overdose."

A flutter of recognition flittered though my brain. I was transported back to Dunlap the day before the Winter Ball. Ginger had tried to meet with Nora's father Sterling Jennings, but he'd called off their meeting in a huff when she'd been mere minutes late.

What if Ginger suspected Nora had a drug problem, and that's why she wanted to meet with Nora's father?

But Ginger was conveniently gone, and we couldn't ask her if that was why she'd called the meeting. I bent down to take a closer look at the syringe.

"Don't touch it," Ellie warned, stepping away from her sister.

"I won't," I replied, crouching down. "I just don't see anything else around here that she could have been injecting." Nora's room was fairly neat, her shoes lined up in a row under the wide bay window, her books piled in a tidy stack on her desk. I didn't dare peek into her closet—Truman would have my head for playing unauthorized detective. But it seemed suspicious that there was a syringe and nothing else on the floor.

I bent in half and glanced under the bed, expecting to find the contraband there. But it was as neat as the rest of the room. Nora hadn't even used the space for extra storage, and it was devoid of dust bunnies or errant clutter.

But something caught my eye: a glint of a sequin on the carpet. I craned my head, and saw the source of the decoration. Duct-taped to the bottom of Nora's bed was what looked like Ginger's tablet, the same one she'd dressed in a shiny navy sequin cover the night of the Winter Ball. The tablet that Truman had expected to find near her body but had been conspicuously missing.

My heart pounding, I called Truman.

"I'm already on my way."

While Xavier slumbered on, Nora awoke the next day. I welcomed the news the girl would live, although she'd probably spend the rest of her life behind bars.

"She denied she killed Ginger," Truman said over the cup of coffee I handed him. His eyes were red and puffy, and his shoulders hunched with exhaustion. But he cracked a guarded smile after he took his first sip. "It just feels good to finally get a break in this crazy case."

"And even though she killed Ginger, I didn't

want her to die," I said. "I'm so glad Ellie and I heard her in her room yesterday."

"You got there just in time to save her." Truman solemnly set the cup down in its saucer. "She probably didn't mean to take that much heroin. Then again," he mused, "maybe it was a suicide attempt over her guilt for killing Ginger." He shook his head.

"She hid her habit well. It couldn't have been easy for her to keep her addiction a secret among all those students."

Truman let out a snort. "Oh, she didn't hide it. She advertised it, if anything."

I felt my eyebrows shoot up, and Truman went on. "She was dealing drugs at school, not just taking them. She'd already gotten kicked out of one boarding school for doing it. Dunlap was her last chance. Her father pulled some serious strings to get her in."

"So Ginger knew to watch out for her."

Truman nodded. "The tablet you found under Nora's bed was Ginger's. Ginger wanted to meet with Sterling Jennings to discuss his daughter's expulsion. When Sterling skipped out on their meeting, Ginger must have decided to deal with it after the Winter Ball." Truman shook his head with a heavy expression dimming his features. "That's probably why Ginger called me, as a courtesy, the day before she died. She wanted to tell me about Nora's dealing. I wish I'd been in the office to take that call instead of testifying in court."

"You couldn't have known," I soothed. "And you certainly had no idea a student would take matters into her own hands and murder the headmistress to keep from getting expelled." I shuddered to realize the mousy, shy Nora was a murderess.

"The last piece of the puzzle was trying to figure out how Nora replicated Caitlin Quinn's murder in Los Angeles."

"Leah must have told her about it," I mused.

Truman nodded. "Leah was the one who found Caitlin, and she must have gossiped about the event to her friend. It seemed like the perfect opportunity to Nora. Staging Ginger's death at the Winter Ball when some of the same people who were present in Los Angeles thirteen years ago were together again in Port Quincy would make it seem like Nora was the last person to perpetrate the crime."

I nursed my own cup of coffee and tried to wrap my head around it all. I had to admit I was shocked Helene wasn't behind Ginger's death. "I hate to say it, but I thought Helene Pierce would be prosecuted one day for Ginger's death." She'd been so furious about Ginger's plans to make the school coed that I'd have bet the farm on her as the headmistress's murderer.

Truman leaned back and chuckled, the first sign of mirth I'd seen from him in days. "Helene may be your arch enemy, but I can't see her as a murderess." He grew thoughtful. "I couldn't say the same for Iris Barnes, though. That woman would stop at nothing to advance her daughters."

I was glad that Iris hadn't killed Ginger to get her daughter her position as headmistress. An errant thought skittered through my brain.

"What about Ginger's secret boyfriend? Did you ever find out his identity?"

Truman shook his head a bit dismissively. "No. We thought we'd finally figure it out when we recovered Ginger's tablet. But he used a Google account that we haven't been able to trace yet." He sighed wearily. "I'm ready to retire that angle, since I'm almost certain we'll prove Nora murdered Ginger." He cocked his head in thought. "Some people just like their privacy for privacy's sake alone. We may never know who Ginger's boyfriend was."

Unless it's Owen, I thought to myself.

But Truman was ready to put the case of the murder of Ginger Crevecoeur to bed.

"To solving part of the mystery," he said drolly, and held his delicate cup of coffee aloft.

"To solving the mystery." I clinked cups with the chief of police, the buttercup-covered china ringing out a hollow sound.

I just wish I could be as sure as he is.

The day of the wedding rehearsal dawned fair and bright. Snow still covered the ground, but the sky was a clear, cloudless cornflower blue. The air was frigid enough to singe my lungs with each breath I took, and thankfully I'd be spending most of the day in Iris and Ellie's tropical greenhouse, setting up for the rehearsal dinner.

"It's Friday the thirteenth," Rachel mused. She straightened a plate on one of the charming wrought-iron tables we'd be using to serve dinner and stood back to admire her handiwork. We'd transformed the lush greenhouse into an elegant party space by ferrying china, linens, and stemware from Thistle Park. Iris and Ellie bustled about the space setting up the remaining lacy metal tables we'd rented for the occasion.

"I'm not usually superstitious," I said. "But I'd like to chance it and say that we've dealt with enough for this wedding. I hope our luck is finally turning, despite the inauspicious date." I placed tiny butterfly name placards on each place setting. Dakota and Beau had suggested the design in memory of Ginger, and I'd happily obliged.

Rachel and I oversaw the staff we'd hired to help prepare and serve the food. Everything was in place and ready to go. I stepped back with a smile and observed the fruits of our handiwork. The greenhouse was at once cozy and elegant, dazzling and welcoming.

"I can't wait to transform our greenhouse into something just as wonderful," I gushed to Rachel. For now, the greenhouse looked like the aftermath of a crime scene that it was, the bleeding hearts trampled on and pulled up, roots exposed and dying.

Ginger's killer will be brought to justice, but what about Caitlin's killer and Xavier's attempted murderer?

I pushed away the dark thought and nervously surveyed the dessert and coffee set up for the party.

"Uh-oh." Several brass carts, ornate and shining, stood at the edges of the party space, bearing antique teacups. Carafes of hot water stood at the ready for the culmination of dinner. The tea itself was housed in adorable, delicate metal cages fashioned as birds, each one nestled at the bottom of a teacup. Guests could each take a cup and pour in hot water, rather than using a teapot. It was a charming display, but the loose leaves made me nervous. They were the perfect vehicle for poisonous plants.

"Is this the best idea, in light of what happened to Xavier?"

Rachel rolled her eyes. "I found these tea cages in the butler's pantry. They haven't been used in ages and they're perfect for this party!" She placed a hand on my arm, her face annoyed. "Quit being the Safety Czar," she chided.

I blanched at the title she'd given me last fall when I'd insisted on placing rather unsightly fire extinguishers in each guest's room.

"I don't care how cute they are. I don't think I'll be having any tea."

Rachel shrugged and got back to work. "Suit yourself."

An hour later and the rehearsal dinner was in full swing. Dakota and Beau mingled with the forty or so guests, their faces animated and lively. Rachel gave Beau a wide berth, and the two of us put out small fires all evening. I chastised myself for worrying about the state of Dakota and Beau's union. They actually seemed like a couple in love this evening. Beau was attentive and doting, and Dakota gazed at her fiancé with tender glances.

Maybe I was wrong about them.

Maybe they would have a fulfilling marriage and

many years together ahead. Or perhaps my hunch about them before had been correct, and they had some kind of arrangement for an open relationship. I didn't think Dakota would be into that, but they were the quintessential power couple. Perhaps they were willing to preserve their engagement and marriage at all costs.

Stop being so cynical.

Beau's head jerked up, and I followed his gaze. His eyes seemed to slide over the curves of a pretty waitress, and I felt my stomach contract.

Nope, I'd been right. Dakota and Beau had fooled me again, like the entertainers they were. I predicted a rocky road ahead for the bride and groom. An uneasy feeling stole over me. I didn't take personal responsibility for the couples whose weddings I planned, of course, but I wanted the best for them. I didn't feel like I was merely throwing them a big party. Sometimes I felt like I was launching the public face of their marriage. I wanted to feel good about it. And I felt anything but regarding Dakota and Beau.

"Penny for your thoughts." Owen appeared at my side looking just as miserable as I was sure I did.

"I hope they're happy," I mused.

Owen appeared pained, his hipster good looks dampened and muted. His whiskey-colored eyes were sad behind the chunky frames, and even his beard seemed droopy today. It was as if he were going to launch into an early "if anyone thinks these two should not be joined" speech.

Beau chose that moment to amble up to us, his

bolo tie in place and his ten-gallon hat a jaunty, formal black. He appeared to gloat somewhat, and clapped Owen on the back a little too hard.

"I can't believe that gorgeous gal is mine," he opined, his counterfeit twang out in full syrupy force. He sent Dakota an exaggerated wink and dug his hands in his pockets, rocking back and forth in his cowboy boots. His breath was redolent with alcohol. I wondered how much he'd had to drink.

"Take care of her," Owen gruffly muttered. He snapped his suspenders in suppressed anger and his eyes scraped the floor.

"Oh, I will," Beau said with a triumphant smile. "You can count on it."

"Honey, let's go." Dakota materialized at her fiancé's side, her face grim. She took in Owen's discomfort and tried to put him out of his misery. "Beau, it's time for you to give a speech, remember?"

"Of course." Beau planted a possessive pucker on his wife-to-be and ambled up to the raised dais at the front of the greenhouse to thank the assembled guests for coming. He reached into his pocket and extricated a note card, clearing his throat. A slim piece of metal fell from his pocket and clattered to the ground next to his cowboy boots.

"I want to thank y'all—"

"Oh, no." Dakota's gasp was loud enough to direct all eyes from Beau to her. She stared in horror at his feet as if she'd just seen a rat.

But it was much worse.

There, at Beau's feet, rested a shiny red butterfly clip.

The kind Ginger always wore.

A pin dropping, or a butterfly clip as it were, could be heard in the greenhouse.

"Now, this isn't what it looks like." Beau's face turned as beet red as the scarlet clip, and he bent down, his inebriated state making it hard to pick up the delicate, winged hair decoration. He fumbled around and swore, finally scraping the scrap of red metal into his palm.

The room began to buzz with the chatter of anxious and confused guests.

Owen finally found his voice.

"You killed Ginger, didn't you."

Chapter Eighteen

Dakota's hand fluttered to her mouth in disbelief, the enormous diamond on her ring finger glittering in the greenhouse's bright grow lights.

"I gave Ginger a set of those clips for her birthday last year." Her chest rose and fell as she dragged in ragged breaths. For the first time in a while, she didn't seem to be performing. I watched her transform, phoenix-like, and she went from shocked to chagrined to horrified to supremely angry. Her words were tinged with pure, white-hot rage.

"Beauregard Wright, you have a lot of explaining to do." Dakota's assembled guests swiveled their heads from her anguished visage to Beau to take in his response.

"It isn't what you think." The folksy affect was gone, his New Jersey accent back in full force. Beau rocked unsteadily on his cowboy boots and took a step back. "I can explain."

The din of the forty or so guests got louder. Beau stared at the mutinous crowd and gulped.

"I'll be right back." He executed a wobbly hop from the edge of the dais and shuffled through the doorway to the side greenhouse Rachel and I had used as a prep room.

"Time to text Truman," I murmured to my sister. *Perhaps Nora didn't murder Ginger after all.*

"See!" Rachel was glowing with I-told-you-so vigor. "Maybe now everyone will finally believe that I didn't hit on that no-good, rotten cheating bastard."

"Let's keep an eye on him." I cocked my head in the direction of the prep room, where Beau was having a heated argument with Dakota. She paced in a circle around him like a tiger, throwing up her hands and gesticulating wildly. The counterfeit country star cringed and cowered in the face of her wrath. Dakota finally tore at her left hand and sent her engagement ring sailing into a koi pond, the large stone sending up a small geyser of water upon impact.

"I never want to see you again!" Her voice was loud enough to resound through the greenhouse. Beau slunk away from his fiancé, choosing to hide behind a small ornamental lemon tree. Dakota whipped around and left him in the side greenhouse, storming off to get some air. Ginger's butterfly clip lay on the dais like a scarlet red letter.

Dakota and Beau's guests seemed to be enjoying the show. They'd arrived this evening to celebrate the impending marriage of the starlet and the singer, but now had been treated to fireworks of an unexpected variety.

"Where in the heck is Truman?" I stared at

my cell phone in annoyance. "He needs to get here *now.*"

The noise level in the greenhouse grew to epic proportions. There was a crescendo of gossip much like a horde of mosquitoes buzzing around the glass structure.

Truman finally parted the small sea of guests and reached my side.

"I came as soon as I could." He seemed mildly annoyed. "What is it now?"

"*That.*" I pointed to the dais and the butterfly clip. "That barrette belonged—"

"To Ginger." Truman swore. "How did it make its way to that stage?"

Rachel and I filled him in on Beau's aborted speech and spilling of the clip, and Truman rushed off into the farthest depths of the greenhouse jungle in search of Beau.

"He's getting away!" Truman shouted from the back of the greenhouse as a loud clatter announced a scuffle. Rachel and I raced to the end of the glass space and saw Beau kick a prostrate Truman on the side. The chief of police moaned and struggled to get up.

"Hasta la vista." Beau swept up his hat and placed it on his head before slinking toward the door.

"I don't think so." Rachel pulled a thin coil of leather from her purse and unfolded it with a snap. It was the whip, and she crashed it down through the air, snaring Beau by the ankle. She gave a sharp tug, with all her might, and he landed in a heap.

Truman crawled over and cuffed Beau behind

the back, limping and leading him out past a cheering group of partygoers.

"I owe you an apology." Dakota appeared at Rachel's side, a sheepish look stealing over her exhausted and shell-shocked face. "I can handle his cheating." Her voice was low and hollow. "I've dealt with that before, and I've even come to expect it." A pool of tears collected in her famous violet eyes and spilled over, twin rivulets dampening her cheeks. "But I can't handle the fact that he murdered my best friend."

Rachel reached out and put her arm around Dakota. Ellie put her arm around her friend as well.

I rolled up the whip with a smirk on my face and deposited it back in my sister's purse.

"I introduced Beau and Ginger a year ago." Dakota shook her head. "In the space of an hour I've gone from mourning Ginger to finally recognizing her betrayal with Beau. It all fits now." A knowing cast came over her face. "Beau went on a few trips with his friends, and it was always at a time when Ginger was unavailable. They must have been seeing each other." She gulped and accepted the tissue Rachel handed her.

"I thought Beau flew in on the red eye that first day we filmed for *I Do*. I arrived in Pittsburgh the night before. He probably arrived the night before too, on a separate flight, and just pretended to come in the next day."

"That explains the two wineglasses at Ginger's house," I muttered. "Beau lied and flew in a day earlier, and spent the evening with Ginger."

"And it explains why Ginger was so secretive

about her new man." Ellie shook her head. "I'm so sorry, Dakota."

The actress drew herself up to her full height and wiped the tears from her eyes. "There's only one good thing that's come of all this." She offered us a shaky smile. "I won't be marrying Beau tomorrow."

"Amen to that." Ellie returned Dakota's tenuous smile with one of her own, and the two friends set off to comfort Roxanne. The would-be mother of the bride seemed more upset about Dakota's broken engagement than the bride herself. Roxanne sat at a table, her head in her hands, sobbing as if the world were ending.

"At least Ginger's memorial tomorrow will get to take center stage," I said to Rachel. "It'll get the proper dignity befitting it, with no wedding celebration immediately afterward."

"If a woman who cheated with her best friend's fiancé deserves any dignity," Rachel sniffed.

"True. But she didn't deserve to die." I pictured Ginger slumped over my desk the night of the Winter Ball and drew in a sharp breath. It was a vision I'd never scrub from my brain.

"Why do you think Beau killed her?" Rachel shuddered and drew the pretty metallic pink sweater she'd donned for the rehearsal dinner closer around her shoulders.

"I think he really needed this marriage to Dakota," I theorized. "His star is fading, and hers is ascending." I felt my mouth twist down in a disapproving frown. "Ginger may have threatened the golden goose, his marriage to Dakota, so Beau took her out." A wave of disgust crested and crashed over me. "He must have been the one sending her the bouquets of flowers. He's been cheating on Dakota for over a year, and he thought he'd have his cake and eat it too. His relationship with Ginger, his marriage to Dakota, and a revived career as the cherry on top."

"I hope I broke his ankle," Rachel spat.

Owen was now comforting Dakota, his arms around her in an embrace that plainly announced to all his romantic intentions. Rachel shrugged and turned to get a long-awaited cup of tea.

"Are you okay with this?" I tilted my head in the direction of Dakota and Owen, wondering for the umpteenth time how my sister's date with the foundation owner had gone.

Rachel beamed, a peaceful look on her pretty face. "I spent the night with Owen," she said, taking in my shocked face, "just *talking*." She giggled and took a sip of tea. "He's an honorable guy. Iris is right—he never got over Dakota. He wants the best for her." My sister took in my surprised face and laughed. "Owen may be the only guy who ever got away." Rachel seemed wistful that her wiles hadn't worked on Owen, but if she was right about him pining for Dakota, she'd never really had a chance.

I'd been wrong about Owen's involvement with Ginger. I blushed thinking of how I'd basically accused him of being her killer to anyone who would listen. My instincts weren't always correct, and I needed to remember that. Maybe it was time I stuck to wedding planning rather than sleuthing.

The party bizarrely went on into the night. Guests who'd watched the catastrophic blowup of Dakota and Beau's engagement now congratulated the actress on avoiding her marriage. I groaned as I thought of the carriage house and the props that awaited us there for Dakota and Beau's wedding that wasn't to be. We'd ordered hundreds of silk flowers in every shade of pink, red, cream, and white imaginable. Tablecloths in magenta and petal pink awaited in neat piles for us to spread out and top with a feast of gourmet comfort food. Rachel's peanut butter chocolate cake was a work of art that now wouldn't see the light of day. Hundreds of glittery snowflakes were to be hung later tonight from the carriage house ceiling. And it was all for naught. There would be no wedding. It was the first wedding I'd planned that wouldn't go off. I'd even managed to make my jettisoned wedding to Keith happen for someone else, and I found myself growing a little wistful.

I made my way over to the tea station, admiring Rachel's use of the antique bird tea cages. They were a hit with the guests, and I was glad she'd found them in the butler's pantry and put them to good use.

I selected a tea cage labeled DARJEELING and poured hot water from the carafe over the trapped leaves. The tea smelled heavenly, but I paused before I took a sip.

"This is a great party." Owen sidled up to me, his grin infectious. The spring had returned to his hipster-booted step.

"All's well that ends well," I mused. We clinked teacups and I started to take a drink, then stopped.

"What's wrong?" Owen asked. "You don't like the tea?"

I shook my head. "I just think I shouldn't get caffeinated. It's been a crazy day, and I want to make sure I sleep tonight." It was near midnight, and a caffeinated cup of tea wasn't the best idea.

"You can have mine," Owen gallantly offered, proffering his cup. "It's chamomile, and I haven't even taken a sip yet. I promise."

I thanked him for the herbal tea and took a grateful gulp, the hot liquid soothing after the frantic and frankly freakish day.

"I just have to ask you one thing," I blurted out. "You and Ginger . . . you were never an item?"

Owen tipped his head back and roared with laughter, his glossy auburn hair falling onto his forehead. "Nope. She was my best friend. We really were the four musketeers, me and Dakota and Ellie and Ginger. But I never dated her."

Owen's effervescent laughter faded.

"Are you okay?"

He realized even before I did, from the look on my face, that something was wrong.

My vision began to swim, the vivid tropical colors of the greenhouse plants swirling together in a dizzy kaleidoscope. My heart rate accelerated, the thunderous pounding in my chest like the hooves of a hundred racehorses. The blood rushed in my ears and I was falling, falling, falling.

"Mallory!"

It all went black.

Chapter Nineteen

"You're lucky to be alive."

Rachel held my hand as I lay in my hospital bed.

Dakota and Beau's engagement party had gone out with a bang, or so I was told. I wasn't conscious for the end of it. But I did start to come to in the breakneck ambulance ride from the Barnes's nursery.

I'd arrived at the McGavitt-Pierce Memorial Hospital in record time and promptly had my stomach pumped.

"You were breathing all funny," Rachel went on, twin tracks of tears staining her face. She brushed them and a few streaks of magenta eye makeup away. She gulped and sniffled. "Iris was screaming that it was probably belladonna, since that's the only plant in the nursery that's poisonous enough to cause a reaction that quickly."

The hospital had admitted me and administered physostigmine on the hunch Iris was correct. I wouldn't feel like myself for some time. My doctor wanted me to remain in the hospital for observation, and I was happy to oblige. I was certainly safer in the hospital than I would be roaming the streets of Port Quincy, or trying to plan a wedding for a couple and a bridal party in which nearly every member was a potential murder suspect. I rubbed my aching head and tried to make sense of it all.

"But the wedding!" I rocketed up in bed, causing my heart rate alarms to beep in clanging annoyance. I'd forgotten it was tomorrow.

How in the heck am I going to pull this off?

A nurse popped her head in my room as Rachel gently pushed me back to my pillow and the alarm abated.

"Don't let her get too excited," the nurse warned my sister.

Rachel gave me a sympathetic yet incredulous look. "Did the poison affect your memory, too? There isn't going to be a wedding, Mallory."

Oh yeah.

It all came rushing back. The clip falling from Beau's pocket as he moved to make a speech at the rehearsal dinner, and Dakota telling him off, once and for all.

I rubbed the bridge of my nose and closed my eyes.

"Someone tried to murder me." My voice sounded small and scared. "But *why?*"

Rachel clasped my hand. "Maybe the killer thinks you know something."

It was possible. I'd run my theories by too many people, apparently, in my quest for justice for Ginger and Xavier. I could have tipped the killer off that I was onto them. Although it must have been inadvertent, because other than Beau killing his lover Ginger, which I was pretty sure of, the rest of the crimes were a mystery. Someone had murdered Caitlin Quinn thirteen years ago and poisoned Xavier this week. And we were no closer to catching the perpetrator of either crime.

A happy thought skittered through my brain. "I don't think I was meant to drink that cup of tea with the belladonna, Rach." I clued her in on my cup switcheroo with Owen mere seconds before I'd taken a near-fatal swig.

"So Owen was just being gallant and offered you his cup." Rachel nearly swooned. She may have been okay with his unrequited love for Dakota, but my sister was still somewhat smitten with the philanthropist hipster.

"Fair enough. But if the belladonna wasn't meant for me, why poison Owen?" I wished I had my legal pad to sketch out the list of suspects. Rachel used her sister sixth sense and bent to her side to hold my purse aloft.

"You brought my bag. You're the best sister ever."

Rachel returned my weary grin. She pulled out a yellow legal pad with a flourish but gently batted away my hands. "Uh-uh, I'll write out the suspects this time. You need to rest."

I acquiesced and leaned back into the anemic hospital pillows. Rachel perched on a chair next to me, pen at the ready.

"First, there's Beau. He already murdered Ginger, so we know he has it in him to kill someone." I shivered.

And his next victim was almost me.

"And what's his motive?" Rachel busily scratched away on the yellow paper.

"He was probably jealous that Dakota still seems to be in love with Owen." Jealousy could make a person do irrational things, even commit murder.

"But all he had to do was keep it together for one more day," Rachel mused. She put down her pen. "If Beau hadn't dropped Ginger's clip, they'd be settling in for their last night as an affianced couple. And then tomorrow they'd seal the deal."

"That's true." I frowned. "But even if they got married, that might not stop Dakota from leaving Beau someday to be with Owen. Or maybe Beau thought she'd call off the wedding at the last minute? She was showing signs of cold feet."

"And Beau's music isn't as popular as it was. He only puts out greatest-hits albums," Rachel chimed in. "He needs this marriage to Dakota."

Dakota's star was rocketing through the stratosphere with her string of acclaimed indie roles, while Beau's was definitely dimming. Their union had been as much about business as it was about love or affection. I nodded as my sister jotted it down.

"Beau had just as much access to the belladonna as we all did. And he had access to the plant encyclopedia in the library with the page marked for the belladonna entry." I remembered the day I'd reached out to brush the soft, mauve-belled plants with the lustrous black berries and had been firmly rebuked by Iris, and how I'd later marked the page.

"Well, if he did it, that would be convenient. He's probably in the Port Quincy jail right now being booked for Ginger's murder. Ooh!" Rachel set aside the pen with a clatter and it rolled off the legal pad. "Beau disappeared for a few minutes before he rubbed his impending wedding in Owen's face. Maybe he was doctoring Owen's tea then?"

I nodded at my sister's reasoning. It was looking like Beau had probably inadvertently poisoned me.

"Although . . ."

"There's still Ellie," I finished for my sister. "She's obviously in love with Owen despite their broken engagement."

"And it's her family's nursery. Maybe she put too much belladonna in the tea and was hoping Owen would drink it close to the end of the rehearsal dinner, go home, and not wake up."

We both were silent for a few beats as we realized that could have been my fate.

"Maybe Ellie was secretly despondent that Owen was still holding a candle for Dakota," I suggested.

"But then why didn't Ellie just go after Dakota?" Rachel had a point.

"That's true," I admitted with a frown. "That would make more sense, but nothing about this wedding has made much sense at all. And if we're considering Ellie as a suspect in my—I mean Owen's would-be poisoning, then we have to consider Iris, too."

Rachel retrieved the fallen pen and scribbled some more on the legal pad. "Iris couldn't have been happy that Owen broke her daughter's heart. Especially because he was still pining after Dakota, who was always besting her daughter. But then again, why didn't Iris just go after Dakota herself, freeing Owen for Ellie?"

"And what if"—my voice grew small—"the poisoner is Dakota herself?"

Rachel's green eyes grew wide, and she added Dakota to the list of suspects. "Dakota could have wanted Owen all to herself."

"And she could have thought that once she married Beau, Owen might go back to Ellie. And she couldn't let that happen."

"Because if she can't have Owen, no one can." Rachel shivered.

My head was swimming and eddying with a horrible host of never-ending suspects. "And if we have to consider Dakota, we need to consider Roxanne." I paused to press the palms of my hands against my eyes. My throbbing headache had returned, and I wasn't sure how much longer I could play murder detective with my sister.

"I should go," Rachel declared. She stood and started to tuck the legal pad back into my bag.

"No!" My voice was louder than I'd meant it to be. "Let's finish this." I gulped. "Before someone else ends up dead."

"Okay." Rachel reluctantly perched on the chair. "Roxanne. She wanted Dakota to marry Beau more than Dakota herself, it seemed."

"To enhance her daughter's brand," I said with disgust. "She knew her daughter was still in love with Owen."

A shiver of knowledge doused my nerves in icy water. This line of thinking seemed more plausible.

"She'd been deathly afraid in the past of her cash-cow daughter throwing in the towel on acting and moving back to Port Quincy permanently," I breathed out in a somber tone. "Maybe she wanted to remove him from the equation once and for all."

"Owen kind of looked like he was about to make

one of those 'speak now or forever hold your peace' kind of speeches tonight," Rachel agreed.

"We're forgetting one thing though." I stopped my sleuthing and my mouth broke open in what felt like a cheek-splitting yawn. "What if Owen meant to poison me?"

It was the simplest explanation, and the only one we'd yet to consider.

"Why?" Rachel was as flummoxed by this possibility as I was.

"It all goes back to where we started." I yawned again. "He might think I know something that I don't even know I do."

"Well"—Rachel smiled mischievously—"Truman will probably have this sorted out in no time. The camerawoman was wandering around all night filming. Maybe she caught whoever put the poison in Owen's cup on film."

The thought cheered me. Maybe this debacle of a wedding show would soon be behind us, the murderers and perpetrators all neatly ensconced in the Port Quincy jail.

But then I remembered Dakota and my spirits dimmed. "How is Dakota taking her breakup with Beau?"

"She'll be all right." Rachel waved her wrist in an offhand manner and started to pack up my legal pad.

A wisp of a horrible thought danced through my brain.

"Rachel. What if Dakota knew Beau was stepping out on her with Ginger?"

"And Dakota killed her?" A knowing look stole over my sister's pretty features, darkening them.

"She is a phenomenal actress," I continued. "And Nora is denying she killed Ginger. If my best friend were canoodling with my fiancé, I'd go nuts too."

"Ahem."

The nurse was back. She cleared her throat and offered us a not unkind smile. "It's time you got some rest." Her voice was warm, but she also meant business.

"Thanks for visiting, sis."

Rachel bent down to give me a bone-crushing hug, her perfume redolent of jasmine and cupcakes and roses. "Anytime."

"Is it too late for a visit?" Garrett's gorgeous face broke out into a relieved grin as he crossed the small hospital room in a few large steps. "Thank God you're awake, Mallory."

"See you soon, Mall. Promise to sleep? No more sleuthing?" My sister raised her perfectly shaped brows in expectation. I crossed my fingers beneath the white blanket and solemnly nodded.

Rachel slipped from the room and my boyfriend sat on the bed.

"I thought I'd lost you when I heard what had happened." He brushed a curl from my forehead and ran his finger down the side of my face to my chin.

"I'm going to be fine," I promised. A well of emotion crested and crashed, and I found myself brushing away a set of tears.

"I love you, Mallory."

"I love you too."

The exhaustion of the day finally caught up with me, and I closed my eyes.

* * *

An hour later, I awoke to a nurse poking and prodding my arm. She murmured an apology and explained she was getting a blood sample.

"Just keep resting, sweetie," she counseled as she left the room.

Yeah, right.

I felt safe from the marauding murderers of Port Quincy all locked up in my hospital room, but there was no way I'd be getting rest anytime soon. A steady stream of nurses and orderlies trooped up to my bed at regular intervals to read my vitals and make sure I was okay. I was grateful for their care, but I also needed some sleep.

"You're awake!" Dakota peeked her shining red head into the room and let out a squeal of relief. "I had to see for myself that you're all right." She placed a hand on her heart and sat down in the chair.

I smiled at the would-be bride.

I don't really think she's a killer.

"I'm just glad you're going to recover," she gushed as Roxanne joined us. She gave me a cool nod as she settled into the other guest chair against the wall. The big bag at her feet yapped and rustled, and I let out a weak giggle.

"You snuck in Miss Pixie," I guessed.

Roxanne broke into a rueful smile and let the Shih Tzu out of the bag. Pixie hopped up into Dakota's lap and gave a doggie grin.

"I'm lucky the poison took effect so quickly," I mused, watching Dakota and Roxanne's faces carefully. "The person who put it in Owen's cup probably thought he would get a little woozy, go home, and never wake up."

Dakota gasped and her hand, sans diamond ring, flew up to cover her plump lips. Pixie picked up on her stress and let out a little bark. "It was that rotten, no-good bastard Beau, I bet." Her accusation came out in a heated staccato hiss.

"We should let Mallory rest," Roxanne admonished.

That's the best thing I've heard all day.

Dakota gave me a hug and started to leave the room. "I'm going to go see Xavier, Mom. Meet you later in the car?"

"He's awake?" I gasped and tried to sit up, then thought better of it when the roaring headache gripping my temples accelerated.

"He awoke earlier today, and he's getting discharged tonight." Dakota beamed at finally having some good news to report, and she slipped out the door, Pixie ensconced in the big bag on her shoulder.

Roxanne gave her daughter a regal nod and remained in her chair.

We were alone.

"I should be more upset that my daughter isn't getting married to Beau, but perhaps it's for the best," she mused.

"Um, he probably murdered Ginger," I said, my voice high with incredulity. "And at the very least, he was having an affair with her." My blood pressure began to rise, as evidenced by the louder beeping of one of the monitors.

Roxanne stood and took a step toward my bed. A cold wash of panic stole over me.

"Sleep well, Mallory."

She was peeved, a barely suppressed current of anger running through her like an electrical charge.

I wish Dakota had left Pixie behind.

Sleep was the last thing on my mind, now that I'd taken an hour's catnap, basking in the glow of Garrett's declaration that he loved me. Now my mind was recharged and racing.

Fat chance I'll be able to sleep until you leave this room.

A stray thought blew through my mind like a snowflake in a blizzard.

"You have some experience with that, I've heard."

"Excuse me?" Roxanne stiffened and stopped her exit from my room.

"Getting people to sleep. I know you used to drug Dakota with sleeping pills." My voice was stronger and clearer than I felt. I wanted to keep up the pretense that I was recovering more quickly than I was.

A jolt of alarm marred Roxanne's preternaturally smooth, Botoxed face.

"Is that a threat, Mallory?" Her smile was cold and hard. She crossed the room and shut the door.

A bead of sweat trickled down my neck.

Chapter Twenty

"You killed Caitlin, didn't you."

It was a declaration, not a question.

Roxanne didn't blanch, but simply cocked her head to one side. "You don't know what you're talking about, my dear." But a cold cast of clarity shone in her eyes.

"You needed *Silverlake High* to go on," I mused aloud.

Where is a nurse when you need one?

Surely it was only a matter of time before one buzzed into my room.

Right?

"It was a shame Caitlin had to die." Roxanne's remark was flippant and sent a chill coursing through my limbs.

"You spend your daughter's money like water." It hit me. "You've been embezzling from Dakota, haven't you? That's why you needed this marriage to happen. So Dakota wouldn't know you've been bilking her out of her money."

I had finally gotten to her. Accusing her of murdering Caitlin hadn't shaken her, but the accusation about money had rattled her to her core.

"You were probably mismanaging your daughter's money even back during *Silverlake High*," I whispered.

"Caitlin was holding out," Roxanne spat. "She was trying to get more money for herself when my Dakota was the real star of the show."

"So you sped up the process to get rid of Caitlin once and for all. But you made a mistake. You didn't count on the network canceling the show upon the death of its true star."

Roxanne shook her head, her silver earrings jangling. "You don't know the whole story. And I don't have to stay and take this." She backed up from my bed. I peeled back the covers with excruciating exhaustion weighing down my arms.

I have to keep her here.

"Xavier said he was laid up on NyQuil the week Caitlin died. You and he had the flu, right?"

Roxanne stopped in her tracks and wheeled around to face my bed. Her counterfeit youthful face twitched in admission.

"You were known to drug your own daughter with sleeping pills when you thought her insomnia was affecting her work. So you just drugged Xavier and murdered Caitlin while he was out of it with the flu."

My eyes dropped to Roxanne's careworn hands, aged prematurely by chemicals and hard work, no doubt when she'd toiled as a cleaner to launch her daughter's career.

"And you knew," I whispered, "about the dangers of mixing ammonia and bleach."

"That's enough!" Roxanne stepped closer to my bed and my heart rate sped up. The machine began to beep. She viciously unplugged it from the wall with a harsh yank.

"I *did* crush up sleeping pills in Dakota's food. I'm not proud of it, but her insomnia was making her forget lines and mess up on camera. But I never did it again after that horrible week Caitlin died." She shuddered and sat down where Rachel had been an hour ago. I cringed and backed up on the pillow.

"Oh, I'm not going to hurt you," Roxanne said wearily, finally looking a bit more her age, exhaustion and disgust permeating the Botox mask.

"Someone took a page out of my own book the week Dakota's friends were visiting, and drugged *me*."

It was a likely story.

"That's awfully convenient, when you're the one with the history of crushing up sleeping pills."

Roxanne shook her head and grabbed my hand. I yelped and extricated it from her clammy grasp.

"Xavier gave me a taste of my own medicine," she whispered. "He even used his own sleeping pills so I wouldn't figure it out."

I threw back my head and laughed, the chuckle making my head spin.

"That's rich. Xavier is Mr. Crunchy. He would never take a pharmaceutical."

Roxanne grabbed my hand again and this time wouldn't let go. "Xavier is into his image and wouldn't want anyone to think he was taking them. But make no mistake, he's addicted to sleeping pills and can't rest without them."

A stray thought skittered through my head. I recalled my search of the B and B rooms with my sister, and the little bottle of all-natural herbal sleep aids in Xavier's possession.

"He hides the sleeping pills in melatonin bottles," I whispered.

Roxanne nodded, giving me an appraising look.

"How do I know you're telling the truth?" Roxanne could have drugged Xavier that fateful week in Los Angeles, as Xavier claimed, or she could have been drugged by him.

Roxanne finally let go of my arm and stood, tears pooling in her eyes. "You don't." A fervent look burned in her eyes. "Just please don't implicate him, Mallory. I'm begging you."

It was her declaration that convinced me. Roxanne was still in love with Xavier after thirteen years.

She's still protecting him.

She stole from the room at last, and I slowly peeled back the covers. If what Dakota said about Xavier getting discharged was true, I didn't have much time.

I slipped the monitor from my fingertip and placed my polka-dotted hospital gown in a neatly folded pile on the bed. It was hard to dress myself. I fumbled with the ornate buttons of the pretty lilac dress I'd worn to the rehearsal dinner, cursing my choice not to wear something with a zipper. My equilibrium was off from the belladonna. I was woozy and exhausted. The lights seemed too bright when I stood. But I pressed on.

Truman and Rachel and Garrett will be so ticked.

I brushed the thought away and finished slipping on my silver flats. I was glad I'd worn sensible shoes to work the rehearsal dinner. I didn't think I could manage heels in my current state.

The hallway was clear when I slipped out of my room. I gathered up every ounce of reserve encrgy I had to shuffle calmly down the hall to the elevators. I leaned against the wall when I'd finally made it in and rested my eyes.

"Are you okay, miss?"

"I'm fine." I offered the worried visitor what I hoped was a convincing smile and dragged myself to the front desk when we reached the first floor.

"I'm here to visit Xavier Morris," I announced. The attendant tapped away at a keyboard.

"He's in room 303. Visiting hours end soon. And it looks like he's getting discharged momentarily."

I dragged my foggy-headed self back to the elevator, resting in the hallway outside his door.

Am I really doing this?

I felt around in my purse for my cell phone but couldn't find it in the flotsam and jetsam at the bottom.

"Mallory, what a pleasant surprise."

Xavier sat in a wheelchair, ready to be discharged. A small bag sat next to him. He wore a beatific yet weary smile. His skin had finally lost the luminescent glow, I guess because he'd been fed intravenously this week rather than consuming his special smoothies.

"Roxanne is just getting the car now," he declared as he folded his long fingers in his lap.

"You woke up." I leaned against the doorjamb and tried to look natural. I didn't want to telegraph that I was probably too unwell to confront him.

"I can't imagine why someone tried to poison me." He offered me a chilling smile.

"Oh, I can think of a half dozen reasons."

His smile dropped from his face in degrees. He swallowed and sat up straighter in the wheelchair, his Adam's apple dancing.

"I know you take sleeping pills instead of melatonin," I spat.

A look of relief stole over Xavier's face. "Oh? So what?"

"You drugged Roxanne thirteen years ago when you both had the flu. While she was sleeping, you slipped onto the set of *Silverlake High* and locked Caitlin in Dakota's dressing room."

Xavier dropped the pretense and deflated in the chair. "Very good, Mallory." He looked as exhausted as I did, though he'd spent the week in a coma. "That little wretch was ruining everything." He dragged a hand down his weary face before returning it to his lap.

"So you mixed bleach and ammonia together because it was on hand in the janitor's closet. And it pointed to Roxanne, since she was a cleaning woman for a time while she was trying to get Dakota her start."

Xavier nodded. "The Los Angeles police zeroed

in on Roxanne, but lucky for her, they couldn't make it stick."

"Because you murdered Caitlin!" I took a deep breath and struggled to remain standing. "And you locked her in *Dakota's* dressing room to make it even harder to trace back to you."

"Caitlin was the golden goose," Xavier raved from his chair. "She made the show what it was. But she was willing to bring it down with her unreasonable demands."

"But the show ended anyway. You chose the wrong course of action. You not only murdered an innocent young woman, but your crime caused the show to go off the air."

Xavier gave a bitter nod of his head.

"Rachel and I are no longer interested in the destination wedding show, by the way," I wryly announced. I didn't think Rachel would mind me speaking for her if she knew Xavier had killed Caitlin Quinn.

"And now I'm going to the authorities." I leaned forward and wobbled. A knowing look stole over Xavier's face.

I may have played my hand too soon.

"Be that as it may," he mused, "this is all your word against mine. The Los Angeles Police Department closed the case. They could never figure it out, and it's not like you were there."

"There's no statute of limitations on murder," I muttered. "You're going down for this."

"This is just a cockamamie theory on your part." A superior look stole over the director's face and deepened as he watched me hold the doorframe for support.

"Now if you'll excuse me." He wheeled the chair toward the door.

"I don't think so!" I flung myself at the wheelchair in a last-ditch effort before I collapsed. Xavier and I landed on the floor in a tangle of limbs.

"Gerroff of me!" he mumbled and I twisted over and tried to pin him as Truman had done last night with Beau. Too bad I didn't have Rachel's Indiana Jones whip.

Loud footsteps slapped on the linoleum floor. "What did your sister tell you about getting some rest?" Truman leaned down and hoisted me up in one fluid movement, placing me in Xavier's wheelchair. He straddled the director's back and cuffed him. A befuddled candy striper stared at the melee from the hall, her mouth dropping open.

"I thought I'd come back to check on you. I knew you wouldn't stay in your room." A rueful smile perked up the corners of Truman's mouth. "Nice work, Mallory."

Chapter Twenty-one

It took some major convincing, but the hospital eventually let me go. I had to swear up and down I'd take care of myself, and I had a doctor's appointment scheduled for Monday to make sure.

I felt like a sitting duck in the hospital, what with people like Xavier in my midst. I liked my chances better on the outside. Truman actually lobbied for my release, and Rachel picked me up in the Butterscotch Monster in time for a quick shower back at Thistle Park.

"So Xavier murdered Caitlin to save *Silverlake High*," my sister mused. "I'm glad we won't have anything to do with that destination show." She handed me a cup of tea. I stared at it for a moment and let out a barking laugh.

"You're not trying to poison me, are you?"

A flush of pink stained Rachel's cheeks. "I should have offered something else. How about some hot cocoa?"

We set off for the apartment kitchen, a cheery

white, yellow, and turquoise space designed by our mother. I sank gratefully into a chair while Rachel bustled about.

"But Caitlin's murder was all for naught. The show was cancelled *because* he killed her." I shivered. "And Dakota must have told her former fiancé, Beau, about what went down in Los Angeles thirteen years ago so he could replicate the murder to kill Ginger."

Rachel shook her head in disgust. "So if anyone put the pieces together, they'd think maybe Dakota was behind it instead of Beau." She set down two steaming mugs of hot cocoa and we drank in sad but companionable silence.

"Are you sure you're up for Ginger's memorial?" Rachel cocked her head and gave me a careful once-over.

"I'm shocked Ginger and Beau were having an affair," I began. "But I'd still like to pay my respects."

We gathered our coats and a few silk bouquets from Dakota and Beau's scrapped nuptials. The carriage house was a sea of red and pink and white, awaiting a wedding that was never to be. The metallic magenta snowflakes flapped delicately in the breeze from the open door. The tables were set with silver and white china, the stemware sparkling and ready for champagne. I closed my eyes against the perfectly appointed space and turned out the light. I would deal with disassembling the trappings of Dakota's wedding when the effects of the belladonna had entirely worn off.

Rachel and I slipped into the last row of the packed auditorium at Dunlap Academy. Dakota, seated on the stage, waved to us, as did Ellie. Ginger's parents spoke first. Then it was Leah's turn to eulogize Ginger. She described the former headmistress as her teacher, mentor, and friend. She broke down in tears halfway through her speech, but carried on. Dakota and Ellie spoke of their friend, the third musketeer. Dakota's speech was particularly impressive given that she'd just found out her fiancé had been involved with Ginger for a year without her knowledge.

"That was a beautiful speech, darling." Iris clucked like a mother hen at the reception after the memorial and smoothed Ellie's hair. The grown woman ducked from her mother's ministrations and blushed. "Um, thanks, Mom."

"As was your speech, Leah, dear." Iris patted Leah on the head like a child as well, and she rolled her eyes as her mother flattened her spiky purple bangs.

"Leah has good news," Iris continued, puffing up her chest with unsuppressed pride. "She got her acceptance letter to Harvard yesterday!"

It felt good to finally have something to celebrate amidst all the doom and gloom and murder.

I smiled up from the chair where I was resting. "That's awesome news, Leah."

Iris wandered off to spread the news of her daughter's acceptance far and wide. Leah let out a breath.

"I'm just excited to have done something on my own." She broke out into a smile, her dark lipstick in bold contrast to her bright white teeth. "Ellie was always going to be an actress, and my mother just pushed her at first, not me." She frowned and picked a piece of lint from her Dunlap issue sweater. "But this achievement is all mine."

I nodded in agreement, thinking of how hard it was to be a sibling sometimes. Rachel and I were very different. When we were growing up, it felt like we were headed in different directions. It was amazing we'd ended up working together on our joint business venture. I was happy it had turned out that way and wouldn't change it for the world, but I understood Leah's excitement and relief in stepping out from Ellie's shadow.

The reception went on for another hour, the young women and teachers of Dunlap Academy celebrating the life of their former headmistress with laughter and tears. But word of Beau's arrest made its way around the room like a dark undercurrent, somewhat sullying the celebration of Ginger. It was ironic that today was to be Dakota and Beau's wedding day, but instead, Beau was languishing in jail, and the woman he'd killed was being memorialized.

"Mallory." A cool hand gripped my arm and I jumped as far as I could in my weakened state. I peered up at Becca Cunningham.

"What in the heck are you doing here? You're supposed to be in St. Kitts." I stared at Becca as if she were an apparition.

She winced, her princess-cut engagement ring twinkling in the lights, sans wedding ring.

"Our flight was cancelled due to the blizzard," she moaned. "Helene caught us at the airport and exacted a promise."

I closed my eyes and shook my head. I was no fan of the woman who'd been involved with my once fiancé, but I'd worked hard on Becca and Keith's elopement and I was invested in Becca getting one over on Helene.

"What kind of promise?" My voice was small, from tiredness over my near poisoning, or because I could see where this was headed.

"She said she'll disinherit Keith if we don't hold a big wedding, here in Port Quincy." Becca's distraught eyes pleaded with mine.

Oh, heck no.

"And-I-was-wondering-if-we-could-have-it-at-Thistle-Park," Becca went on in a rush, the tic having returned to her left eye. "You're one of the few people on the planet willing to stand up to Helene."

I closed my eyes and tried to wish Becca away. But when I dragged my eyelids up, she was still there.

"You're my only hope."

I thought back to Helene running roughshod over my wedding to Keith and vowed to help Becca. It would be an unlikely partnership.

"I'll do it."

Please don't let me regret this.

I spent the rest of the event sitting off on the sidelines, recuperating from my near-deadly cup of tea. I was grateful when the reception wound down. I was ready to put this whole sordid affair in the rearview mirror.

* * *

Rachel and I filed out of the reception room. We wended our way through the hallways of Dunlap, lost in a sea of students and parents and teachers. The sun was finally setting outside the floor-to-ceiling windows. It was going to be a frigid night, with temperatures in the single digits. I shivered and pulled my cardigan closer around my shoulders, though it was warm and toasty in the school.

"I wanted to thank you for figuring out Xavier murdered Caitlin all those years ago." Dakota sidled up to me as we moved through the hall and gave my arm a squeeze. "I've learned a lot this week about the people I thought I knew and loved." Her pretty face twisted in a stony frown.

And she doesn't even know the half of it.

"Dakota, when we get back to the B and B, we need to talk." I would need to reveal to her that her own mother had been embezzling funds from her, but now was not the time nor the place.

But Dakota thought otherwise.

"Tell me what's going on, Mallory." Her violet gaze was intense as she pulled me into a side vestibule. I barely had time to tell Rachel I'd meet her at the car before Dakota shut the door.

Okay, here goes nothing.

"I think Roxanne is doing hinky things with your money. That's why she's so hot and bothered for you to take every gig and do everything you're offered." I told her about the issues with the bank I'd overheard on the porch and how Roxanne hadn't denied it when I'd confronted her last night.

Dakota stood as if she'd just been slapped. She slowly nodded, the pieces fitting together. "I feel like an idiot." Her hand floated up to touch the side of her face. "Beau's cheating was in plain sight, and I was going to settle for him just to improve my brand. I was going to marry him because Roxanne wanted me to. And all this time she's been stealing from me?"

The door to the little room we were in flew open, and Leah tumbled in, another student hot on her heels.

"You promised me a realistic paper, but you wrote an A. I never get As. I paid you a lot of money to make it look like—"

"Stop." Leah whirled the girl around to face us. Her classmate went silent, a crimson flush blooming on her face. "Forget it," she muttered and exited the room.

What was that all about?

"I hear you got into Harvard." Dakota offered Leah a rather distant smile and the three of us left the room.

I walked with Ellie and Dakota as they accompanied Leah back to her dorm.

"I'd better get going—Rachel's waiting. Congrats again."

Leah sent me a smile as Ellie and Dakota and I left her room. On a whim, I stayed behind to ask her about what I'd heard.

"Leah? What were you talking to that student about?"

Leah's eyes strayed to the open door and she got up to shut it with a soft *snick*.

"I'm not sure," she stammered. "I think she was confused."

It dawned on me. "You're writing papers for other students, aren't you?"

Leah opened her mouth, then closed it, then gave up the ruse. "Yes," she said simply. "What of it?"

I let out a sigh of relief. It wasn't as if she was dealing drugs like her classmate Nora had.

"I remember your mom said she was sure you had a good shot of getting into Harvard, but that she wasn't sure how you'd pay for it."

Leah nodded, a bit of relief flooding her eyes. She pushed back a lock of purple hair behind her glasses frames and sat on her bed.

"That's highly creative," I mused aloud. "Unethical, but creative."

"And not illegal," Leah added. Her face glowed with pride. "I write for more than the students here. I have my own online business. I take orders from all over the world."

"That's quite entrepreneurial," I said. A thought skittered through my head. "This is why Owen said your work was slipping at the foundation. You've been too busy keeping up your own grades and writing papers for your paper mill to volunteer."

Leah shrugged again. "I do what I have to do."

I turned to go. Leah's room was the mirror image of Nora's, with the same thick, luxurious carpet, dark wood furniture, and sweeping views of the arctic landscape outside. My mind did a quick replay of the day Ellie and I had found Nora, complete with Ginger's tablet taped to the underside of her bed. I suddenly felt infinitely tired. Maybe coming to Ginger's memorial was a bad idea.

My eyes swept the room as I headed for the door.

Oh my God.

A shiny strip of gold gleamed on Leah's bookshelf. The book was hard to miss. It was taller and wider than the textbooks it was nestled next to. Leah had turned it with the spine toward the back of the shelf so no one could read the title, but I was betting on knowing that book. It was the plant encyclopedia my contractor had given me. The one in which I had turned down the pages for the entries on belladonna and bleeding hearts.

I gulped and tried to suppress my galloping heart rate.

"Congrats again, Leah."

I hustled into the hall of the dormitory, relieved to see groups of girls standing there. I slipped my cell phone out of my purse to text Truman.

Chapter Twenty-two

I'd figured it out too late. I hurried from the Dunlap dormitory, shutting the door behind me. The night was cold and clear, with a waxing moon high and luminescent in the sky like an ivory coin. I took in a steadying breath, the air so cold it seared my lungs. Rachel must be wondering by now what was keeping me. I held up my phone to continue my text to alert Truman.

"Don't breathe a word." Leah pressed a gun into my spine. I felt the butt of the weapon push through my coat. "Keep walking." She gave me a harsh push, and I stumbled off the cobbled walkway. She grabbed my wrist and gave it a painful twist, leaving me gasping. "You won't be needing this." She tossed my cell phone into the bushes by the dormitory door. It sank into a mini snowdrift, out of sight.

Crap, crap, crap!

We trudged around the side of the dormitory and headed for the ice-skating pond. My little flat velvet shoes were no match for the crusty snow. Ice bit into exposed flesh on my feet and ankles. It seared and burned, feeling more akin to fire than snow.

I stumbled over a lump of snow and landed on my face in the white stuff.

"Get *up!*" Leah demanded. She roughly hoisted me to my feet and we began our brutal march, the pond spread before us.

Ellie wasn't the only one in the Barnes family with acting chops. Leah had fooled us all.

"You seemed so devastated when your mentor Ginger was found dead at my desk," I breathed out, my voice sounding labored. "Who would have ever thought you'd killed her?"

Leah snorted and dug the weapon harder into my back. "Ginger found out about my paper-writing business and was going to expel me. I told her I could provide her with the name of a student who was dealing drugs in exchange for a chance to remain at school."

"Nora." We had finally reached the pond. I desperately wanted to turn around to see if anyone had realized where we were. But the gun nestled in my ribs through my pea coat prevented that.

"Ginger said she didn't operate like that, and besides, she already knew about Nora. She was planning on expelling both of us at the same time—can you believe it?" Leah gave a bitter laugh. "I convinced Ginger to let me attend the Winter Ball before she went through with it, and she granted me that wish." Leah offered me a crazily triumphant smile. "Ginger made a mistake. She should have just expelled me. I filled a Winter Ball flower arrangement with bleach and ammonia from Thistle Park. It wasn't hard to do—you have a cleaning supply closet by your office."

I nodded for her to go on, hoping to buy myself some time. My teeth began to chatter, as much from fear as from the frigid conditions.

"I took her tablet and her phone and locked her in your office. No one heard her banging to get out with the loud DJ."

I was sickened by the matter-of-fact way Leah described how she'd murdered her mentor and headmistress.

"I stole the tiara to make it look like a reason for Ginger's death. I mailed a piece of the crown to Dakota just to mix things up and to make Dakota think this had something to do with Caitlin's death so many years ago." Leah paused and let out a low laugh. "And then I buried the tiara in your greenhouse to make you look suspicious."

"What about Xavier?" His was the only unsolved attempted murder, but I had a hunch the perpetrator was standing behind me.

"I tried to blackmail him for what he did to Caitlin," Leah explained, her hand with the gun never wavering from my back. "I had a hunch he was responsible, and I turned out to be right. I don't really remember what happened with Caitlin when I was five, other than everyone telling me I was the one to find her. But he didn't know that."

"So what happened?"

Rachel must be worried sick by now.

"He threatened to tell Ellie and the school that I'd blackmailed him. So he had to go."

A clammy chill spread between my shoulder blades. Leah had callously killed one person and attempted another murder. Who knew what other mayhem had been at her hands? She wouldn't stop to spare me.

"You hurt Nora," I whispered.

I could feel her nodding. She gave a rueful laugh. "Yes. Other things happened that helped get me off the hook. Nora was the perfect fall girl for Ginger's murder, for example."

"You drugged her."

"Oh, she drugged herself. I just waited to give her a little more."

I felt like my limbs were going to fall off and my fingers were a lost cause to frostbite. I didn't have the strength to run away and Leah knew it. I feared I would crumple to the icy ground soon, but I had to know the whole story, no matter what happened.

"And you ended up poisoning me instead of Owen," I whispered. "He was on to you, wasn't he?" It made sense. He'd mentioned Leah's volunteer work was slipping at the foundation.

"That punk!" Leah's voice was a little too loud. It ricocheted across the icy pond. "He doesn't know I was writing papers for money, but he was going to withdraw my recommendation letter. I missed too many volunteer sessions at the last minute. So he had to go." She shrugged, the gun riding up and down my back. "And you are always poking around into everyone's business. Can't you leave well enough alone? I wasn't too upset when you drank Owen's tea."

It wasn't the first time my nosiness had gotten me into hot water. But I realized, with a gulp of subzero air, that it might be my last.

"And now I finish things."

Leah pushed me onto the ice. I hoped it would hold, but it must not have been cold enough to freeze beyond a few inches deep since the mini heat wave before the blizzard. I crouched on my belly, trying to distribute my weight, as Leah pushed me farther out onto the ice. I had nowhere else to go.

The surface cracked.

Oh no.

It sounded like a shot from a gun and I dimly wondered if she'd pulled the trigger on me as well. The crack spread and I went in, the water shocking me as much as a live electrical current. Each nerve in my body screamed as the frigid water attacked my senses. I opened my eyes and saw black, black, black. I kicked in the brackish water and breathed in a lungful of the cold stuff. Each nerve ending in my body seared with icy, chilly pain. I bobbed up one last time.

Figures struggled on the shore. Someone hit Leah, and she tumbled to the ground. More ice cracked, and people swore. Strong hands lifted me up and pulled me out.

"Mallory, stay with us."

Epilogue

I didn't object this time when I landed back in the hospital. I stayed for three full days, recovering from frostbite and hypothermia and the lingering effects of the belladonna. Truman was torn. He was happy I'd figured out Leah was responsible for murdering Ginger and the attempted murders of Xavier, Owen, and yours truly. But he wasn't okay with how it had all gone down.

Garrett had stayed by my bedside, tenderly taking care of me and, more importantly, making sure I stayed put. But he needn't have worried. I promised him my sleuthing days were over.

It turned out Leah hadn't even had a gun. She'd pressed a flashlight into my back, but I couldn't have known. She'd planned on letting me drown in the icy water, and with my shock, it wouldn't have taken long. Leah's own sister, Ellie, had clobbered her on the shore of the skating pond and Dakota had fished me out.

Adrienne Larson paid a visit to me the last day of my stay in the hospital. Her impressive ring was gone, as was her prissy stance. She'd lost her fiancé to what I hoped would be a life sentence back in Los Angeles. She'd also possibly lost her job hosting *I Do*, since we'd probably just filmed the last episode.

I'd heard from Truman that they'd finished processing Adrienne's release and dropped the charges against her for Xavier's attempted murder just as they led Xavier into jail. The scene hadn't been pretty, with Adrienne mourning the loss of her relationship, but also berating her new fiancé for killing Caitlin Quinn.

"I wanted to thank you." Adrienne spoke the words in a low tone. "For figuring out Xavier's role in Caitlin's death." She shivered. "I'd rather know the truth than be married to a killer."

She'd spent the rest of her time in Port Quincy bonding with Summer before she left for Los Angeles. She'd lost her fiancé, but she had gained a new relationship with her daughter.

Three months later, I had a new wedding to prepare for. The days had turned balmier, matching the artificial humidity and warmth of the Thistle Park greenhouse back in February. Our winter of discontent had melted into mellow spring.

Leah and Xavier were languishing in jail, she in Port Quincy, and he extradited back to Los Angeles. Beau was free and working on a new album. Dakota and Owen were to be married under the stars in Thistle Park's garden.

Their three-month engagement had been fast, but I had a feeling this marriage would last. Roxanne was grudging but accepting. Dakota had forgiven her mother for funneling away her millions and refused to press charges. She'd installed a new, professional money manager, and Roxanne was left to dote on Pixie, no longer in charge of mismanaging Dakota's earnings or pushing her to take every gig. Dakota joined the board of Dunlap Academy and cast the tiebreaker vote in favor of merging the girls' boarding school with the boys' private school. She also purchased the Winter Ball tiara and donated it to the Carnegie Museum, commissioning a replica to be made for subsequent balls. She'd fulfilled Ginger's wishes and ticked Helene off to boot.

Night fell on a warm day in May. Twenty guests gathered in the backyard, seated before an arched trellis wreathed in pink roses and silhouetted by the setting sun. Roxanne and Pixie the Shih Tzu walked Dakota down the aisle. Dakota wore a long, pink, gauzy strapless gown. Pixie wore a matching pink tutu, and Owen had consented to wear a suit jacket over his skinny jeans and suspenders.

Ellie was the only bridesmaid, and there was no host, no cameras, no fanfare. Guests held sparklers and fireflies buzzed in delight.

"Now this is a wedding I can get behind." Rachel beamed as we surveyed the guests noshing on the gourmet comfort food menu we'd selected so many months ago. Dakota and Owen cut into their peanut butter cake, and soon were dancing the night away beneath the stars.

"All's well that ends well." I slipped my hand into Garrett's and we surveyed the merrymaking before us.

The next day, we bid a fond farewell to the married couple. They were leaving for their honeymoon in Montreal.

"Thank you, Mallory." Dakota enveloped me in a crushing hug, then switched off with Owen. "For everything. I'm so happy." She beamed, her smile genuine, her face carefree for once.

Dakota was going to semi-retire. She'd still take roles, but not at the breakneck pace dictated by Roxanne. She and Owen planned to divide their time between Los Angeles and Port Quincy, and they'd run Owen's foundation together.

The footage of the wedding from hell was to be spliced together into an episode of *I Do*. It was ironic that this was projected to be the most-viewed episode of *I Do* ever, and Xavier wouldn't be free to see that he'd succeeded in resurrecting his show after all. His ploys had led to the permanent cancellation of *Silverlake High*, but worked for the reality wedding show. The tabloids had covered Dakota and Beau's dissolution, and everyone wanted to watch the infamous episode. Adrienne had just been named director of the reality show, and the next season would feature a new host.

I headed over to the greenhouse after seeing off the newlyweds.

"What do you think of these?" Summer held up a tray of seedlings. "They're peas."

We were planting only edible flowers and veggies in the resplendent glass space. We didn't want to take our chances on ever again providing a would-be killer with ready-made poison mere steps from the house.

"I think they'll be delicious." I slung my arm around Summer and together we planted in the sun.

Recipes

Peanut Butter Banana Cake

2½ cups flour
2 cups white sugar
1½ teaspoons baking soda
½ cup milk
½ cup banana puree
1 teaspoon vanilla extract
¾ cup water
½ cup coconut oil
¼ cup vegetable oil
¾ cup peanut butter

Preheat oven to 375 degrees. Grease two nine-by-nine cake pans.

Combine flour, sugar, and baking soda. Combine milk, banana puree, and vanilla. Pour milk and banana mixture into flour mixture and mix well until combined. Heat water, coconut oil, vegetable oil, and peanut butter in a pan on medium heat and stir frequently until mixture is smooth. Add peanut butter mixture to flour mixture and stir until smooth. Pour batter into two greased and floured nine-by-nine cake pans. Bake for twenty-five to thirty minutes. Cool cakes and frost cake with chocolate icing.

Chocolate Icing

5 tablespoons coconut oil
¾ cup light brown sugar
3 tablespoons milk
1¾ cups confectioners' sugar
1½ tablespoons cocoa powder
2 teaspoons vanilla extract

Heat coconut oil and brown sugar in a saucepan, stirring frequently until smooth. Add in milk. Remove from heat. Combine cocoa and confectioners' sugar. Add cocoa mixture and vanilla to coconut oil mixture and beat well.

Cranberry Sunflower Muffins

2 cups flour
1 cup brown sugar
1 teaspoon baking powder
1 cup vegetable oil
1 cup chopped cranberries
1 cup sunflower seeds, shells removed

Preheat oven to 350 degrees. Line a muffin tin with foil or paper cupcake liners.

Combine flour, brown sugar, and baking powder. Add vegetable oil to flour mixture and stir well. Mix in cranberries and sunflower seeds. Fill paper liners three-fourths full. Bake for thirty to thirty-five minutes or until a knife inserted in the center of the muffins comes out clean.

Blueberry Scones

4 cups flour
1/3 cup sugar
4 teaspoons baking powder
1/2 teaspoon salt
1/2 cup chilled coconut oil
1 cup milk
1 cup blueberries

Preheat oven to 375. Line cookie sheets with
parchment paper.

Combine flour, sugar, baking powder, and salt. Use
fingers to mix in cold coconut oil until mixture
resembles coarse sand. Add milk to dry ingredients.
Divide dough in half. Gently work in blueberries.
Form each section into a nine-inch circle. Cut
dough circle into eight wedges. Bake for twenty to
twenty-five minutes, or until scones are lightly
browned.

Cherry Chocolate Martini

1 ounce vanilla vodka
1 ounce chocolate liquor
1 ounce heavy cream or half and half
1 ounce grenadine
maraschino cherries
chocolate syrup
ice

Drizzle martini glass with chocolate syrup. Combine
ingredients and shake. Pour over ice. Garnish with
a maraschino cherry.

Please turn the page
for an exciting sneak peek of
Stephanie Blackmoore's next
Wedding Planner mystery

GOWN WITH THE WIND

coming soon wherever
print and e-books are sold!

Chapter One

"You're either a saint, or completely crazy." My sister Rachel put down her wand of electric blue mascara and tried to catch my eye in the rear-view mirror. "You can still back out, you know."

I kept my eyes on the road, a slalom-like dip of pavement retreating from our Italianate mansion B and B, toward the other side of the town I'd come to call home. Port Quincy, Pennsylvania, rose up before us at the top of another steep hill. Pretty painted lady Victorians flanked both sides of the brick street in shades of lilac, butter yellow, and petal pink, like little girls in Easter dresses. The turreted and gingerbread buildings gave way to wide craftsman bungalows and squat Cape Cods. Ruby geraniums, winking black-eyed Susans, and lush magenta impatiens bloomed in profusion in front yard flowerbeds. The sky was an overturned bowl of rich robin's egg blue, with a scrape of cirrus clouds scattered like feathers. I rolled down the window of my ancient tan Volvo station wagon, a vehicle I'd christened the Butterscotch Monster. The air was sweet and warm, carrying the scent of a recent rain. It was a gorgeous late May afternoon. Summer was upon us, but spring still held sway, the world around me dewy and fresh and new.

"I think I'm a little bit of both." My heart rate accelerated as I turned to follow the road next to the roiling Monongahela River, away from Port Quincy and toward the countryside. "I can't just leave Becca hanging. What I would have given to have some help standing up to Helene last summer." I shivered despite the warmth of the late-day sun and recalled when I'd been in Becca's position. When I'd been engaged to Keith Pierce, Port Quincy's favorite son, about to go through with my inflated albatross of a wedding. Back when I was an attorney. Before I'd found out about Keith's cheating, called off the wedding, and inherited his grandmother's mansion, Thistle Park.

So much had changed. I was now a wedding planner and B and B purveyor, working with my sister to make brides and grooms' dreams come true. I loved my new career and my life in Port Quincy. I felt like I'd found my true calling, and had the good fortune to stumble upon a place I could call home. The only glitch was occasionally running into my ex-fiancé, Keith, his mother, Helene, and his new fiancée, Becca Cunningham.

"Well I know *I* wouldn't even give Becca the time of day, much less plan her wedding to Keith." Rachel had moved on to the lipstick portion of her car face-painting routine, and she carefully applied a swath of rose gloss to her lips.

"She extracted a promise in a moment of weakness." Just this past February I'd tried to help the man whom I'd once thought I'd marry, and the woman he'd been cheating with, elope. But a blizzard stymied their plans to jet off to St. Kitts. Becca had acquiesced to Helene's demands for a big Port Quincy society wedding, and I'd taken pity on the bride. I was once in her position, fulfilling Helene's every wish for my wedding, against all my own wants and desires. I'd felt sorry for Becca, and though she was once the other woman, no one should have to stand up to Helene without reinforcements. I squared my shoulders behind the seatbelt and glanced at my sister.

"We're lucky the Norris party cancelled their event. We can get Keith and Becca's wedding out of the way, and in two weeks, this will all be behind us."

Becca and Keith were on a waiting list to be married at my B and B, and they had accepted the slot from a recent last-minute cancellation. Their nuptials were to be the first week of June, and then I'd be done with them for good.

Rachel rolled her eyes in apparent disbelief at my proclamation as we reached the development of mega mcmansions nestled in the rolling green countryside. I approached the cul-de-sac Keith and Becca called home and stifled a giggle. I parked the Butterscotch Monster behind Keith's familiar navy BMW in the circular driveway and cut the engine.

"Holy heck." Rachel dropped a compact of

bronzer in her lap and yelped as a spray of tan talc covered the worn leather bench seat.

"I warned you." I couldn't tamp down the grin I felt spreading across my face as Keith and Becca's hulking colossus of architectural wonder stood before us. The bride had designed the house, a busy collection of cubes and rectangles jutting out at improbable angles. The structure was a dark red brick edifice that would rival any creative toddler's Lego construction. Floor-to-ceiling glass block windows glimmered in long, unpredictable slices peeking out from under a shiny copper roof. Severe and precise topiary huddled next to the house in random groups.

"If this is a clue to Becca's wedding style, we may be in trouble." Rachel dusted off the last bit of bronzer from her berry colored leather mini-skirt and craned her head to take in every inch of the modernist house.

"Oh, it gets better. Wait'll you see the inside." I advanced up the wide brick path to the double lacquered front doors and took a deep breath before I rang the bell. It was flung open a nanosecond later, and I found myself face to face with a woman I'd never met before.

"You must be Mallory. I'm so glad to meet you." I found myself being gathered into an impetuous hug on the threshold of the house, and I smiled as the woman next embraced my sister.

"I'm Becca's mother, Lana Cunningham. Her father and I are so thrilled you're able to accommodate Becca and Keith so much earlier than we were expecting." I tried to listen to Becca's mother and take in my sister's reaction to the interior of the house at the same time. Rachel's pretty green eyes grew round as she did a double take.

The inside of the house was a study in nineteen-eighties boudoir finery, with yards of white, cream, and ecru chintz and silk. Gold and sea foam accents were scattered throughout the cavernous open floor plan, and everywhere the eye landed, there was peach. Peach tile, peach ceilings, and peach pillars. Even the kitchen cabinets were a shade of apricot. It took my eyes a few seconds to adjust to the glow of the room. A room that had my nemesis Helene written all over it. I wondered how Becca liked living in this split-personality house, where she'd designed the outside, but had to acquiesce to her fiancé's mother with regards to the inside decor.

But I wouldn't be dealing with Helene today. Becca and Keith were keeping it a secret from the reigning queen bee of Port Quincy that they were to be married in two weeks' time. She would never consent to having the wedding at Thistle Park, and they were going to reveal their plans to marry the very week of the wedding. I wasn't sure how I was going to keep their ceremony under wraps until then, but I would try. I didn't want to face the wrath of Hurricane Helene.

Rachel and I followed Lana through a maze of white and peach furniture to the sleek black deck at the back of the house. I shielded my eyes as we stepped outside, briefly noting the spare obsidian rock garden beyond the low, rectangular pool. It was before Memorial Day, but the wide expanse of blue water appeared ready for swimmers.

"You're finally here." Becca leaned down to give

the side of my face a cool air kiss, and I stifled a wince as she pulled away. We were not friends, if not exactly enemies, and I didn't need to exchange pretend pleasantries.

"I'm glad we were able to move your wedding up," I said in a neutral voice.

Becca gave Rachel a brief nod. The bride to be had donned a pretty pink tea dress and pearls worthy of Betty Draper for the occasion. Her large princess cut diamond engagement ring was front and center as she folded her left hand over her right. She wore her ubiquitous flats, the better to attempt to match Keith in stature now that she was engaged. Her hair was its usual fall of shiny flaxen tresses, her trademark stripe of dark roots standing out at her part.

"You must have a lot of cancellations if you were able to accommodate us so quickly," Keith Pierce said with a glint in his eye. My once fiancé was clad in his best prepster wear for this wedding planning meeting. He wore a navy blazer with gold buttons, a pink check dress shirt to complement Becca's sundress, and he completed the outfit with khakis and boating shoes. A bead of sweat dripped down from the bald spot forming atop his head and landed on his shoulder with a plop.

"The first cancellation this year," I responded, trying and failing to remove the frosty tone in my voice.

"And we're glad luck was on our side to move up the wedding." A sprightly woman of an indeterminate age, somewhere between eighty and ninety, clutched my arm with warm, gnarled hands. She had a slight stoop bringing her height under five feet, but her grip was firm. A fluffy corona of shocking white hair graced her head, and her blue eyes twinkled merrily like those of a young woman.

"I'm Alma Cunningham, Becca's grandmother," the woman gushed. "And this is my son Rhett."

A short, portly man shuffled forward to grip my hand in a surprisingly hard handshake.

"Pleased to meet you, Mallory." Becca's father had a little button nose, an amused smirk, and the same twinkling eyes as his mother Alma. His hair was a longish iron gray, the ends nearly brushing his shoulders. He reminded me a bit of the Quaker Oats man. I couldn't help but swivel my head from Rhett Cunningham to his wife Lana. Becca definitely favored her mother. Lana Cunningham and Becca towered over Rhett by an easy foot. Both mother and daughter had a sophisticated, if brittle kind of grace. Lana wore a coral shift dress, her frame willowy and tanned and toned.

"And I'm Samantha, Becca's sister." A slight, short woman seemed to emerge from the shadows, dressed simply in a businesslike black shirtdress and strappy sandals. "Pleased to meet you." Her lips parted and she gave a bright smile, and it was then that I saw her resemblance to Becca. Samantha favored her father Rhett and grandmother Alma, with her short frame and merry blue eyes. But her hair was dark, the color of Becca's roots.

"My twin sister, actually." Becca slung an arm around Samantha and bestowed her with a winning smile.

"Twins?" Rachel squinted at the sisters.

"Fraternal," Samantha qualified. "I've been overseas in Colombia, working as a human rights

attorney," she added. "I couldn't make it back for
my cousin Whitney's wedding last October. It's so
good to be home for Becca's wedding." I found
myself warming quickly to the sweet woman, who
obviously loved her twin sister.

"Shall we get started?" Keith's droll voice cut
through the air, and he glanced officiously at his
fancy watch.

"Of course."

I accepted the chair Rhett pulled out for me
and opened the book of ideas I'd fashioned for
Becca and Keith.

"You wanted a Japanese cherry blossom inspired wedding, to mirror your backyard, but also
to take advantage of the grounds at Thistle Park."
I pulled out a photograph of the gazebo at the
back of my property. It was festooned with cherry
blossoms and stands of orchids, lit from within by
red lacquered lanterns.

"Oooh . . ." Becca shimmied in her chair as I slid
the book toward her. Keith continued to look
unimpressed, but I felt all my misgivings melt away.
Becca seemed pleased with my vision, and I relaxed
by degrees. I was going to give Keith and Becca a
beautiful day, and maybe earn some karma points.

Rachel took over the food portion of our planning reveal. "The wedding will be a joint catering
effort between our cook and the restaurant
Fusion. For appetizers, we'll have sushi and a variety of spicy spring rolls. Dinner will feature ginger
beef short ribs, coconut curry risotto, and Thai
chili mint chicken."

"And the cake will be a five-tiered cherry and
almond vision in pink," I revealed.

The doorbell chimed somewhere deep within the house, solemn and gong-like.

"We've arranged for a small replica of the meal from Fusion for you to taste."

Rhett licked his lips appreciatively as Rachel and I emerged several minutes later with trays of food bearing appetizer-sized bites of the wedding menu.

"And what about the dance floor?" Becca set down a half-eaten spring roll and delicately touched the sides of her mouth with a cherry-blossom patterned napkin. "I don't want just a boring white tent."

Ah, that's more normal.

Becca's usual imperious tone had returned. I knew it was only a matter of time.

"We'll rent tents with a bamboo thatched roof, and the sides will be mosquito netting," I smoothly promised. I pulled out the brochure of the company in New York that had agreed to let us rent the tents at extremely short notice. "They will be translucent and will look lovely with the torches we place around the grounds."

Becca seemed to love the idea in spite of herself.

"And what about—"

"Well, well, what do we have here?"

Becca went silent as all of our heads swiveled in unison to take in Helene Pierce, standing in the doorway of the deck in one of her trademark Chanel boucle jackets. Her face was a malevolent smirk, her pageboy haircut fanned out above her ears like a king cobra.

"I see you opened the pool before Memorial

Day," she tsked as she made her way to the table. "A savage move, but not unexpected."

"Mother—" Keith rose to greet Helene, carefully stepping in front of a seated Becca, as if to shield her. Becca frantically grabbed at the idea book of her wedding and shoved the large tome under the table.

"What's this?" Helene nimbly retrieved the book and did a cursory flip-through, her papery cheeks growing red and mottled under her peach blush.

"This looks like Thistle Park." Her voice was quiet and quaking, the volcano about to erupt. "And just when were you planning on carrying out these clandestine plans to wed?"

"In two weeks," Samantha answered brightly. She seemed to have misunderstood Helene's hot face for excitement, not barely controlled anger.

"Not on my watch!" Helene tossed the idea book into the pool, where it broke the smooth expanse of blue and sent up a splash. "And at Thistle Park, no less? You!" She turned to me, her index finger a mere inch from my nose. "You are behind this, once again?"

"Calm down, Helene." I took a step back from my once mother-in-law to be and bumped into Rachel, who sent Helene a powerful glower. "Perhaps if you had been a bit more understanding, Becca and Keith would have included you in their plans." Helene was a pistol, but I didn't think she'd ever resort to fisticuffs, no matter how mad she got.

"You little—" Helene lunged for me. I'd miscalculated.

A flash of white materialized at my elbow, and I barely comprehended the wooden cane that nimbly tapped Helene behind the knees, setting her off balance. Helene grabbed at my elbow as she went down and nicked the edge of the large silver tray laden with appetizers.

The beautiful plated pyramid of elaborate sushi made a quick return to its marine beginnings, toppling into the pool with a satisfying splash. Edamame and a rainbow of sushi rolls bobbed upon the waves like a mini school of fish come to the surface. The contents from upended bowls of wasabi drifted around in the water like green algae.

And above it all was Helene's frantic caterwaul. She continued to carry on, splashing and screaming, channeling the melting witch in the Wizard of Oz.

"I can't swim! Help me!" She bobbed under the water again and resurfaced, gasping and gulping in huge breaths of air. Her gray locks finally succumbed to the effects of the water despite a prodigious amount of hairspray. Wet clumps of hair hung limply on either side of her face.

"You're in the shallow end. Just stand up." Becca's voice was spasmodic and high-pitched. I wondered if she was upset, when I realized she was trying to hold back gales of laughter. She finally gave up and began to hysterically giggle, tears rolling down her face, leaving inky trails of mascara.

Keith looked at his bride in disgust and shrugged off his navy sports coat. "I'll fish you out, mother." He leaned over the edge of the pool and meekly offered his hand. Helene grasped it like a drowning woman and nearly pulled her son into the pool. Keith hoisted her up and out of the water, careful not to get too wet himself. Helene stood quaking with rage, a puddle of cold water forming below her now ruined pale blue suede kitten heels. Rivulets streamed down the sleeves of her sodden wool boucle Chanel jacket, and her plaid skirt clung to her frame.

"This is all your fault, Mallory Shepard." She crooked her index finger in my direction, the large sapphire wobbling. I took a step back and bumped into Rachel. It was our cue to leave.